DOWN CAME THE RAIN

DOWN CAME THE RAIN

A Roxanne Calloway Mystery

RAYE ANDERSON

Doug Whiteway, Editor

Signature
EDITIONS

Cover design by Doowah Design.
Photo of author by Michael Long.

This book was printed on Ancient Forest Friendly paper.
Printed and bound in Canada by Hignell Book Printing Inc.

We acknowledge the support of the Canada Council for the Arts and the Manitoba Arts Council for our publishing program.

Library and Archives Canada Cataloguing in Publication

Title: Down came the rain / Raye Anderson ; Doug Whiteway, editor.
Names: Anderson, Raye, 1943- author. | Whiteway, Doug, 1951- editor.
Description: Series statement: A Roxanne Calloway mystery
Identifiers: Canadiana (print) 20220166773 |
Canadiana (ebook) 20220166781 |
ISBN 9781773240992 (softcover) |
ISBN 9781773241005 (HTML)
Classification: LCC PS8601.N44725 D69 2022 |
DDC C813/.6—dc23

Signature Editions
P.O. Box 206, RPO Corydon, Winnipeg, Manitoba, R3M 3S7
www.signature-editions.com

Dedicated to the memory of my grandfather,
Andrew Rankine Hynd, who taught me to love stories and
patrolled the streets of Dundee as PC Hynd in the 1920s
with his faithful Airedale, Major, at his side.

Down came the rain and washed the spider out.

—from "Ipsy Wipsy Spider"
Children's Nursery Rhyme

1

MO MAGNUSSON DROVE up and down long gravel roads searching for a lost dog. She knew, roughly, where it was, running loose in the area northeast of Fiskar Bay, a lakeshore town in Manitoba's Interlake. Someone had posted a photo on Twitter. Mo drove up one road and down the other, watching for a glimpse of a yellow dog, maybe a young lab. Chances were that it wouldn't be out on a field, not on this day, early in April. The farmland was awash in spring melt, the ditches overflowing. She just hoped it hadn't holed up among the trees, out of sight.

It had been a long winter. Just last week, a late storm had dumped a foot or so of wet white stuff on land that was already waterlogged. The frost had gone deep into the ground this past year, freezing it solid, and it hadn't had time to thaw, so all the fresh, melting snow lay on the surface with nowhere to go. During the day the temperature rose but it still dropped below zero most nights. Icy snowbanks remained, unthawed, at the edge of the roads. It was no place for a lost dog to be out alone.

Mo drove a big white van, Mo's MUTT RESCUE emblazoned on the sides. She came well-equipped. Inside was a crate with bedding, a long pole with a noose at the end, an assortment of leashes and a collar, a bag of smelly dog treats and, if those failed, another of dried meat scraps. She also had binoculars resting on the seat beside her, powerful ones. But right now, her attention was focused on the road in front of her. It was slick with yellow mud, the gravel long since pushed to the side. She took her time, careful not to skid. Hardly anyone else drove this way, even in the middle of the afternoon. She didn't want to get stuck out here, alone. Above her the sky was grey, reflected in fields that had turned into ponds. The trees were drab shades of brown, the ditch water grey and dirty, as were the snowbanks. Nothing was growing, not yet.

She passed a small Ukrainian church, its black onion dome pointing to the sky. This area was dotted with them, built by settlers who had first farmed this land. Most of them had fallen into disrepair, some had been demolished, but this one looked well cared for. It must still be in use, but right now, on a Thursday, it was deserted. "Desna Ukrainian Orthodox Church," read a blue sign, designating it as a heritage building.

Mo stopped at the next intersection and scanned in each direction. The roads ran north and south, east and west, straight as a die over the flat land. Up ahead, she could see a stand of willows, their branches a comfortingly warm orange on this bleak day, and a row of dark spruce, sheltering a farmhouse. She drove in that direction and pulled into the farmyard.

It was a typical prairie farm, small house, big outbuildings. Large round hay bales were stacked under a corrugated metal shelter. There must be cows in the big red barn beside it. A pair of dogs, one a Rottweiler cross, the other a Blue Heeler, loped toward her, barking, as she opened the van door.

"Shush!" Mo commanded, and they did so. Dogs paid attention to Mo. They slunk back and watched as a farmer, weathered and as suspicious as they were, emerged from a Quonset hut. Mo explained her purpose.

No, he hadn't seen any yellow dog. His own dogs would have let him know if it had been hanging around here. He looked through narrowed eyes at her leather jacket, black jeans, knee-high, thick-soled boots, the ring in her nose and her bright pink hair. He knew who she was. That Magnusson girl, the one whose mother had got herself killed early last year. She'd been left a pile of money, he'd been told. Bought the old Axelsson place and was soft on animals.

Wouldn't last long, he'd bet. His mouth was a tight line. He had nothing to say to her. He watched her walk back to her van and drive off, his dogs barking behind her as far as the roadway, then walked up the steps of the farmhouse. There, he came face to face with his wife, watching from a porch window, framed by tomato seedlings in peat pots.

"What did she want?" she asked. She went back into the kitchen to put on the kettle, once she'd heard. "More money than sense, that one. Did you see the hair? At least she had the right boots on."

Mo watched the dogs trot back home in her rear-view mirror. She wasn't surprised that Farmer Kuryk had told her nothing. She was usually ignored by men like him around here and that was fine with her. The people of Fiskar Bay tolerated her, just. The town had been founded by Icelanders, displaced over a hundred years ago by a volcanic eruption in their homeland, and she was a Magnusson, descended from one of the founding fathers. Not only that, her own dad was Erik Axelsson, another of their own, and word was that she'd done all right by him. Bought him out of his farm, paid cash, and moved him into the city, given him a job caretaking an apartment building that her mother had left her. She looked weird, so did her boyfriend, the one that lived with her, but they could put up with her, especially if she spent her money in their town. And she did. She'd hired local tradespeople to fix up the old place. Bought all her cat and dog food from the local vet's. If she wanted to blow all her mother's money on saving lost pets, that was her lookout.

Mo turned the van at the next corner and headed north. KURYK ROAD read a sign. Roads around here got named for the families that lived on them. On her left was a stand of poplars, interspersed with scrub oak, some ash. An eagle flew over, back from wintering in the south, dark wings spread, its white head bright against the grey sky. She was glad the missing dog was not a small one. A bird like that would soon snatch up one of those for its dinner. To her left, a sodden field was streaked with lines of dark earth, black as liquorice.

Her eyes returned to the road. She was approaching the next intersection. The ditch ended there in a pool of water, dead brown grass covering the bank above it. Lying among them was something solid, blue and brown and large.

Mo stopped the van. Was that what she thought it was? She reached for her binoculars and focused them, saw a grey head, vacant holes where the eyes had been, a jaw hanging open. An arm, clad in navy blue, stretched out, the hand spread. The other lay by the side of the body, which lay half submerged in water. She could make out the legs, spread-eagled on the bed of ice that lay under them, a foot or so down. The jacket was open, so was a shirt underneath; she could see the top of the belly. It had been opened and gutted.

"Shit," said Mo and lowered the glasses. She took her phone out of her pocket and called 911.

SERGEANT ROXANNE CALLOWAY received the call. She was back in uniform. She had left the RCMP's Major Crimes Unit five months earlier, after a dangerous incident while she was investigating a murder case, convinced by her sister that she should find a safer job, one that would keep her out of harm's way and make sure she saw her young son grow to adulthood. Roxanne had worked in Fiskar Bay the previous year, on the Magnusson case, and had heard that Sergeant Bill Gilchrist, team commander of that detachment, was about to retire. She'd just had time to squeak her application in.

She had inherited some of Gilchrist's team, including Constable Ken Roach.

"We're getting Foxy?" he had sneered when he'd heard that she would be replacing Sergeant Gilchrist. He'd aimed an imaginary gun into the distance and mimed pulling the trigger as he moseyed off toward the lunchroom, his sidekick, Sam Mendes, following in his wake. Roach remembered Calloway from the Magnusson case. Now here was that skinny redhead, didn't look like a cop at all, coming back to run the show.

Roach might resent her presence and call her Foxy Roxy behind her back, but the town was coming round to having a woman in charge of the local police. She'd worked on that during the winter months, while she and her son settled into their new life. Finn was six now, in grade one. She'd bought a small house on a tree-lined street, an easy walk to the school and to her workplace, and made a point of saying hello to her neighbours as she passed. She used to wear her hair in a neat, red cap but she'd grown it. Regulations required her to wear it off her face so she couldn't entirely hide the red scar at her neck, a constant reminder of the attack that had spurred her to make the move, but it did conceal the missing ear lobe she had sustained at the same time.

Finn had had trouble adjusting. He missed his cousins in Winnipeg, and he still needed the occasional weekend visit, but he liked hockey and the more he played the more he was accepted. She was too. She did her bit as a hockey mom, took her turn carpooling small boys to games on weekends and showed up at all the town's fundraising events. Roxanne knew how to make this work. She'd grown up near a small prairie town in Saskatchewan. She'd never have the status that came with being an Icelander in Fiskar Bay, but as the sergeant in charge of the local RCMP, she was noticed. The mayor and council were polite. Friendly, almost, to her face.

It had been a quiet few months, a good time to figure out how her new job worked. The only excitement had been an occasional drunken fight on the weekend, the inevitable drug issues, thefts, accidents out on snowy highways. It would get different in the summer, Sergeant Bill had warned her, when the town's population swelled with cottagers and tourists. They came to have a good time and sometimes they behaved badly. "No end of trouble," he had told her when he heard she would be replacing him. But meantime, life had been uneventful. And that was okay by her, Roxanne told herself. Nevertheless, when Mo Magnusson told her there was a dead body lying in the ditch out on Kuryk Road, Roxanne felt an old frisson of interest.

"Be right there," she said, reaching for her jacket. "Ravi." She popped her head around the lunchroom door. "You're coming with me. Sam, you too. Bring a second car."

Ravinder Anand had arrived in Fiskar Bay shortly after her, last year. He was a rookie, straight out of the Depot, the training centre for the RCMP in Regina. He was having a harder time being accepted than she was. Mounties wearing turbans still raised a few eyebrows in rural areas of the province, but the mayor had told people to get over it. "Don't want people thinking this is the boonies," he had said.

Kathy Isfeld lifted her eyes from her computer screen as they hurried out the door. Kathy had been the civilian in the Fiskar Bay detachment forever. She'd talked about retiring at the same time as Bill Gilchrist, but Roxanne had persuaded her to stay on, for the winter at least. Kathy knew everything about what had happened in the detachment and her ear was tuned to the town grapevine.

"Wonder what that's all about?" she said.

"Some woman called Mo wanting to talk to her," Aimee Vermette, the constable behind the front desk, told her.

"That right?" Kathy lifted her phone and called Mo's Mutt Rescue. Roberta Axelsson answered. She volunteered there regularly.

"She's out," she said. "I'm not sure what's going on. She went looking for a stray dog. Someone just called here to say they've spotted it and I'm trying to get hold of her, but she's not answering her phone. I'll let you know if I hear anything."

MO MAGNUSSON WAS leaning against the side of her van, phone in hand, when the RCMP cars rolled onto Kuryk Road. She pointed toward the next corner along, two or three hundred feet from where she was parked, as they approached. They could see the body lying in the water. Ravi drove past Mo and pulled in at the side of the road. Sam Mendes walked to the edge of the swollen ditch, his mouth hanging open in shock and surprise.

They stood, side by side, and stared at the grey face. The man's hair was almost white, close cropped. His mouth hung open and his eyes were dark voids. The face had been pecked at, by ravens, probably. They'd taken out his eyes first. The belly had been emptied as well.

"The coyotes have been at him?" Ravi hadn't seen many dead bodies yet on the job, far less one as mutilated as this. "Who do you think he is?"

Roxanne knew. The body was still recognizable as that of her predecessor, retired Sergeant Bill Gilchrist, until November of last year team commander of the RCMP detachment at Fiskar Bay.

2

SAM MENDES HUNKERED down at the edge of a snowbank, grey icy water between him and the body. "What's happened to him? What was he doing out here?"

"Did anyone know he was back?" Roxanne asked. Sam shook his head. He hadn't heard anything. Bill Gilchrist and his wife, Julie, had left for Arizona late November, soon as he'd quit his job. They owned a house on the lakeshore, just north of Fiskar Bay. Their summer home, Bill had started calling it. Now that he was retired, they were going to become "snowbirds" —Canadians who wintered in the southern U.S., away from the arctic blasts you could expect in Manitoba. They'd bought a trailer in one of the parks set up for people like them down south, with retirement activities on tap and a golf course nearby. This way he could golf all year round, Bill had bragged at his retirement party.

"They would have been due back around now," said Sam. Bill and Julie couldn't stay across the border more than six months in the year if they wanted to maintain their Canadian residency. He stood up again and stepped back across a pile of frozen snow, grim-faced and unusually pale. Roxanne had her phone to her ear already. Inspector Schultz, her old supervisor, was not thrilled to hear the news.

"You're sure it's him? Jesus. How'd he get there?"

Roxanne had no idea. There was no sign of a vehicle having been at the roadside, but there had been a big snowstorm last week and any tracks that might have been left were long gone. Could he have walked there? It might take an hour to walk the long roads between the Gilchrist house and this lonely spot, but was it likely? Bill Gilchrist had preferred wheels, loved driving. Even on the links he scooted around on a cart.

"You'll secure the site until someone from the MCU and Ident can get there, right?" It was more of an order than a question. Ident was the Forensic Identification Unit. She could.

"And Roxanne," Schultz continued. That was new. When she'd been in his direct line of command, he'd always called her "Calloway." "Once our guys get there, they're in charge, right?"

She got the message. Hands off. She wasn't in the Major Crimes Unit anymore. Still, the body was on her turf. She'd need to be kept informed. She hoped she would. "We'll be available to provide support as needed, sir," she said.

"Hrrmph," her old boss replied.

Roxanne looked up to see Sam pocketing his own phone. "Who did you tell?" she asked.

"Just Kenny."

Of course he had. Roxanne should get back to the detachment and deal with the fallout from the news. This was going to shake up her team. Sam had worked under Gilchrist's command for years and he was obviously finding this difficult. He needed to be kept busy for now. She sent him to get rebar so they could hang crime tape. It would need to be hammered into the frozen ground. Then she'd send him home.

Mo Magnusson was watching them intently. Roxanne walked back to where she stood.

"We'll need a statement," she said. "But someone can come by your place and take it down later. Meantime, you should go home."

"Good. I've got a new stray to take care of." Mo didn't appear to be alarmed by her discovery, but that could be an act. Roxanne had seen Mo play it cool before, when she'd been investigating the death of her mother. Mo pointed a chin at the body in the ditch, hands tucked into the pockets of her short leather jacket. The temperature was dropping as the afternoon wore on.

"That's the cop that used to have your job, right?"

So, she had recognized Bill Gilchrist. Mo had been around the detachment at Fiskar Bay, last year. She'd been taken in for questioning then, but she would only have seen Sergeant Bill in uniform. Roxanne had hoped she might not have recognized the body, but no such luck. Mo was observant and she'd had plenty of time to look. And maybe take photographs.

"You need to keep quiet about this for now," Roxanne told her.

"Darn it, Sergeant. Told someone where I am already." Mo waved her phone at her. Then she grinned. "Relax," she said as she walked back to the driver's side of her van. "I didn't send out a Tweet or anything. No pictures." She tipped her head in the direction of Gilchrist's body. "Wasn't going to post that online. What do you take me for?" She climbed inside and waved as she drove off.

Roxanne called Kathy Isfeld.

"Bad news, Kathy," she said.

"I heard already," was the terse reply. "Roach told us. Do you want Sigrid to pick up Finn after school?"

She did. Sigrid was Kathy's granddaughter and lived a couple of streets over from Roxanne. She was seventeen, in grade twelve at Fiskar Bay High and was like Kathy, quiet, serious, and reliable. Having access to a babysitter that close and easily available was one of the perks of living in a small town and Sigrid was always happy to earn an extra buck or two.

Meantime, someone, probably herself, should go talk to Julie Gilchrist, to tell her they'd found a body and it might be Sergeant Bill. Make sure Julie wasn't alone and find out how long it was since she had seen him. Roxanne looked up at the sky, blackening in the west. It was going to rain, last thing they needed. And it was definitely getting colder. She hoped it wouldn't snow again.

THE MISSING YELLOW dog had been picked up by a school bus driver. The bus drove up and down country roads once the kids were let out of class, dropping them off at their driveways. There had been two more stops to do when the driver spotted the Labrador, skittish but hungry. One of the kids hadn't eaten half of his lunch sandwich. Corned beef had done the trick. She listened, agog, as Mo, with cheerful disregard for Roxanne's advice, described what she had seen out on Kuryk Road. So did Roberta Axelsson, while she bedded down the pup. Her shift was almost over. She couldn't wait to get home and call her friend Margo Wishart.

"It's Bill Gilchrist? The big white-haired RCMP sergeant? The one that retired?" asked Margo. She lived in Cullen Village, a few kilometres south of Fiskar Bay. Margo had helped Roxanne Calloway out on a couple of murder cases in the past. She'd had occasion to drop by the Fiskar Bay detachment back when Bill Gilchrist was in charge. She was quite friendly with Roxanne. They had lunch occasionally in Fiskar Bay. "She moved out here to get away from investigating murders and coming into contact with the dangerous people that do them. Wants to raise her boy, Finn, in a quiet town where there's less trouble."

"Ha!" Roberta snorted. "She can't avoid that. She's still a Mountie, right?"

"Yes, but she's not in Major Crimes any longer." Margo looked out the window toward the lake, smooth, grey and still. A couple of raindrops hit the pane. "She won't get to investigate this case."

"What do you wanna bet?" asked Roberta. "She'll stick her nose in. Bound to."

A FEW HOURS later, Roxanne got back to Fiskar Bay, cold and tired.

"They've gone over to Roach's house," Aimee Vermette told her, still behind the front desk. The phone lines were busy already. The word was out. Roxanne called home. Sigrid answered.

"No problem," she said in a quiet little voice that sounded remarkably like that of her grandmother, Kathy Isfeld. "Finn's in his pj's already and I brought my homework with me."

Roxanne found the rest of her team in Ken Roach's basement, beers in hand. They'd eaten most of a plate of sandwiches. His wife, Janine, took her coat and said she'd make her a fresh one. Would ham and cheese do? Roxanne didn't feel like eating but when she bit into it, she discovered she was ravenous.

"They all done out there?" Roach opened the door of his beer fridge and passed her a bottle. Sam had changed out of his wet uniform before they'd got together at Roach's. It was where they usually met. If they'd gone to the bar to drink and talk, all of Fiskar Bay would have known that the cops had been out, drowning their sorrows. Sam was well into a few beers. So was Pete Robinson, a corporal by now and her second-in-command. Ravi nursed a can of Coke.

Roxanne had watched the Ident team put up a tent as the rain teemed down. She knew Corporal Dave Kovak, who led them, and Dr. Abdur Farooq, the provincial medical examiner. He had examined the body where it lay and shaken his head. Most of the internal organs were gone and a lot of the blood had drained out. But some would remain in the extremities and there was hair, teeth and bone to help him figure out how Bill Gilchrist had died. The lungs still remained within the chest cavity, although the heart had been torn out. One leg was skewed at the knee.

"Saw that." Sam rolled his beer bottle between his hands. "So he'd been hit by something?"

"Maybe," Roxanne replied. "Or he could have tripped and fallen. On ice."

"Nah," said Roach. "Sergeant Bill curled in the winter when I first came here. He was good on his feet, on a rink. I've seen him, back in the day."

Roxanne drank some of the beer. She'd only have one since she was driving. Sam and Pete had walked to Roach's house, knowing that they'd have a few. "He might have been distracted by something. If he was close to the edge of the ditch he could have toppled right in."

"And lain there with a broken knee, waiting to die?" asked Sam Mendes. They all sat in gloomy silence.

"Did you talk to his wife?" Pete finally asked. Roxanne had not. The Gilchrist house had been locked and dark.

"Did Sergeant Bill have a phone on him?" Sam looked across the room at her.

They hadn't found one on the body but it could be lying in the watery ditch. Or buried in a snowbank.

"I don't get it," Roach complained. "What was he doing, out there in the middle of nowhere? How did he get there? Has somebody done him in?"

"We don't know that," Roxanne said firmly, although that thought haunted all of them. "We'll know more after the autopsy. For now, it's a suspicious death. And the MCU is taking over."

"We knew him best," Roach persisted, his jaw jutting out. He'd served with Sergeant Gilchrist almost six years. Pete had been in Fiskar Bay for five of those years and Sam had arrived close after him. Kathy Isfeld had known Bill Gilchrist the longest. Kathy had gone right home not long after she had heard that he had died, saying very little, but that was Kathy. She was private and she didn't drink with the guys. Roxanne felt a twinge of guilt. If Sigrid wasn't babysitting her son, she'd have been able to visit her grandmother. The two of them were close. She bit her lip. It couldn't be helped.

"Who knew that he was back in Fiskar Bay?" she asked. They all looked blank.

"Thought he was still down south," said Sam.

"No one's seen him? Talked to him?" They shrugged, frowned, shook their heads, no.

"How long's he been in that ditch?" muttered Roach. No one knew for sure. Janine Roach interrupted them from the top of the stairs.

"The rain's beginning to freeze out there. Roads'll get bad real soon. Maybe you need to get home."

"There's a great end to the day," said Roach. Freezing rain would encase the town in ice. Commuters started driving toward the city at around six-thirty in the morning. The municipality would have sanding crews out by then, but the highways would have to be patrolled. Some cars would end up in the ditch for sure. The RCMP had a busy day ahead of them.

Roach's question remained unanswered. Ice pellets stung their faces as she, Pete and Sam slid their way to her car. She would drop them both off home. It was no night to be out walking.

"How's Izzy McBain taking it?" Sam Mendes asked from the back seat as she nosed the car carefully along the street toward his apartment building. The night was pitch black, the road surface slippery, shining already in the orange glow from the street lights.

Izzy had spent three years working under Sergeant Gilchrist. She had been the first person in the MCU to reach the Interlake. She and Matt Stavros had just moved into a big, new house that they had built near Cullen Village. Izzy had been on her way home from Winnipeg when she got the call, so it hadn't taken her long to reach Kuryk Road. She'd teared up when she first saw Sergeant Gilchrist's body sprawled at the road end. Roxanne had watched her as she wiped the tears from her eyes with both hands, blinked hard and got to work, just like the rest of them. It was the only way to cope with this.

MATT PUT A mug of hot chocolate down on a coffee table. Izzy had held herself together while she worked. She'd watched while Sergeant Gilchrist's body had been loaded into the back of Dr. Farooq's big white van and the Ident team had hacked out chunks of ice from the ditch. Its layers would help them determine how long the body had lain there. By the time they were finished, the outside of the tent that they had erected and the area surrounding it shimmered with ice. The clouds had cleared, a waning moon and starlight made the landscape gleam. It would be a treacherous drive back to the city.

It had been almost 2:00 when Izzy slithered to a stop outside the back door of her house. Matt had waited up for her. She'd taken one look at him and burst into tears.

"He was my first real boss!" she had wailed, pulling the tie off her ponytail so her blonde hair fell around her face. "He taught me so much and now he's dead!" Izzy seldom cried, if ever, but when she did, she bawled. Usually she was cheerful, a smile on her round face, her blue eyes bright, but now they streamed tears.

She huddled up on the one sofa in the wide, open room that was the ground floor of their house. They had brought all the furniture they owned from the apartment they had shared during the winter in the city. It didn't begin to fill the space.

"It's Sergeant Bill for sure?" Matt sat beside her. She had texted that she would be late, that something had come up, but hadn't said what it was. She'd wanted to tell him herself but the news report on CBC had mentioned human remains being found in the Interlake. Before he went to law school Matt had worked in the RCMP too, at Fiskar Bay, under Sergeant Gilchrist. That was where he and Izzy had met. He'd been online. He had already discovered who had died.

Izzy described the scene, her tears abating.

"Dave Kovak thinks he's been there since before that storm last Wednesday. There's still a lot of ice below the body, from that cold spell we had, end of the month." An unseasonal polar vortex had settled over the prairies, in March. The temperature hadn't risen above minus twenty for weeks, until a sudden spring thaw. "He wasn't dressed for the cold. Dave thinks it might have happened just before, when we had that warm patch. He'd been there long enough for the coyotes to get at him. Dave says maybe it was two, three days before he got buried in the snow. So, it could have been the weekend."

"Can they tell how he died?"

She shook her head. The hot, sweet drink was warming her up. "It could have been an accident. But why was he out there, all by himself?" She looked at Matt, perplexed. "And who would want to kill him?"

3

ROXANNE DROPPED HER son off at school the next morning. The road surfaces were melting, sanded and salted already, and so was the path to the school door, but the kids preferred to slide around the playground where it was still icy. She watched Finn, confident on his feet. All those hockey practices were paying off.

Slippery highways had made for a busy morning already. Pete Robinson and Ken Roach were out at the scene of an accident. Traffic heading toward the city had been slow and an impatient driver had overtaken a car, lost control on the ice, sideswiped a van coming in the opposite direction and rolled. His car had landed upside down, and they had had to wait until he could be extracted from the wreck. Cars were still being rerouted around the crash site. Aimee Vermette wasn't due at work until later, Sam was still out on patrol and Ravi Anand was working the front desk. The phone had been ringing non-stop, some people wanting to know about the state of the roads ("They don't know how to check the internet?" Kathy Isfeld muttered from her desk) and others to ask if it really was former sergeant Bill Gilchrist's body that the RCMP had found the day before.

Kathy was surprised that the Gilchrists were back from Arizona already.

"They said they wouldn't be back until later this month," she said. "Bill wanted to be sure that all the snow was going to be gone first. And where is Julie?" So far, no one knew.

"One of the daughters lives in Grunwald." Kathy tapped on her keyboard while she spoke. That small town lay half an hour south of Winnipeg. "Fern. Went to school here. Got married right after she graduated. The other one's called Hazel. She's at university in Toronto." Fern had married a guy called Wiebe. He sold tractors. John Deeres. Worked at a big country dealership. Bill hadn't emailed, as far as she knew, and he wasn't one to use social media. "Too busy playing golf, probably," but Julie might have. She had some friends around town. She was into quilting. Went to yoga. Maybe she had been in touch with some of those folks.

Roxanne had expected Izzy McBain to come breezing into the detachment by now. There was an office upstairs that they had used as an MCU incident room last year, during the Magnusson case. She'd thought they might move in there, but so far Izzy hadn't appeared. She texted, telling her what she'd learned so far. Izzy might have been called into Winnipeg. Not knowing how the Major Crimes Unit was planning to handle the case was frustrating. But meantime, Roxanne figured, she could help by doing some basic groundwork. Julie Gilchrist was a local resident and needed to be tracked down. There was no reason why she, Roxanne, shouldn't use her contacts to do that. She called Margo Wishart. Margo went to yoga classes, so did Julie Gilchrist.

"Is it true that her husband's dead?" Margo asked. They couldn't say, Roxanne replied. That news wasn't official yet.

"Well," Margo responded. "It's all over my newsfeed already. All of the Interlake must know by now." She'd last heard from Julie in February. "She was going to phone me at the end of this month so we could get together, so they must have been planning to be back by then. I'm writing a book about women in the Interlake who make art using textiles, and I'm hoping to get a show together later this year. Julie said she'd like to be involved. She's an amazing quilter. She goes way beyond your usual piecing."

Most people made quilts according to traditional geometric patterns. They stitched scraps of fabric together, padded the back and made blankets and other useful objects. "I'll send you her email address. She hangs out quite a bit with Susan Rice, our yoga instructor. You could talk to her. She lives near me, in Cullen Village. Do you want her number, too?"

"Sure. And tell me where to find her house," said Roxanne.

Live interviews were often more informative than a phone conversation. She could drop by and see if Susan Rice was home. She put on her jacket and walked to the parking lot outside the front door but didn't get any further. A big grey van pulled up alongside her and a woman jumped out.

"Aren't you the policewoman who replaced my dad!" she yelled. "What is going on?" She marched up to Roxanne, blocking her way. "I've been getting calls since early this morning, saying my dad's dead! It's all over the internet, and nobody from the RCMP has even called me." A child, strapped in a car seat behind the driver's seat, started to wail. "Hey, Oliver," said the woman, turning to attend to him. "I'm not done talking to you yet!" she barked at Roxanne over her shoulder as she reached in to unbuckle her son.

"Sergeant Roxanne Calloway." Roxanne introduced herself as the woman lifted a small boy, about two years old, out of the van. "You're one of Bill Gilchrist's daughters?" It was pretty obvious. She was taller than Roxanne, round-headed, small nose above a familiar square jaw. She looked just like her dad.

"Fern Wiebe," snapped the woman, wiping snot off her son's face. "I called the RCMP at headquarters in Winnipeg. Got some idiot cop who put me on hold, can you believe? Then he said someone would be getting back to me. Took my name and number, but did anyone call? No, they didn't."

Roxanne understood that the Force would want to tread cautiously given the death of a recently retired member, but even so she was surprised that no one had spoken to Fern as the only available family member. It had been eighteen hours since the body was discovered.

"Come inside," she said. "I'll tell you what I know." She escorted Fern Wiebe toward her office. Kathy Isfeld raised her eyes from her screen. They widened in recognition.

"Coffee?" Kathy asked, reaching for her coat. The detachment liked to get its drinks from the Timmies on the corner opposite. When she came back, she brought a bag of muffins as well.

"Thought you could use those," she said, putting it and a tray with coffee containers down on Roxanne's desk. She'd bought one for herself and tea for Ravi, too. Fern Wiebe peeled her son out of a snowsuit while Roxanne told her where the body had been found. Fern wore a long skirt, almost to her ankles. Her hair was drawn back from her face and pinned at the back of her head. She was about the same age as Izzy McBain but looked older.

"You saw the body? You knew it was him?"

Roxanne had. There was no doubt of the identity.

"He's been taken to Winnipeg for an autopsy so we can figure out how he died," she said. "This may have been an accident. Did you know your parents were back in Manitoba?"

Fern lifted her son onto her lap and gave him a chunk of muffin to keep him happy. "I didn't think they'd be back for another two weeks," she said. She hadn't heard from them for a month, but that wasn't anything unusual. "We don't talk to each other all that often," she said, faintly defensive. "And it's usually Mom. Dad's always busy." She had both their cellphone numbers. She'd tried both. Got voice mail and neither of them had called back. "He was loving the golf in Arizona, didn't want to leave until he had to, last I heard."

She didn't have a key to the house. "They have a security system on it while they're gone. But I know where they usually leave one. Do you know where my mom's got to? She must have driven back with him."

"We don't know, but we need to talk to her," said Roxanne. "I need you to stay away from the house for now."

"You don't really think it's an accident?" Parallel creases appeared between Fern's eyebrows.

"Like I said, we don't know yet." Fern busied herself by wiping her son's face with a napkin. Roxanne couldn't see the expression on her face anymore. "Are you planning to stay for long in Fiskar Bay?"

Fern had an old school friend she could go visit. But she needed to be back in Grunwald by 3:30, when school got out. She had three other kids. Her sister, Hazel, was in Toronto, at York University, doing an MBA.

"I'll call her," she said as she zipped up the snowsuit again, ready to lug her child back out to her van. "Maybe Mom's talked to her. If she knows anything I'll let you know." Roxanne gave her a business card and watched her go. It occurred to her that Fern Wiebe hadn't cried at all. She had shown no dismay or grief at the news that her father was dead. Kathy Isfeld had noticed, too. She waited, then said,

"Probably thinks he's gone to a better place. To be in heaven with Jesus. The Wiebes are a religious lot."

Roxanne left yet another message for Julie Gilchrist to call her, right away. Then she called Izzy. Still no answer.

She changed her mind about going to visit Susan Rice. Instead, she went to a cupboard and found protective clothing, a plastic suit, double masks, gloves, head and foot coverings. Then she drove out to Heron Haven. It lay at the end of a road that ran toward the lake from the highway, a couple of kilometres north of town. Only three houses stood there, in a row, facing out toward the lake. They had all been built by a Winnipeg company, Isbister Homes, four years ago, using the same materials but to different designs. The Gilchrists had been one of the first occupants, after they sold the old family home in Fiskar Bay. Each was separated from the rest by treed lawns and driveways, and they all had large, built-in garages. They were locked up, only occupied in the summer. Each had a sign in the window saying that it was protected by Denny's Cottage Alert, with a Winnipeg phone number. Roxanne called, explained who she was and asked for access.

"Can't do that, ma'am," said a young, male voice.

"I need to get inside as part of an RCMP investigation."

"And how do I know that you are who you say you are?" was the slick response. "I need to see your ID."

"No camera surveillance?" she asked. "I'm in uniform."

"No," he replied. What he could do was fax a form to her office and she could send it back.

"And how long until I get an answer?" she asked.

"We do our best, ma'am," was the smooth reply.

"Well," said Roxanne, exasperated. "I am going to enter that house. If the alarm goes off in the next minute or two, you'll know it's me."

She ended the call before he could respond. She looked around her while she suited up. The three driveways all faced west. They lay in the shadows of the houses, and they were still ice-covered, but the snow that had covered the ground last week was almost gone. There were no footprints or car tracks to be seen. She held her boot coverings in her hand and walked across a lawn covered in crisp, ice-coated grass to the doorway. It tinkled under the soles of her shoes. There were gardens plots on either side of the front steps, shrubs growing behind them, edged by a row of stones, decorative ones. Under one of them, as Fern Wiebe had told her, lay a key.

She opened the door and was met with silence. The alarm system had been deactivated. The house was warm. The furnace clicked on as she walked down a hallway. She checked a thermometer on the wall. It was set at a comfortable twenty degrees. The heat would have been turned off while the Gilchrists were in Arizona. They must have come back and turned it on. A large fabric wall hanging was suspended on a white wall in front of her, where the hall turned and opened into a large living space. The room was cathedral-ceilinged, with tall windows along one side that opened out onto the lake. Blinds were pulled halfway down, but Roxanne could see a large deck and grounds that stretched toward the water. A skin of ice remained on the lake, shining blue in the sunlight, all the way out to a big floating white slab, solid ice, several feet thick, what remained of the covering that had formed on the lake during the winter months.

A stone fireplace lay between the windows. On either side of it were brown leather sofas with embroidered cushions arranged on them. More quilted hangings hung on the walls and the dining chairs were upholstered in needlepoint. It was a bright, comfortable room despite its size.

Roxanne walked carefully, touching nothing unless she had to, using her phone to photograph as she went. An open kitchen area faced the window wall, on the far side the room. There were a few unwashed dishes in the dishwasher, not enough for a full load. She turned on a tap. The water would have been disconnected for the winter so the pipes wouldn't freeze, but someone had turned it on again. To the left, a wooden staircase led upstairs and to her right, another hallway. She opened a door. It led into a washroom. Another, behind the kitchen, revealed a utility room. There was a laundry basket full of unwashed clothing, male and female. At the very end of the corridor there was a door. It opened into a double garage.

Inside was a blue GMC Yukon, in need of a wash, and an empty space beside it, large enough for another car. Bill Gilchrist's golf clubs leaned against the wall. A door opened into a workshop area, with tools neatly arranged above a workbench. A riding mower was parked there. Steps led upstairs. The room at the top was vast, above both the workshop and the garage, stretching to the back of the house. There were windows back and front. Shelves lined one wall, stacked with folded fabric and boxes of sewing supplies. A large table at the centre and two smaller ones bearing sewing machines lay along a wall. On the bigger table there were bags filled with new supplies, some bought in Arizona but others in Fargo, North Dakota. They hadn't been unpacked.

Another door led back inside the house itself, upstairs. The master bedroom lay off a corridor. The bed was made up. On the floor were two large suitcases, both open, partly unpacked. There were toilet bags in the ensuite bathroom, an electric toothbrush on a shelf and a razor plugged into the wall. Why only one toothbrush?

Julie Gilchrist had been in this house. She hadn't stayed long enough to finish unpacking or do a load of laundry. Both she and her husband had eaten, dirtied a few dishes and drunk some coffee. Then Julie and her car had disappeared. But had that happened before or after her husband had died?

4

IZZY MCBAIN FINALLY called, from her car, on the radio.

"They're stalling," she said. "Arguing what to do." She'd been summoned, first thing, to HQ in Winnipeg, to meet with Inspector Schultz. Izzy was a confident driver on icy roads, but the accident on the highway had delayed her. "It started off badly. He was pissed off that I was late. He hadn't heard that Matt and I weren't living in Winnipeg anymore. That we had moved back to the Interlake. Then I could see his little brain figuring out how much money he could save if he didn't have to pay for an investigator from the city to stay in the hotel at Fiskar Bay. So I get to stay on the case for now. They're hoping it's just an accident. A hit and run, at worst. They're shit scared that it really is murder, and that someone Sergeant Bill locked up has killed him. That it's revenge from an old case gone wrong."

Having a past arrest resurface often meant it would be scrutinized for a miscarriage of justice, especially by the press. The RCMP didn't need one of those.

"If it is a murder, Schultz is hoping it's local," Izzy continued. "Wanted to know if there were any rumours kicking around Fiskar Bay about Sergeant Bill. Had he made any enemies in town? Was there someone who might hold a grudge? He thought I might know since I worked under him. And he knows I grew up there. But I can't think of a thing that sticks out. Can you?"

Roxanne couldn't. "There's only been two murders that I know of. The Magnusson case and that gang killing, the one where a kid got stabbed one summer, but the Major Crimes Unit worked on those. Sergeant Bill didn't solve them." She was also driving, was almost at Cullen Village, finally on her way to find Susan Rice. She pulled over onto the shoulder of the road so she could talk some more.

"It could be something from years back," she said.

"Maybe." Izzy's engine revved as she pulled out to pass an elderly farmer puttering along the highway in a beat-up old truck. "Sergeant Bill stayed in the office and played nice when I worked for him. We were the ones out on the street, locking up drunk summer visitors and the druggies."

That meshed with what Roxanne had seen in the few weeks she had worked out of Fiskar Bay the year before. Sergeant Gilchrist had managed his team from his desk. He'd lunched with local politicians, played golf with the mayor. He'd said more than once that putting a good face on the detachment was his main job, that was what community policing was largely about, especially in small prairie towns and villages, and Roxanne tended to agree with him. She tried to follow his example, except for the golf.

"They haven't told the family yet. Fern Wiebe came looking."

"Really? Haven't seen her since we were seventeen." Izzy and Fern had gone to school together. "I suppose they want to know more before they tell them, but still. Someone should have got hold of her already. They maybe want to speak to Julie first."

"There's still no sign of her. I'm on my way to ask some of her friends if they've heard from her," said Roxanne. "That's okay with you?" Asking permission of Izzy McBain was strange. Roxanne had been Izzy's superior, on two previous murder investigations. But now Izzy was assigned to the case, not her.

"Be my guest. Wonder where she's got to? That is weird. Hope she's okay."

"Do you think she could have got into a fight with Bill?"

"Julie? No. She's a little mouse of a thing. Wouldn't say boo."

"But it makes sense, doesn't it? She could have run him over with that big Yukon of theirs and then taken herself off in her own car. The guys say she drives a little green Mazda. It's not in their garage."

"I'd better let Schultzy know about that. We've got to get on top of this. I'm almost at Fiskar Bay." Izzy was on a faster highway, one that was further from the lake and ran parallel to the one that Roxanne was travelling. "Let me know what you find out, soon as."

"I MET MATT Stavros in the grocery store this morning. Lovely guy." Roberta Axelsson sat on the window seat in Margo Wishart's house, a mug of hot tea in her hand. Behind her, the trees dripped water. The morning's freeze was over. The lake's surface was covered in broken shards of ice, stirred up by the motion of the water, but the white flat pancake of ice remained, stretching out to the horizon. "I told him about that nice yellow Lab at Mo's place. How she's pregnant and needs a foster. He said he wasn't sure about looking after a litter of pups, but he'd go have a look. I think it was just a good excuse to find out exactly what Mo saw in that ditch yesterday." They were waiting for Sasha Rosenberg to arrive so they could discuss an idea for their art project. Sasha had called to say she was running late.

"Anyway." Roberta swallowed a mouthful of tea. "Mo called me, just before I came here. Matt showed up at her place, right after he talked to me. The barn's set up as dog runs now, you know? And he walked up and down, looking at what was there. There's only six in right now. And the one he stopped at was Joseph. Ugliest dog you ever saw. Little beige thing with a black muzzle, got an underbite. Matt hunkered down and Joseph came right to him, wagging his tail, and that was it. Love at first sight. Mo's so happy. She thought nobody was ever going to take that dog. But no, he's off home with Matt. Trotted out to the truck with him and hopped right in. Mo said she could have cried."

The door banged open, and Sasha finally arrived, her own dog loping in ahead of her, big basset ears flapping. Margo opened the back door and let him outside, to play in her fenced yard with her black mutt, Bob.

"Roxanne Calloway's car has just stopped outside Susan Rice's house," Sasha reported. "Wonder what that's about?"

Margo could guess, but she wasn't saying. She poured a mug of tea for Sasha. "We got the arts grant," she said, steering the conversation onto other ground. "So we can go ahead and plan this show." Her project was to involve different women artists who lived and worked in the Interlake, many of them included in her new book. There was enough money to pay some artist fees, to rent a space for an exhibition and cover promotional costs. The idea was to have ten to twelve participants each create a piece that reflected what the lake meant to them, in their chosen medium.

"I guess Julie Gilchrist won't be joining us, now that her husband's been found, dead." Sasha took the mug and found a seat at Margo's long rectangular table.

"We'll have to wait and see. Meantime we need to firm up what we want to do with this project before I invite other artists to commit to it."

"Word is that she's gone missing." Roberta was not ready to let that subject go. She reluctantly left the window seat. It was her favourite spot in this room. "Her daughter Fern's in Fiskar Bay, looking for her. Mo told me."

"They don't know where she is?" Sasha asked. "Maybe she's dead too. Or do they think she's maybe responsible? That she's done him in?"

"I don't think so!" Roberta knew Julie. Sometimes she dyed fabric for her when she needed a specific colour for a quilt that she was making. "Julie would never hurt anyone. She's not like that."

"You never know." Sasha stirred sugar into her tea, ever the cynic.

"I don't think that being in Arizona suited her." Margo fetched her own mug, paper and a pen. "She emailed me a couple of times. She didn't like the heat or the lifestyle. Lots of socializing. Not Julie's thing at all. She's a bit of a hermit, isn't she? Happy up there in her loft all winter long. Just her and her quilts."

"Have you seen it? The loft? It's massive. Looks out over the lake and has great light." Roberta sighed, remembering. She could never afford that kind of workspace herself, or the kind of equipment Julie Gilchrist had. She worked out of a cluttered little house. In the summer she expanded into the porch, but during the winter months her rooms got filled up with bags of wool and half-finished projects. "She must have hated having to leave it. It was her husband who was keen to go south."

"She does yoga, right?" Sasha occasionally went to tai chi at Susan Rice's studio. "Bet that's why the police are over at Susan's. Why haven't they talked to you yet?" She saw Margo hesitate. "They have, haven't they?"

"I don't know any more than you do," Margo told them, quite truthfully.

"But he's dead and she's disappeared? Geez," said Sasha.

SUSAN RICE WAS home. The house smelled of incense. Dreamcatchers hung in the windows, some with crystals in them that sparkled when the sun shone. Bead curtains separated the rooms. Statues lay on the tops of shelves and on small tables, mostly of the Buddha and of Kwan Yin, but there were also ones of Kali and of Ganesh. They were surrounded by bells and beads and decorative stones. In one corner, pride of place was given to a fairy garden, with a tiny, steep-roofed house at its centre. There was a large sofa and big armchairs that all looked comfortable and well-used. Susan took Roxanne's jacket and indicated one of them. Roxanne sank into it. It was so soft and low that it enveloped her.

Susan Rice was tall and thin. She wore magenta Thai pants and a loose, pale beige tunic. Her soft brown hair was tied into a large knot on top of her head and her only jewellery was a wedding band. On her feet were thick socks and sandals. She taught yoga classes in her house. Another room was her studio, she told Roxanne as she moved between the kitchen and the room where Roxanne sat. She led classes three days a week and a friend came out from the city once a week to teach tai chi. She put a plate of lemon slices and a pot of honey on a low table in front of Roxanne. Then she brought a teapot and two small china bowls.

"I made ginger tea," she said, "since it's turned cold outside again." She kicked off the sandals and sat down on a cushion on the floor at the other side of the table in one graceful, fluid movement, then tucked her legs up under her. Roxanne watched her and wondered, not for the first time, if she should take up yoga herself. But she hardly had time to run these days, between work and caring for Finn. Running had always been more of her thing, anyway.

Susan had two children at school in the village and her husband, Steve, worked as a counsellor. She mentioned a clinic in Winnipeg, one that Roxanne recognized. It had a solid reputation among members of the RCMP that investigated the drug trade.

"So." Susan poured the tea. "How can I help you?"

"I believe you know Julie Gilchrist," Roxanne began.

"Indeed, I do." Susan turned to indicate a fabric hanging on the far wall. "That's one of Julie's. She gave it to me as a birthday gift."

"Have you talked to her since she returned from the U.S.?" Roxanne sipped the tea. It was gingery and bitter. Susan pushed the lemon slices toward her.

"Most people like some lemon and honey with it," she said. Every movement she made was smoothly executed and unhurried. "I have," she continued. "About two weeks ago. They had just got back home. May I ask why you need to know, Sergeant?"

Roxanne busied herself with the honey pot to hide her surprise. Was it possible that Susan Rice did not know that Julie Gilchrist's husband had been found dead? News like that travelled fast in

Cullen Village. The whole neighbourhood must have heard by now. Margo Wishart's house was just along the street. She and her friends were all active on social media, and they talked. But perhaps Susan Rice was not.

"We found human remains yesterday, just north of Fiskar Bay," Roxanne said. The tea still wasn't great but now it was drinkable.

Susan Rice's eyebrows arched. "Not Julie, surely?" she asked.

"No, but we do need to talk to her."

"Ah, well." Susan folded her hands in her lap before she spoke again. "That might be difficult, Sergeant. I believe Julie has gone into retreat."

"She has what?" Roxanne put down her teacup.

Susan smiled gently at her. "She told me in confidence," she said.

"And confidentially," Roxanne responded, "the remains are those of her husband, William Gilchrist. So, it is urgent that we reach her."

Susan Rice's lips formed a round O.

"She called me." Her brown eyes became large with concern. "It was a Friday. They had spent the previous four days driving back from Arizona and they weren't long home. She said she needed some time alone, and I told her that a friend of ours was conducting a meditative retreat at the Sunnywell Arts and Culture Centre, starting the very next day."

Roxanne had heard of the Centre. It was located between Cullen Village and Winnipeg, at the southern tip of the lake, in the grounds of what had once been a convent.

"I gave her a number to call, and I haven't heard from her since. That's not surprising. If that is where she is, she's been sworn to silence these past two weeks. She'll be talking to no one."

5

IZZY MCBAIN HAD trouble tracking down her old schoolmate, Fern Wiebe, Bill and Julie Gilchrist's daughter. It took two or three tries before she found the friend that Fern had visited, someone else who had been in their year at Fiskar Bay High. Fern was long gone.

"Awful news about her dad. Did someone really kill him?" the woman probed, baby on hip. Almost all the girls they had gone to school with were married with kids by now, as Izzy's mother liked to remind her.

"We don't know how he died yet," she said, not that that would scotch any rumour that was flying around town. "Did Fern say if she was going straight home?"

She had talked about going to have a look at her parents' house. That sent Izzy racing up the road to Heron Haven. The last thing they needed was Fern and a sticky-fingered toddler handling things in what might turn into a crime scene.

Fern's appearance when she opened the door shocked Izzy. She had put on weight and she looked dowdy. The long skirt and the tied-back hair didn't help but neither did the thick stockings and baggy cardigan. Makeup must be forbidden in the sect that she now belonged to. Fern had been pretty when she was seventeen but now she looked tired and older than her age. Maybe that wasn't surprising? She'd had four babies inside ten years.

"Izzy McBain!" A toddler waddled up behind her. She stooped to pick him up. Izzy could see her own appearance being checked out in turn. "You haven't changed at all. Have you found my mom yet?"

Izzy shook her head. They hadn't, but did Fern have a few minutes to talk?

"Sorry!" Fern couldn't stay. She needed to get home. The school bus would drop off her other three kids at her driveway before 4:00. She was cutting it fine as it was.

"I already spoke to your boss." She picked up a child's jacket from the floor by the door and tucked his arms into it. He resisted. "Hold still, Oliver!" she told him and put him back down so she could use both hands. She looked up at Izzy. "I told her everything I know. It's not much. Did you get hold of my sister?" They hadn't done that either. "It's the end of term." Fern succeeded in zipping up the jacket and picked up a small boot. "I've tried too. She's probably writing a paper and turned her phone off. Sit down," she told her son and seized a foot. "Do you know what they're doing with my dad's body?"

Izzy hunkered down beside her and helped with the second boot. They were waiting for the autopsy to happen, she said. The body had been frozen and it was being thawed slowly. It would take time. Izzy held the squirming child while Fern buttoned herself into a long, padded coat.

"We need to find your mother," Izzy said.

"I don't know where she is." They both looked at each other, perplexed.

"She didn't tell you?"

Fern shook her head. "I haven't heard a word. You'll let me know, soon as you find her?"

"And you call us if you hear from her."

The child was finally ready. They exchanged contact information.

"You're going to stay here?" Fern asked, ready to leave.

"Sure am." Izzy held the door open for her. She saw Fern look behind her, into the house. "I need to have a quick look around.

Don't worry. I'm not going to dump out drawers or anything. I won't leave a mess." Not yet, she thought. That might all change if Julie Gilchrist didn't show up soon.

Once Fern had gone, Izzy walked through to the spacious living room. She looked out a big window. A lawn stretched down to the lakeshore. Last time she had been here was for a barbecue, Bill Gilchrist out on the deck, flipping burgers, people milling around, a table full of salads and desserts, buckets of cold drinks and beer, wine bottles.

How long would it be before they put out a missing person call for Julie? If Izzy had her way, it would have been out on the airwaves already. Everything about this case was going too cautiously for her. She tapped her foot in frustration. She continued to check the house but didn't learn much new, except that the Gilchrists had both been here for a short time before he had died and Julie had disappeared.

She headed up Heron Road and across the highway to the site where the body had been found. The rainstorm the previous day had swollen the ditches even more, but the sun was shining. Patches of water gleamed like mirrors on the flat landscape. The grass looked faintly green. A pair of ducks, back from wintering in the south, paddled toward the corner where the body had lain, undeterred by festoons of yellow tape. Someone had left a bunch of roses. Yellow, no label to say who they were from. Someone must miss Bill Gilchrist. Her phone buzzed, a text, from Roxanne Calloway. BACK AT OFFICE. TALK SOON? She drove straight back to Fiskar Bay.

Roxanne's office door was closed when she got there. Sergeant Calloway was suddenly busy with another problem, Aimee Vermette reported.

"We just heard that there's ice jams happening south of the lake on the river. They've asked for assistance sandbagging tomorrow. And they're keeping a watch on a couple of creeks up here. They might get jammed up and flood too."

When the ice on a river broke up, chunks of it were swept along and sometimes impacted at a bend into a solid pack. Water backed up behind it and could cause extensive flooding. Izzy stuck her head around Roxanne's door.

"Sorry. This just happened." Roxanne raised her head from a sheet of paper, putting together work schedules that would free up some of her team to go help out tomorrow. The dams at the south end of the lake were out of her area, but all the RCMP detachments nearby were expected to pitch in during an emergency like this. "I'm going to have to get this organized. But I have found out where Julie Gilchrist probably is." She related what Susan Rice had told her. "And the Sunnywell Centre is right in the flood zone. I could send Pete and Sam there tomorrow, to help with sandbagging and I could drop by and visit, if you like. But right now, I need to get this done."

"Do you want to come over to our house later?" said Izzy. "We can order Chinese. Bring Finn. We can park him on Matt and talk about this case."

"You sure Matt won't mind?"

"No, he likes kids. I'll tell him."

Roxanne knew Matt Stavros. He'd worked the Magnusson case with her, alongside Izzy. He reminded her a bit of her late husband, Jake, though not in looks. Matt was darker and built more squarely than Jake, but they were alike in manner. Kind, considerate men, both of them.

It was evening when she drove up the driveway to Izzy and Matt's brand-new house out on a country road west of Cullen Village. She had been there before, walked around the veranda, had a peek at the mudroom, been shown all four bedrooms and three bathrooms.

"It's just made for a family," she had overheard Izzy's mother declare at Bill Gilchrist's retirement party. Matt had inherited the land from an aunt. It had been built some distance away from where her house had once stood. That area was now grassed over, still damp with snow melt, two mountain ash trees planted at its centre.

"They're supposed to ward off evil spirits," Izzy had told her.

The sun was going down behind Roxanne's car, a blaze of red and orange, turning the wet grass a fleshy shade of pink. The trees sent out long-fingered shadows that reached toward the new house. Roxanne had picked up an order at the Chinese restaurant in Cullen Village on the way. She let Finn out of the car and carried a couple of bags to the house.

Matt opened the door, a small, scruffy dog at his heels.

"What have you got there?"

"This is Joseph." Matt grinned. Finn fell to his knees and stretched out a hand. He wanted a dog, badly. Any dog. But he was in school all day and Roxanne was at work. It wasn't going to happen. "I found him at Mo Magnusson's."

"He was supposed to come home with a real dog." Izzy appeared in a doorway and rolled her eyes.

"What happened to his teeth?" Finn rubbed the furry head.

"Don't know. Maybe they just grew that way," said Matt. They walked into the kitchen. Matt spent most of his days now studying for exams at a table beside the window. His books had been cleared for now and were stacked on the shiny new floor, in a corner. Roxanne dropped the bags on the kitchen counter.

"You hungry, Finn?" Matt opened them up. "How's about we get ourselves a plateful and take Joseph next door."

"I just want wontons," said Finn, helping himself to a handful.

Izzy opened the fridge door. "We've got wine and we've got beer."

Roxanne loaded up a plate with noodles and vegetables and sat at the table. She watched her son follow Matt and the dog into the living area. Someday, Matt Stavros would make a great dad.

"This case is going so slow!" Izzy passed over a glass of wine and joined Roxanne, her plate loaded with lemon chicken, battered shrimps and pork ribs. "It's going to be another day at least before the body's thawed and that's Sunday. It'll be forever before we get results. Meantime, they've got a couple of guys glued to their computers going through every case they've got on record that Sergeant Bill was ever involved in, just so they'll be ready if this all really does go sideways."

"But you're to ask questions around here? Right now?"

"I'm supposed to be discreet. Whatever that means." Izzy bit into a large shrimp. Her favourite. "And it's still just me on the job."

"Do you want some help?" Roxanne offered.

Izzy grinned. "Sure. Helps to have someone to talk to about it."

Roxanne put down her fork. Chinese food did not come with chopsticks out here. "What if it really was an accident?" she asked.

"Don't think so. You know there's damage to his knee? They're not sure how much but it's possible it was a hit and run."

"Yes, but just suppose," Roxanne insisted. "Think about it. He could have gone for a long walk. It would take twenty minutes max to reach the highway from his house. It's three intersections more to get to Kuryk Road, so an hour at the most if you walked at a decent pace. The temperature was at seven, eight degrees the end of that week in March, that warm spell before the snowstorm blew in, so he wore a spring jacket and opened it up when he warmed up from the exercise. But there was still snowpack on the roads back then, and it iced over at night. It thawed where it caught the sun but stayed frozen in the shade. So he could have been striding along, stepped on a slippery patch, fell over. Cracked his leg on a lump of ice or a rock as he went down. Right?"

"No." Izzy sat back in her chair, unpersuaded. "Can you imagine Sergeant Bill going for a walk all by himself? Not a chance."

"He'd just got back from a four-day drive from Arizona. The golf courses aren't open around here yet. Maybe he needed the exercise. And some fresh air."

"Nope," Izzy repeated. "He never walked if he could take the car. You've seen the belly he had on him. Too many lunches and doughnuts with his coffee. He worked at a desk all day and parked himself in front of the TV at night. He gave up curling because he hated being on his feet for that length of time."

"What if he needed to get out of the house? Did he and Julie get along okay? Could they have had an argument?"

"Don't think so," said Izzy. "They seemed to get along just fine. She's pretty quiet."

"But Susan Rice says she needed to get some space to herself, soon as they got back. What was that about? It's possible, right? That they had a fight and he stomped off? Maybe someone saw him walking. If it happened on Sunday, someone might have been around at Desna Church."

"Could be." Izzy got up and fetched a paper pad and pen from Matt's stash. "Ukrainian Easter was the weekend after. They might have been getting the church ready."

"Who else lives out there?"

"Besides the Kuryks at the farm? There's a couple that built a new house, further along Desna Road. Then there's Jenn the Potter and her husband the Dopehead. They're on the next block."

"What about the farmhouse, over in the other direction, to the north? You can just see it from the place where he was found."

"I don't think anyone's living there anymore." Izzy took notes.

Finn ran into the kitchen with the dog at his heels. "We're going to make popcorn," he called to his mother, "and play a game." He disappeared into the washroom. The dog ran in with him.

"He's doing fine," Matt assured Roxanne as he took a packet of popcorn out of a cupboard and put it in the microwave. "Nice kid."

"If it was a hit-and-run, someone has a dent in the front end." Izzy lifted her head, ignoring the interruption. "We could check to find out if anyone's had a repair done."

Roxanne shook her head. "It's the weekend. There won't be any service staff working at the garages around here."

"Lots of guys do repairs on the side," said Izzy. "Remember Erik Axelsson?" Roxanne did. Erik had been married to Roberta and was Mo Magnusson's birth father. He had made money on the side by repairing cars. "I'll ask my dad. Or my brother. They'll know."

"Find out if they've heard of anyone badmouthing Bill Gilchrist lately while you're at it. I'll get my guys to ask around too." Roxanne made a mental note to herself. "I still think it's more likely that someone's done this deliberately."

"That someone killed him? Bill Gilchrist got along with everybody out here. He made a point of it."

"Won't Kathy Isfeld know?" Matt stood listening at the microwave while the corn popped. Finn and the dog ran past him toward the sofa. "She was working in the detachment before he ever moved here."

"She's off for the weekend," said Roxanne. "But she lives just behind me. I could ask her."

"What's happening with Finn tomorrow?" Matt asked. Finn had a hockey game, first thing, but it was another mom's turn to drive. Roxanne could free herself up for the morning at least. "Where's he playing?" he volunteered. "I'll go pick him up. He can hang out with me and Joseph, rest of the day, if you like."

"You sure? Sigrid Isfeld's my regular babysitter but I think she's got a game herself, tomorrow."

"She has," said Izzy. She had once coached that same team and she kept in touch. "Plays on the forward line. She's good."

"That's settled then." Matt took the bowl out of the microwave and went into the living room. "Hey, Finn," they heard him say. "Want to come over here tomorrow? Help me build some bookshelves?"

Roxanne was pleased. If a murder investigation was looming, having Matt available to care for her son was going to make it easier for her to work outside her regular schedule, should that need ever arise.

6

SANDBAGGING WAS WELL underway at the Sunnywell Centre by 9:00 on Saturday morning. Roxanne noticed Pete Robinson heaving sandbags off the back of a truck, parked close to the riverbank. "Hi, Sarge," he said when he saw her. "Come to help?"

"Not yet," she told him. "I have to talk to someone first."

Each bag was being passed along a row of volunteers to be stacked on a growing wall. It needed to be three feet high at least when it was finished, and watertight. They were halfway up and fighting a battle against time. The river roared by, filled to the top of its banks with fast-moving, murky brown water, sweeping chunks of ice and broken tree branches along with it.

Up ahead, where it curved, Roxanne could see the source of the trouble, piled ice, wedged into a solid dam, stretching from one bank to the other.

"It's like that all the way around the bend," a sturdy, thick-set woman, one of the organizers, informed her. Roxanne's presence wasn't questioned. Her uniform gave her the authority to be there, watching. Pete and Sam Mendes were wearing theirs, too. Being seen to do community work boosted the RCMP's profile and that was encouraged by the Force. "They're trying to break it up from the far end, but it's hard going. The ice is unstable and it's piled three feet thick in most places."

The Sunnywell Arts and Wellness Centre still showed evidence of its roots as a convent. The Sisters of the Sacred Heart had lived there for more than a hundred years, until their number dwindled to a handful, all elderly, and they retired to the mother house. The diocese had tried to run religious programs for a decade or so after they left. The chapel had not been deconsecrated until around the turn of the century, when they had finally decided to sell. It was presently owned and operated by the widow of a man who had inherited old Winnipeg money and invested it well. She had informed him, at his deathbed, that she would put his accumulated wealth to good use. He was in no condition by that time to argue.

Mrs. Benedict now lived on-site, in what had been the main building of the convent. She maintained a suite of rooms on the first floor, with a view over the treed and grassy grounds to the riverbank. It was usually a tranquil scene, but not today, as more trucks arrived, leaving tracks across the lawn, and volunteers in thick-soled rubber boots stomped all over the grounds.

Bea Benedict liked to think of herself as an arts benefactor. She served on several boards, including that of the Prairie Theatre Centre and the local symphony. She had converted the chapel into a small performance venue—the acoustics were superb—and knocked down walls to create spaces for workshops and artwork display. She liked to tell her friends and potential funders that she "nurtured creative projects and the artistic souls who dreamed them up."

It had not taken long to discover that these activities were too much of a drain on her resources, but the convent's religious roots and its normally peaceful surroundings, less than a half hour's drive away from the outskirts of the city, made it ideally suited for gatherings of a spiritual or therapeutic kind. The wellness community was eager to rent the centre's facilities as a venue for meetings, gatherings, conferences and events and many of its members also had the resources to pay for it. Mrs. Benedict had expanded her mandate and the centre's name accordingly. The Sunnywell Arts and Wellness Centre did well enough, now, to pay its bills and to keep its patron happily occupied.

Seeing an RCMP sergeant walk in the front door on this particular Saturday morning did not surprise her. Like everyone else, she assumed that Roxanne was there because of the sandbagging. The barricade needed to be completed by nightfall or the east side of her property could be submerged. More sandbags were needed to protect the house in case that happened and the basement started to fill up with river water. She had pumps at the ready. Keeping the volunteers fed and on task was imperative. An army of women was in the kitchen making sandwiches and chopping up vegetables for soup. Fortunately, there was only one group of meditators in residence, and so far they hadn't complained about the ruckus outside.

She was surprised to discover that Sergeant Calloway was not there because of the flood. She did not know if a woman called Julie Gilchrist was one of the meditators.

"We don't handle individual registrations," she said, folding her hands under her ample bosom and speaking in the fluting tones of a woman who was used to being listened to. "We rent out rooms and provide meals and accommodation, if required. The organization tells us how many attendees to expect and pays us in one lump sum."

Roxanne explained that a death had occurred. Bea beckoned Roxanne into her office, behind the front desk.

"Ask someone to bring us some coffee, Mary," she ordered a young woman who was working there. "And some nice biscuits." The front hallway was spacious, with tall ceilings and polished wood. A staircase rose at its centre. The room behind it was also large, with an imposing desk and solid oak bookshelves. The nuns who had lived in this house watched from photographs that hung on the walls.

Mrs. Benedict led the way to a chintz-covered sofa and matching armchairs in front of a window. She pulled the curtains almost closed and lit a couple of lamps, so they did not have to look at the havoc that was happening to her lawns. Then she arranged herself in one fat armchair, crossed her legs and indicated that Roxanne should take the other.

"Now," she said. "Do tell me all about this." Her lips pursed as she listened, and her brow furrowed. The coffee arrived, in a tall china pot with matching cups and saucers and a plate of short-bread, carried in by Mary, on a tray. The nuns had been known to be frugal. Mrs. Benedict saw no reason to continue that tradition.

"Mary," she said. "Could you ask that Sheila person who is with our current rental to please join us? They're a quiet group," she continued as she poured. "Got here two Saturdays ago. Some kind of Buddhists, I believe. Silent meditation. They have a teacher that they call Lama John. He holds a communal session every afternoon in one of our larger rooms. They chant, then he talks. Most of them come to the dining hall for meals. They can take food back to their rooms if they prefer. They eat without saying a single word to one another. It's all quite peculiar."

Mary ushered a woman into the room. Her grey hair was shorn almost to her skull, she wore a long cotton skirt and had a woven shawl draped around her shoulders. Round beads hung from her wrist. She smiled.

"We asked not to be disturbed, Mrs. Benedict," she stated, without changing her expression, then stopped when she saw the uniformed RCMP officer in the room. "Oh!' she exclaimed, her forehead creasing with concern. "Is something wrong?"

Roxanne was introduced. The woman's name was Sheila Bond. Mrs. Benedict sent Mary off in search of another cup.

"I need to talk to Julie Gilchrist, who, I believe, is meditating with you," said Roxanne.

Sheila Bond sat in the middle of the large floral sofa. A streak of light shone through a crack in the curtains and illuminated her oval face. "That is quite impossible, Sergeant," she said, tempering her remark with that mild, benign smile. "We guarantee that our attendees will not be disturbed."

Bea Benedict responded before Roxanne could open her mouth. "Her husband is dead!" she declared. "And it is a matter for the RCMP. You must make an exception!"

Sheila Bond blanched, but the gentle smile did not waver. "I don't know," she said, equally insistent. "Lama John gave strict instructions that the participants in the retreat were to remain silent, regardless of the circumstances." There was a loud clanging of metal outside the window and voices shouting. Another truck had arrived and dropped its tailgate, right outside the window.

"In that case, I need to speak to Lama John myself," said Roxanne. Sheila Bond's pale eyes grew anxious and her hand reached over to finger the beads on her opposite wrist.

"He must not be disturbed," she said, articulating each syllable, her face serious, the smile gone.

Roxanne decided that confrontation was going to get her nowhere. Better to back off and try again. "But Julie Gilchrist is with your group?" she asked. Sheila Bond seemed to be temporarily appeased.

"I think she's on the list," she said, rising from the sofa. "I'll go and check." They watched the door close behind her.

"Some of these groups have strange ideas," said Mrs. Benedict, "but I suppose we do have to give people what they have paid for." There was more banging and shouting outside. Sheila Bond returned, carrying a spiral notebook. She sat once more and ran her finger down a list.

"Julie Gilchrist registered late, the day before we started," she said. "She paid by credit card, in full, over the phone. And she arrived on Saturday." She pointed to a check mark by Julie's name. "She must have been here by lunchtime. She's staying in one of the cabins, and they were all filled up by the afternoon."

Half of the retreatants were housed in rooms above them, in the main building, but the option that offered greater privacy was to stay in one of ten wooden cabins, constructed at Mrs. Benedict's own expense on the far side of the property.

"Meditators love them," she said. "So do writers." Lama John was staying in one of them too. "They are in our woodland, separate from each other. Very private. Come. I'll show you. Perhaps you can talk with her when they stop for lunch."

Good, Roxanne thought. Then she could meet Julie Gilchrist without alarming the rest of the group or violating their rules. They left the big building. Sam Mendes stood by a large truck, wielding a shovel. He raised a hand in greeting and watched her go, obviously curious as to what she was doing.

The cabins lay down woodland paths, surrounded by oak trees interspersed with clusters of spruce. The nuns had walked the Stations of the Cross here. The statuary remained at each turn in the path, but the cabins had been situated between them, so that the residents did not have to look at images of an agonized Jesus when they sat out on their porches, and each had been given a zodiacal name. The Centre, like Susan Rice, aimed to embrace all spiritual beliefs. The cabin that Julie Gilchrist had been assigned was called Orion. It had a small porch with a bench under the window. Empty wooden planters stood each side of the door and an ample supply of firewood was stacked at the far end.

"Strange," said Mrs. Benedict. "It doesn't look like any of it has been used."

Roxanne tried the door handle. The cabin was unlocked.

"Should you be going in there?" Sheila Bond inquired. She had wrapped the scarf around her head to protect her scalp from the air. It was still quite chilly. Roxanne ignored her comment and entered.

There were only two rooms; no plumbing, so the residents used washrooms in the main house. Water bottles were supplied and one had been drunk, the empty bottle returned to the crate.

"That's funny." Sheila suppressed her scruples and followed her in. "Most of our meditators bring a cushion to sit on and they usually set up a shrine."

There was no sign of either. A fabric tote bag, probably of Julie's own making, was propped against a padded chair, beside the window. It contained sketchbooks, drawing materials, swatches of fabric. The wood stove was set for a fire.

"It doesn't look like it's been lit at all." Bea opened the front of the stove and peeked inside. "Strange. It gets quite cold in the evenings."

The bed in the other room was made up. A night shirt was neatly folded and placed under the pillow and a knitted cardigan hung in the closet. There was no sign at all of Julie Gilchrist.

A knock at the door startled them. Constable Sam Mendes opened it. "A word, Sarge," he said. Roxanne joined him on the deck. "We just heard there's another ice jam, up at Edgeware Creek. They're scared it's going to flood the north end of Cullen Village."

7

ANOTHER TRUCK LOADED with sandbags stood in Sasha Rosenberg's driveway. Hers was one of the houses under threat of flooding. Edgeware Creek was normally a peaceful stream, home to ducks and teals and the occasional blue heron now arriving back from winter migration. It travelled from western farmlands to the north end of Cullen Village, ran through culverts, under a roadway into the marina, and from there out into the big lake. But not today. A brown torrent surged along its path, carrying ice and debris with it.

Broken ice had piled up at its mouth, where it flowed into the culverts. Constable Ken Roach stood on the roadway above them, looking down onto sharp pointed white and grey shards, wedged between the rushes that edged the creek's banks. Village Counsellor Freya Halliday gesticulated beside him. They disagreed as to how the emergency should be handled and were equally certain that each one of them was right. Men with ice augers had congregated on the other side of the road and clambered down onto the wooden piers that ringed the marina. From there, they drilled holes into the ice to weaken it. The noise made it difficult for Roach and Counsellor Halliday to make themselves heard. It did not stop them. They just spoke louder.

Behind the ice pack, the water was backing up. Ten houses were at risk, all of them on the south side of the creek. They were the ones being sandbagged and the village had turned out in force to help. Margo Wishart had put in over an hour already. She found it heavy work. She'd been relieved when a couple of girls' hockey teams, their game over at Cullen Village arena, had shown up to help and she'd been sent inside to assist with the food instead. Now she was in Sasha's kitchen, making sandwiches.

"The RCMP's searching for Julie Gilchrist." Sasha filled a large thermos with coffee. One of her neighbours had a large deck. It had been commandeered as a warm-up station. Sasha's job was to help keep it supplied with hot drinks and food. "That's what Roxanne Calloway was doing at Susan Rice's house yesterday." Sasha screwed down the cap on the thermos. "Questioned her for ages. Susan thinks Julie's gone away on some kind of retreat."

"She might have. Julie's always been into that kind of thing," Margo said, laying meat slices onto bread. "She meditates a lot of the time. It's only two days since they found her husband's body. Maybe she doesn't know that he's dead."

"Or she does. She could have bumped him off and then done a bunk," said Sasha.

"Julie?" Margo looked skeptical. "Have you met her? She's a quiet little thing. And she's nice."

She looked out Sasha's window, across the back garden. A metal gazebo frame stood in the centre of a grassy square, bordered with shrubs. At the far end was a large shed, converted into a studio, where Sasha plied her art. An upside-down canoe lay beside it. Sasha like to paddle the creek on warm summer nights. One of her few extravagances was to rent a berth at the marina so she could use the clubhouse during the summer months. It amused her to leave the canoe among the motor launches and expensive sailboats that usually moored there. Margo could glimpse brown water, burbling along. It had risen a good two inches since she first arrived. Another foot and the garden and studio would be swamped. She wrapped stretch film over the sandwiches. "I'll take these over to next door," she said.

UP ON THE neighbour's deck, the village mayor was shaking hands, thanking people for their participation in the rescue effort.

A reporter from the local newspaper stood by, camera on hand, ready for a good photo op.

"Guess the RCMP sent us Roach," said a round-bellied man, chomping on a Rice Krispie square. "Too bad Bill Gilchrist isn't still around. He'd know how to get people organized without getting up their noses."

"Freya's dealing with him." The mayor was good at delegating out jobs he'd rather not do himself. He figured that Counsellor Halliday was a match for Ken Roach when it came to being assertive.

"Bad business, that, about Gilchrist." The man popped what was left of the square into his mouth. "He was a good guy. Where's that woman who's replaced him? Shouldn't she be here?"

His wife stepped out the glass door behind him, carrying a crockpot full of hot chili. "Maybe she's got other things to do. Like looking for whoever killed him," she said, handing the pot to him. "Find somewhere to plug that in, will you? Those girl hockey players that are sandbagging are due a break and I'll bet they're starving."

THE DINING HALL at the Sunnywell Centre was thronged with noisy, hungry volunteers. They ate in shifts. Lunch started early. It would take three hours to feed them all.

Lama John sent a request, in writing. His group wished to eat together in the large room where they usually met so that they could remain quiet.

"They haven't offered to help sandbag?" Roxanne asked. Bea Benedict waved a dismissive hand.

"This retreat is a big deal for some of them. They take time off work for it. Nothing gets to interrupt it. But it's all right. We have enough helpers out there."

"Maybe I could speak to all of them at the same time," said Roxanne. "When they stop to eat." Sheila Bond was informed. Her beatific smile was strained but she conveyed the message.

Information regarding Julie Gilchrist's presence, or lack of, had been hard to find. The notebook in the tote bag that she had left in the cabin was blank.

"She brought work with her, here?" Sheila had sniffed her disapproval when she saw it. The meditators were not permitted to bring books or use phones while they were in retreat. They were instructed to leave their devices at home or to lock them in their cars. Roxanne fired off a text to Izzy. Julie Gilchrist must have taken her phone with her, wherever she had gone.

The registration form that Julie had completed had asked if a parking space was required. She had said yes, but the Centre had not asked what make of car she drove or taken down the registration number.

"We usually have plenty space for parkers," Mrs. Benedict sighed. "But not today." The Centre had two parking lots, both full, because of the sandbaggers. The driveway was lined with cars nose to tail.

Lama John's group began their communal lunch. Roxanne met the lama in the hallway outside the room where they were eating, first. He was a small, rotund man, head either bald or shaved or a combination of both. She was surprised to see that he wore street clothes, comfortably baggy. Given his title, she had expected to see robes. A string of beads hung around his neck and his feet were bare. On his face was the same bland smile as that of his minion. He bowed, hands together, when they were introduced.

He did not know Julie Gilchrist personally, he said. She had been referred to him by Susan Rice, who sometimes meditated with him.

"You don't know what she looks like?" Roxanne wished she had a photograph. He did not. Could she keep her remarks to a minimum, he requested, so that the equilibrium of the retreatants should not be disturbed too much? They were eating mindfully, as a part of their practice.

The meditators each sat on a cushion, well-spaced. On the floor, in front of each, was a bowl of soup, a sandwich on a plate, and a glass of water. Some lifted a spoon slowly to their mouths, drank the soup and lowered it just as slowly. Others raised the sandwich, bit a small mouthful and returned it to its place. When they had swallowed, they paused, gazing off into the middle distance. The only sound in the room was that of chewing. The hubbub continued outside, but they seemed oblivious to it.

Lama John's cushion was on an elevated platform, in front of them. He did not sit but stood beside it, hands folded, and nodded to Sheila Bond, who rang a bell. Twenty-some pairs of eyes were raised toward him. The chewing stopped. All spoons and half-eaten sandwiches were returned to their places

"I regret having to disturb you," said the lama. His voice acquired a deeper resonance than it had when he had spoken to Roxanne minutes before. "This is Sergeant Calloway of the RCMP. She is inquiring about the presence of one of our participants." All eyes shifted, to focus on Roxanne. No one else spoke a word.

The RCMP needed to talk to Julie Gilchrist, she told them, regarding a sudden family bereavement. Concern registered on some of the watching faces. Julie had signed up for this course. Did any of them know her? Had any of them seen her?

A woman three rows back raised a tentative hand and looked toward Lama John. He inclined his head, giving her permission to speak.

"I've done a quilting workshop with her," she said, "I recognized her. She was here the first day, the Saturday, when we gathered in the evening, Lama John, and you gave us our instructions. I don't think I've seen her since."

IZZY CALLED IN at the Kuryk farm. The farmer was slightly less taciturn with her than he had been when Mo Magnusson stopped by. Izzy was, after all, Dave McBain's kid. Dave farmed south of

Stan Kuryk's place, his son with him, good guys, both of them. And Izzy was a cop. Plus, he had a complaint to make.

"That body was lying on my land," he grouched, hands pushed deep into the pockets of his overalls. "Who says I can't have access to it?" The area around the ditch was still taped off. It took in a tiny fraction of his field. He was just making a point, for the sake of it. Whoever had laid flowers there had ignored the tape and left footprints.

"Soon as we know more," said Izzy and went to talk to his wife instead. Netta Kuryk was more forthcoming. Her kitchen smelled of yeasty bread dough. She covered a bowl and put it on top of the stove to rise, washed her hands and poured Izzy a mug of coffee.

"So nothing was happening around here a couple of weeks ago?" A cookie jar had been cracked open. Izzy chose one. Oatmeal with raisins.

"The week of the storm? Oh yes," said Netta. "That was the week before Ukrainian Easter. We had to get the church ready. I make paska." Easter bread was her speciality. The grandkids used to come out to decorate traditional Easter eggs with her, but they weren't interested any more. She attended the church whenever she could, but they didn't have their own priest these days. The congregation had shrunk and they were lucky if someone came out from the city to conduct a service once a month. But there had been one for the Easter service. Some Ukrainian churches had switched over to a western calendar, but not them. They followed the old ways and celebrated Easter on the traditional date, same as in the old country. They made an effort to make the place look its best.

Had she noticed if Sergeant Gilchrist had walked by?

"No." She shook her head. "What would he be walking out here for?" Had she seen anyone else? No one. Nobody ever walked around here. They drove. Threw their garbage out of their car windows. You should see what ended up in the ditch. Netta looked uneasily in the vague direction of the northeast corner of Kuryk

Road, remembering what had been found there. She bit a cookie. Izzy helped herself to another.

The other people that had worked at the church that weekend, mostly came from Fiskar Bay. They didn't drive past the farm either. Jenn the Potter had been around. Her grandparents had helped build the church and she took an interest. She'd got it designated as an historic site. The church might have been closed and torn down otherwise. They'd done that to one in Cullen Village a few years back. The onion dome ripped off, lying like a giant black eggshell on the ground. Shocking, but that was the diocese for you. Anything to save money. No respect. Izzy should go talk to Jenn. She might have seen something. Izzy took her leave, through a porch lined with racks of seedlings, placed to catch the light. She recognized zucchini, tomatoes, beans, beets.

"These are coming along," she said. Netta's broad face brightened, pleased she'd noticed. She looked hopefully through the window. Patches of uncovered grass were beginning to green up. A square garden plot was waiting for her to fill it up with plants.

"Can't wait to get out there," she said. "Not long now."

THE PASSIVE ECOLOGICAL house that the couple from the city had built was half a mile past the Kuryk farm. It was made of new wood, rectangular, with a sloping roof covered in solar panels, and had a row of south-facing windows, blinds half drawn, looking as if it was brooding over the landscape. The new outbuildings were closed and so was the house. No one was home.

Izzy continued through another couple of intersections, then bumped down a potholed driveway. Jenn the Potter greeted her at the door of a shabby little house. Inside it was warm and colourful, the walls lined with shelves full of books and samples of her work. Her husband was out, working the woodlot. He aimed to supply them with enough logs to keep the stove going all winter and to fuel a brick-built kiln out back. Izzy noticed oil lamps and candlesticks. This house had no electricity, but there was a well in a pumphouse near the back door. She couldn't see any sign of an outside biffy, but she expected there was one.

"I just heard yesterday." Jenn wrung her large potter's hands. "I didn't know a thing about it. And he was lying in a ditch, just past the farm?" Her eyes welled up. Jenn was a sensitive soul. She had seen nothing. No one. "We were snowed in for days after the storm. Kel's tractor died, and it took us forever to shovel it out so he could go get a part." She'd been able to get over to the church that Sunday, but not for long. She liked to take care of the icons. "They're really special," she said. She'd driven back home, along Desna Road. Hadn't seen anyone at all. No car, no nothing.

Izzy drove back along the same route. There were no signs of activity at the church today. Too bad. She'd have liked to see inside. She should have asked Netta or Jenn who had a key. Probably one of them did. One of Izzy's grandmothers had gone to a church like that. Izzy had been taken along at Easter to get her coloured eggs blessed. She remembered a hot stove, a choir singing up above her, spooky old pictures of Jesus, a four-cornered tabernacle that looked like the church in miniature and a service that seemed to last forever.

She covered her feet in plastic when she reached Heron Haven and pulled on latex gloves and a mask before she searched, thoroughly this time. The Gilchrists had given up on a landline long since, but she found no cellphones or tablets or computers. In Julie's loft above the garage a business desk stood in a corner. A drawer contained details of quilts Julie had made and sold, with photographs neatly filed. She kept invoices in a box and maintained a manual ledger. Two shelves above it held books about sewing and quilting. There was a printer and a packet of copy paper, but no computer.

Izzy looked around at all the supplies and the unopened bags, the sewing machines, an ironing table. Behind a screen in the corner, a Buddha sat on top of a small bookcase. The shelves below it held incense holders, an empty vase and a row of silver bowls. Propped against the wall was a large cushion and, beside it, a rolled-up yoga mat.

She looked out the window to the east. The lake was calm, shiny smooth, all the way to the horizon, the ice patch at its edge. Then she heard a car approaching. She reached the window opposite, one that looked out over the top of the garage doors, in time to see a small green car drive up.

She barely made it downstairs and into the hallway, the plastic covers flapping at her feet, in time to see the door open. Two women looked at her. One appeared to be in her twenties. She recognized the other.

"Izzy McBain! Why are you in my house? And is it true that Bill is dead?" asked Julie Gilchrist.

8

JULIE GILCHRIST HAD left Kenora, Ontario, before 10:00 that morning and reached the Winnipeg airport in time to pick up her daughter, Hazel, shortly after noon.

"Someone from the RCMP called to tell me about Dad. Then my sister sent a message." said Hazel. "They said they couldn't find my mother. So I called my Aunt Sherry in Kenora and, of course, Mom was there." She eyed Izzy up and down through black-rimmed glasses, taking in the plastic bootees, the blue latex gloves and the mask dangling at her throat. "Are the police searching for something specific? Do you have a search warrant? This isn't a crime scene, is it? The cop who talked to me said it looked like Dad had been in an accident."

Hazel must have probed, Izzy thought, to get that answer. But still. Whoever had talked to her shouldn't have said that. They still had no idea how Bill Gilchrist had ended up in the ditch.

Izzy unhooked the mask from her ear. "We tried to find you, Julie, so we'd tell you first. How come neither of you got in touch with us? Didn't you hear the news?"

"I'm busy writing term papers, Constable," was Hazel's tart reply. "I'll go get the bags."

Julie hung her jacket in a closet and exchanged her shoes for a pair of felted slippers. "I was staying with my sister. Going for walks and talking and doing crossword puzzles. Taking some time off. I didn't listen to the news or look at my iPad. Exactly what has happened to Bill?" she asked.

Izzy told her what they had found so far. Julie looked dismayed. She walked to one of the big brown sofas and sat, her hands folded in her lap. Hazel joined them. She had last seen her husband on the Saturday morning, two weeks previously, Julie said.

"We got back from Arizona that Friday. I needed some time to myself and my yoga teacher suggested a meditation retreat run by a Buddhist she knows at the Sunnywell Centre. It seemed like a good idea, so I signed up."

Julie's pointed little face was framed by curly light brown hair. It was obvious why people said she was like a mouse. She wore a thin sweater and a quilted vest, in shades of mauve and taupe. Her skin was slightly tanned, not as brown as you would expect after five months in the sunny southern states.

"I left here first thing Saturday morning. It was a beautiful day. And quiet at Sunnywell, hardly anyone around. The retreat didn't start until the evening, so I had the day to myself. I had no idea that I would never see Bill again alive." She stared at the wall in front of her, at a quilted landscape in greens and blues and browns, representing the marsh water along the shores of the lake, but her eyes were blank, like she wasn't seeing a thing.

"I got one of the cabins, in the woods," she continued. "It was very private. I walked a lot that day. Past the Stations of the Cross. Have you been there? Seen them? So cruel and violent. They make me shudder. It was warm enough to sit on the deck, in the sun, but I spent more time by the river. It was just starting to break up.

"Then I went to the first session of the retreat. I knew right away it wasn't the right choice. So earnest and so many instructions. And the lama was, well, intense. Not the right teacher for me. I thought I could just spend some time in my cabin instead. Do some work on a project I was thinking about. But the next morning I decided to drive to Kenora instead and spend a couple of days with my sister. I meant to come back; I'd paid for the whole two weeks. I left some of my things there, but I should have taken them with me because when I got to Sherry's it was so comfortable that I just stayed."

"Not to worry, Mom. I'll call and make sure you get them back." Hazel Gilchrist reached out and gave her mother's hand a reassuring pat.

"You didn't call Bill to let him know where you were?" Izzy asked.

Julie shook her curly head. No, she hadn't. She had told him that she would be in that retreat for two weeks, in silence, unable to talk to anyone. "So, there was no need, I thought."

Hazel wrapped a protective arm around her. The look she gave Izzy over the top of her mother's head was reproachful. "My mother cried almost all the way here."

Julie did look puffy around the eyes and the end of her little nose was red, but right now she was tearless and calm.

"Did Bill have any health issues?" asked Izzy.

Julie looked surprised by the question. "He needed to lose some weight," she said. "His blood pressure was a bit high. But nothing serious."

"No heart disease? Diabetes?"

Julie shook her head slowly from side to side. "You think he had a heart attack?"

Her daughter latched eagerly onto the suggestion. "Or a stroke? That he died of natural causes?"

"We won't know until after the autopsy."

Julie's lip quivered when she heard that. She took a deep breath and composed herself.

Hazel was in her twenties, dark-haired, with features that resembled her mother's but with a sharper edge. Her glasses made her look more like a watchful owl than a mouse. She needed to fly back to Toronto on Monday, she said.

"It's almost the end of term. I can't afford to miss the time. I've a group presentation on Tuesday morning that counts toward my final marks. I've got to be there. If Dad's death was accidental, there hasn't been a crime, right? So there won't be a long investigation? How long will it be before we can get his body back and organize a funeral? Soon as I'm done I can come back here and help Mom out."

"What about Fern?" said Izzy. "Your sister. Can't she help your mom?"

"Fern's not much use," Hazel explained. "She's hardly been near Mom and Dad since she married Cory Wiebe. If you want to talk to her, you'd best try to get hold of her today. It's Saturday. She won't talk to you tomorrow. They belong to a fundamentalist Christian cult that observes the Sabbath."

"She came here yesterday," said Izzy. "To Fiskar Bay. She'd heard about your father, and she was concerned." Julie's mouth dropped open, surprised, and Hazel looked perplexed.

"Really?" Julie asked. "You spoke to her?"

"Yup," said Izzy. "Been a long time. I haven't seen her since high school. She came here, to your house. She had her youngest kid with her." Julie's eyes began to film over. "She was worried. Maybe you could give her a call. You can't go visit, though. We need you to stay in Fiskar Bay for now," Izzy told them. "Until we know for sure how Bill died. It might not take long. We should get autopsy results early in the week."

Julie crumpled. She leaned her face into her daughter's shoulder. Hazel wrapped a protective arm around her. She frowned at Izzy, reproachful once more, and patted her mother's back.

"Don't worry, Mom. I'll come back, soon as I can, and I'll take care of everything."

BY LATE AFTERNOON, the ice dam at Cullen Village had been breached. A gap, two feet wide, had been opened all the way to the culverts. Water began to run through them again. Constable Roach had busied himself keeping onlookers at bay. His car blocked one end of Marina Road, lights flashing. He'd taped off the section of road that bridged the creek and

mounted guard, deciding who should, or should not, be allowed
to drive through.

"Keeps him occupied," Counsellor Freya Halliday commented
to Margo Wishart, a bowl of soup in one hand, a spoon in the other.
She herself had still plenty of work to do. She had taken on the task
of making sure that all the men who still worked to widen the icy
channel were given breaks and got some hot food into them. Once
she had eaten, she'd head down and send another hungry squad
back to the deck. They waved goodbye to a couple of the hockey
players who were just leaving. Those girls had worked hard.

"It didn't rain," Freya said, looking up at the sky. And will you
look at that!" She pointed with her spoon. A rainbow had emerged
in the eastern sky, over the lake. "A good omen, don't you think?"

Margo did not imagine for a second that a woman as practical
as Freya Halliday believed that their good fortune depended on
lucky signs from the cosmos, but she and the others on the deck
did look up and feel a little lighter, seeing that band of colour
curving up from the edge of the water.

The mayor had returned to his office to get ready for a phone
interview with a CBC reporter. The news about the averted disaster
at Cullen Village would be broadcast on the evening news.

AT THE SUNNYWELL Centre, the volunteers had built the protective wall to the required height. The parking lot was almost
emptied as they drove home to their suppers and their beds, leaving a stalwart few to monitor the still-flowing river. There were
pumps at the ready, just in case the water found an unexpected
leak in the sandbagged barrier. Lama John's group gathered together, sat on their cushions and chanted to Tara, female Buddha
of compassion, to invoke her protection.

Bea Benedict walked her grounds. She passed Orion, the cabin
that Julie Gilchrist should have occupied. She knew by now that
the RCMP had found out where she was. A woman who said
she was Mrs. Gilchrist's daughter had called, asking her to set

aside Julie's belongings for pickup, sometime tomorrow. As if she needed something else to take care of.

BY NIGHTFALL, ONLY Ken Roach remained at Edgeware Creek. All the people who lived along its banks were inside their houses, safe once more and tired from the day's efforts. The creek was still swollen. Ice remained on either bank, caught by a thick mat of reeds, but the centre of the stream was running through the culverts into the marina. All was well, for now. He began to spool up the tape that he had put up around the bridge. Traffic could start to move along the road again and soon he, too, could go home.

The streets of Fiskar Bay were almost deserted. It looked to be a quiet Saturday night. Sam Mendes and Ravi Anand were out on patrol, keeping an eye on the traffic around the pubs and out on the highway. Nothing much else was going on. Roxanne drove to Izzy's house to pick up her son. Figures on her car dashboard told her that the outside temperature was a balmy seven degrees. The sky was banded with red and gold in the west. There wouldn't be a hint of frost overnight.

Matt Stavros was out on his veranda, grilling wieners on a gas barbecue. Finn trotted down the steps to meet her.

"C'mon, Joseph!" he called to the dog, but it was not leaving the smell of roasting sausages. They'd built the bookshelves, he told Roxanne, and gone to visit Mo Magnusson.

"She's got a dog that's going to have puppies, Mom!"

"That right?" said his mother.

"Stay and eat." Matt skewered a sausage and held it up in invitation. Roxanne didn't mind if she did. She went to find Izzy.

"Julie's not telling half of it. Why did she did need to take off, soon as they got back from Arizona?" she said and parked herself on a stool by the kitchen island.

Izzy poured a couple of glasses of Shiraz and passed one across the counter. "Bill probably talked non-stop all the way home. For four days. That could be why she needed a break from him."

"Do we know for sure that they got along?"

"We never saw Julie much," Izzy shrugged. "She stayed home and sewed. Showed up when she had to. Christmas parties, stuff like that. Always brought great food. Never said much though. It was Bill that did all the talking."

"She's tidy," said Roxanne. "You've seen her workroom. It's well organized. But she didn't unpack completely or run a load of laundry before she left. It looks like she couldn't wait to get out of there. Then she changed her mind and decided to drive to Kenora and didn't even let him know?"

"Maybe she didn't go to Kenora when she says she did." Izzy went to the fridge and yanked the door open. "She could have come back to Fiskar Bay from the Sunnywell Centre any time that weekend, driven him into the ditch and headed off to Kenora right after and nobody would be any the wiser. No one else was living in the other houses at Heron Haven. They're all snowbirds too and they're not back home yet. There was no one to see if she went back there. Maybe the two of them went for a drive and they had a falling-out." She found the mustard and ketchup containers and kicked the fridge door shut.

"You think so?" Roxanne thought for a second. "Do you think she's capable of murder? People say she's so mild-mannered."

"She is. Well-behaved. Hazel went on about how upset she was, but I didn't see it until I mentioned Fern and one of her kids." Izzy placed squeezy bottles on the top of the island and came around to sit on the other stool. "I can't believe how Fern's changed. We were friends, once. She played on the same hockey team as me, the one Sigrid Isfeld plays on now. Not super smart like Hazel but good enough to go to university. She can sing. Great voice. We did a musical every year and she always got the lead. Played clarinet, too. Our band teacher wanted her to go study music."

"So why didn't she?"

"Cory Wiebe came along. His dad came to Fiskar Bay to run the hardware store. They repaired small engines, snowblowers, chainsaws, stuff like that and Cory worked in the shop. We all thought they were Mennonite at first, like a lot of Wiebes, but it turned out they belong to some weird sect called the Brethren or something. And the Brethren have a choir. They recruit other singers—they do a couple of concerts every year—and it wasn't long before old man Wiebe talked Fern into joining. So, she met Cory and that was that. We were in grade eleven and we all thought it was so romantic. She was pregnant halfway through grade twelve. Must have been six months gone when we graduated, and then she got married. She'd moved in with his mom and dad already."

"And joined the church?"

"Oh yeah, big time. You've seen her. She wears the frumpy clothes. Doesn't cut her hair. Has babies. Her oldest kid's got to be twelve by now. She's got a whole bunch of them."

"Bill and Julie didn't get to see their grandkids?"

"I guess not," said Izzy. "Bill never said."

Roxanne's phone buzzed. "Janine Roach just called," said Aimee Vermette. "She's wondering where Kenny's got to. He's supposed to be home by now. She's got a girls' night out happening and he's supposed to be there to take care of the kids. I tried reaching him and he's not answering."

"Bet he's at Sam's, cutting it fine before he has to get home. Jerk," said Izzy. "Here's our dinner." Matt walked through the door with a platter of hot dogs, a boy and a dog at his heels.

It was an hour later before Roxanne left. Finn was buckled into a booster seat in the back of the car, dozing by the time she reached the road end. He was out cold when she reached the turnoff to Cullen Village. She decided to drive round by the creek and have a quick look.

Soon as she turned onto Marina Road, she saw the lights from Roach's car flashing red and blue. It still straddled the street, south of where it crossed the creek. She pulled in and looked behind her. Finn didn't move. She went to Roach's vehicle. It was unlocked. She turned off the lights. Now there were only the street lights, casting long shadows, and a pale white moon. She checked on Finn again. He was still sleeping, his mouth half open. She walked along the low wooden fence that separated the road from the creek. She could hear water gurgling through the culverts below her. Crime tape ran halfway along, then looped to the ground. A part of the fence was broken. She took out her phone and turned on its flashlight, leaned over and swept a bright beam across the stream from one icy bank to the other. The water was backing up again, not flowing as easily as it should. She swung her beam straight down and saw what blocked it. A man lay in the water, the top of his body crammed into the mouth of the culvert. He wasn't moving. All she could see of him was his booted feet and two wet pant legs. Down the side of each was the distinctive yellow stripe of the uniform of the Royal Canadian Mounted Police.

9

POLICE CARS WAILED their way to Cullen Village, shattering that Saturday evening's peace.

The house four doors down from Sasha Rosenberg had two storeys, tall enough to provide a view over the treetops to the place where Ken Roach's body lay in the water, his head and shoulders in the mouth of one of the culverts under the road. The man who lived in the house stood at a bedroom window. He examined all that was happening through binoculars and kept the village informed via his phone. They were strong enough for him to catch a glimpse of yellow striped legs with chunks of ice and water passing around them. The internet soon buzzed with the news that another Mountie was dead, under suspicious circumstances, just like the one that had been found last week, only a few kilometres away.

"You quit working Major Crimes so you wouldn't get yourself killed and now someone around here is bumping cops like us off?" Izzy McBain asked, looking down over the remains of the broken fence to the body below.

"Never said that was why I left," Roxanne retorted and walked away. That story might have some truth in it, but she wasn't going to admit to it. Izzy and Matt had been among the first to arrive on the scene, in separate vehicles.

"You two take care of yourselves," Matt had said tersely, then scooped up the sleepy Finn and taken him back to their house. She'd watched them go, glad to know that her son was in safe hands.

The Fiskar Bay RCMP team were back at work. Pete Robinson waded through reeds and chunks of broken ice, camera held high above the water. Roach lay face down. His legs stretched toward Pete, slabs of ice, two to three inches thick, jammed up against them, piling up on each other. They would have to get him out of there before he caused the creek to dam up again. The moving water kept shifting the ice around him, but the Forensic Identification Unit needed to decide when and how to move him. They were on their way, fast as they could. Meantime, Pete was making a visual record, while the water swelled.

Another neighbour who lived closest to the road came to the water's edge and offered to rig floodlights from his yard. When they shone, the whole scene was illuminated, casting black shadows. The man aloft sent a video online; film noir, it played live in quiet little Cullen Village.

Sam Mendes had gone to photograph the scene from the other side. He was obviously shaken by Roach's death. Ravi Anand had hung fresh crime tape and had the road blocked. Roxanne had done everything she could here, for now. Someone needed to go talk to Janine Roach.

"You go. I'll take it from here," said Izzy.

Janine couldn't stop crying. She'd heard already that there was a dead body at Cullen Village, that it might be a cop. She was expecting bad news, but hoping it was not. She had no family nearby. They were all up in Robson, more than seven hours north by car. She and Kenny had both gone to school there. They'd been together since grade ten.

"Who shall I call?" asked Roxanne. Janine had girlfriends; she was supposed to be with them now. Within minutes, two cars roared up outside and a bunch of women piled into the house and took charge. One child, a boy aged about ten, had been asleep. His sister was just into her teens. Now they wandered out of their respective rooms.

"How do I tell them?" Janine moaned into the shoulder of a consoling friend. Two of her pals scooped up the kids and drove them away, to their own houses. Yet another tapped away at her phone.

Soon all of Canada knew that the Mountie who had been found dead in that swollen creek in the Manitoba Interlake was Kenny Roach, a veteran member of the RCMP. Married, with two children.

Inspector Schultz's voice crackled on the radio as Roxanne made her way back to Cullen Village.

"What's going on out there?" he growled. "First Gilchrist turns up in a ditch, and now Roach ends up in a creek? I'm putting a team together. Let you know who, soon as. Meeting tomorrow, your place, noon. We need all your guys there." And he hung up.

Izzy heard from him as well, right after. She'd be file coordinator. "I'm too inexperienced to be primary investigator, he says. This case is going to be too important," Izzy told Roxanne, disappointed. File coordinating tended to be a desk job, not Izzy's style. She liked to be out talking to people, like now.

The Ident team arrived, with wetsuits and their own lights. They got the body out of the water, soon as they could. Chunks of ice were sliding on top of it, threatening to block the culvert completely.

Roach was lifted carefully onto a stretcher, then carried up onto the roadway. "He can't have been in there long." Corporal Dave Kovak hunkered down, looking at a gash on his forehead. "He could have got that when he fell," he said. "Or he could have been hit by a moving piece of ice."

Roach had worn a regulation jacket, leather gloves. His hat had fallen off, probably when he fell, and floated into some reeds. It was hard to tell if he had sustained any other injury.

"Abdur Farooq's sending a van to pick up the body. This autopsy is going to have to be a priority. And they need to hurry up with Bill Gilchrist's. If someone's out there killing police, you guys need to get on top of this case right away," Kovak told Izzy. His team examined the road surface and the broken fence to find out how Roach had toppled over.

"He's been hit by a car?" Roxanne asked Izzy when she got back to the site.

"Maybe. Don't know for sure."

Pete Robinson had been sent home to dry off and Sam had gone to talk to the neighbours. Roach had still been around when they had closed their doors for the night, they said. They had all gone inside once the ice jam at the creek was broken up; the volunteers had gone home, and the food remains had been cleared away. No one had seen Roach fall to his death, or seen a car stop at the road and anyone talking to him. They had all been safely inside their houses.

"You can go pick up Finn and go home, if you like," said Izzy.

Roxanne was reluctant to do so. Being at the scene of a crime always interested her. But it seemed there was little else to find out this evening. She'd been doing groundwork up until now, but the case had escalated and someone would be sent to lead the investigation. Six months ago, she would have been a candidate, but now she had other responsibilities. Some of her team might be seconded to the case, but not her. The actual work would be assigned to Izzy and whoever else Schultz brought on board. Roxanne's own role would be to keep things rolling along as normally as possible in her detachment. She suppressed her frustration. This was what she had opted for, wasn't it? She left the scene and drove to Izzy and Matt's house to pick up her son.

SASHA ROSENBERG VENTURED out into her garden, flashlight in hand, to see what was going on. She wasn't alone. Shadows moved on the deck where the volunteers had gathered earlier during the day. She could see her neighbour in his newer, bigger house, further along the creek, up at his high window, still keeping watch. She flashed the light in his direction. His shadow waved back.

"It's all lit up like a Christmas tree out there." She called Margo Wishart soon after. "There's at least four police cars with their lights going, and floodlights. A big white van. I talked to one of my neighbours. They have divers in the water. He saw them lifting the body out. It was in uniform; he could see the yellow stripe down the pant legs. It's got to be that cop that was in charge all day. The one they call the Roach."

"Ken Roach?" Margo was tucked up on her sofa, her dog, Bob, at her feet. "Really? He was a big man. He looked like he could take care of himself."

"Maybe someone caught him by surprise and shoved him off the road."

"First Sergeant Gilchrist and now him?" Margo untucked her legs and topped up the wineglass in front of her.

"Guess someone's got it in for the Mounties," Sasha continued. She had a glass of wine herself. Her own vintage. She had taken up wine making in an attempt to economize. She was drinking it in her kitchen with the lights off so she could still observe the comings and goings at the end of the creek. Her laptop was open in front of her, too, so she could read her neighbour's ongoing newsfeed.

"Looks like it. Julie Gilchrist is back home." Julie had called Margo that evening. "She was worried that the police thought she had killed her husband. This will get her off the hook, so that's one good thing. She'd gone to Kenora to visit her sister. Had no idea that he was dead."

"That must have been a shock. Guess she'll be too busy to be in our project now."

"But she still wants to do it! Her daughter's going to be staying with her. She said she'd come tomorrow." Margo had scheduled a meeting to discuss the lake project for the following day. "I think she's quite happy to be distracted."

"Huh," said Sasha. "Not until she tells us what she knows." She paused to read a Facebook post. "They've just loaded what looks like a body into the back of that white van. Gotta go and look. Talk tomorrow." And she hung up.

FINN CALLOWAY WAS tucked into a sleeping bag on Matt and Izzy's sofa, a pillow under his head, sound asleep, a dog snuggled beside him. Two chairs were ranged alongside to make sure he didn't fall off.

"You can leave him here if you like," said Matt. "He's out cold. And it looks like you and Izzy will be working all day tomorrow. It's Sunday. He can keep me company again."

"You sure? You're supposed to be studying."

"He's no bother. I kind of like having him around. He and Joseph play together. It's too bad we don't have a spare bed. You could crash here too. You look frozen. How about you have something hot to drink before you go home?"

"You just want to find out what's going on," she commented.

"Well…" His eyes crinkled when he smiled. "That too." He reached for a jar of hot chocolate.

"I'd rather have some decaf if you've got it," she said and parked herself on a stool. He boiled a kettle while she told him what they had seen so far.

"You and Izzy do need to make sure you're safe," Matt said when she was done. "We don't want either of you being the next one to be run off the road and left for dead. Have you seen what they're calling it already? On Twitter? The Culvert Cop Killer Case. It got a mention on the national news. And Ken Roach is a hero already. Out doing his job, fourteen years on the Force. Devoted husband and father." They sipped their tea. Matt shifted on his stool. "That's not what people said about him, back when I was working with him. Janine was fed up with him staying out drinking after work, leaving her stuck home alone with the kids." Matt had worked alongside Ken Roach for a couple of years during his days in the RCMP.

"She's pretty upset that he's gone."

"Well, she would be. It's got to be a shock. She's got a couple of kids to take care of too. And I'm not saying she had anything to do with this. She couldn't have if she was home with the kids tonight. But everything gets skewed out of perspective on cases like these, doesn't it?" He wrapped his big hands around the mug in front of him, thinking. "There's a difference between the story that's served up to the public and what's really going on. Do you know who's going to be leading the investigation?"

"We'll find out tomorrow. Schultz has called a meeting for tomorrow morning. They'll want someone with a load of experience for this case."

Matt got to his feet. "Want to see something?" He fetched his laptop from the table nearby. They could hear snoring from the sofa in the darkened living area. The dog, not the child. "I've been checking the places where Bill Gilchrist served before he ended up here at Fiskar Bay."

"I thought you were studying?"

"Well…" There was the Stavros smile again. "I just thought I'd do some research to help you out." He opened a file. "Sergeant Bill had been around. He did a stint in Saskatoon and another in Yellowknife. And look at this." He swung the screen around so that Roxanne could see. It showed a photograph of two RCMP constables, in uniform, smiling for the camera. They had been at a school, attending a party to dole out school patrol awards. One of them was a younger, thinner version of Bill Gilchrist.

"That was taken twenty years ago," said Matt. "In Robson, Manitoba. Bill was stationed there for five years. And you know that Kenny Roach grew up in Robson? I'll bet he was still in high school when Bill was around. Janine's from Robson too. They went to school together. That's how they met."

"Bill might not have known them back then," said Roxanne.

"Maybe not. But Julie would have. She taught home ec in the high school up there."

10

THREE CARS PULLED up, one after the other, outside the RCMP detachment at Fiskar Bay the following morning. Inspector Schultz stepped out first, put his hat squarely on his head, straightened his tie and pulled down the cuffs of his jacket sleeves, ready to address his troops. He was followed by a tall dark-haired man carrying a briefcase and another with brown hair and a more muscular build; both wore casual everyday clothes. They were members of the Major Crimes Unit.

Roxanne's team had met earlier in the lunchroom. Doughnuts and coffee had done little to lift their gloom. Izzy McBain was there too, quieter than usual. Dave Kovak from Ident had booked into the hotel at Fiskar Bay overnight and joined them in the morning.

"He had been hit hard, probably by a moving vehicle," he told them. "Crashed through the fence and landed in the water."

"So he drowned?" asked Sam Mendes. He had got past his initial shock. Now he was just plain mad about what had happened to his best buddy.

"We won't know until the autopsy. It's happening today. They're rushing it through, since he's one of us. This is a big deal. Bill Gilchrist's has been moved up to the front of the queue too."

"You mean they haven't done his yet? Jesus." Sam slapped the table in front of him.

"They were both murdered?" Pete Robinson sat beside Sam and nudged him. They all needed to stay calm. Keep their emotions under control.

"Looks like it," said Dave.

"So someone has it in for us? Going around slamming into police while they're out doing their job? Like Kenny?" Sam folded his arms across his chest, not about to be placated.

"Not necessarily," Roxanne said, knowing that he was not the only one of them thinking that. "It's likely that Ken Roach and Bill Gilchrist were deliberately targeted. But we should be careful. You'll be partnered up for the next week or two. I sent you your new schedules this morning." A couple of them opened their phones to check their messages. "Try not to be alone any more than you have to when you are off duty, too."

"I live alone, Sarge." Aimee Vermette lifted her head from her phone.

"And I do, too." said Roxanne. "I have my son with me, but he's only six. Not much in the way of protection." She smiled wryly at Aimee, trying to reassure. "We're probably quite safe. Both incidents happened when someone was alone, at a roadside, with no one else around. We just need to be sensible. Stay calm and keep your eyes open. Avoid situations like that. Just until we know more. Chances are there's an old case that Kenny and Bill both worked on, and someone has been holding a grudge. Those of you who worked with both of them, think back, and if anything springs to mind, tell Izzy. Or me, if you prefer."

"We should have Kathy in here," said Pete. "She's the one that will remember."

Kathy Isfeld was out at the front desk, keeping an eye on the office. She'd come out from behind her computer desk so she could stand behind the front desk, be more of a presence while she was in charge. Now she pointed Inspector Schultz in the team's direction. They rose as he entered. He gestured that they should sit, marched to the front of the room and took command.

"A crime has been committed against an RCMP officer and a retired sergeant," he proclaimed, standing in front of them, hands clasped behind his back. He was stocky, not tall, but standing with his feet apart, he made the most of his size. Roxanne was used to seeing him behind a desk, like a bespectacled bullfrog. He wasn't wearing glasses today. He placed his hat on the table beside him, revealing a shiny skull. His brows were lowered, the corners of his mouth turned down. He surveyed the room and barked at them.

"This is a bad business. Unprecedented. With the death of Constable Roach, it would appear that someone is responsible. Together, we shall find that person and bring them to justice. All possible resources will be made available to bring this case to a speedy conclusion. The investigative team will be led by Sergeant Mark Cappelli." He indicated the dark-haired man sitting in front of him. "As we speak, a forensic search is being made of records of past cases in which both Roach and Gilchrist were engaged. That line of questioning will, of course, continue here, at Fiskar Bay. Corporal Jeffrey Riordan will lead that endeavour out of this detachment as primary investigator, assisted by Constable McBain, who will be acting as file coordinator."

The smaller of the two men half turned, smiled, and raised a hand in greeting. Roxanne recognized them both. She'd never worked with either of them, but she had seen them around when she had still been in the MCU. Jeff Riordan was popular, considered a good guy, easygoing. Mark Cappelli was another matter. He was thorough, a stickler for detail, a loner with ambitions, fast tracking toward an inspectorship. One team he had once worked with had taken bets on who could get him to smile. No one had won. Schultz couldn't have chosen two men who were more different.

"Normally," he continued, "We would second one or two of you to the Major Crimes Unit for the duration of the investigation, but with the passing of Constable Roach you are one man down already, and Sergeant Calloway has decided that you will be working in pairs when you are on duty, so your numbers are stretched. We will draw on your assistance if required and hope, for now, that it will not be necessary. I believe that there is a logical reason for most suspicious deaths, and this will be no exception. You can help by keeping your eyes and ears open. Listen for rumours. People in places like this notice strangers. It's quiet at this time of year." It would be different in a few weeks when the lakeshore was swarming with visitors. "People talk. If someone out there is harbouring a grudge, we need to know. You need to be watchful. Vigilant."

Heads nodded obediently in response as he drew toward the end of his speech. "I am going to go and speak to the widows of our fallen comrades. As a serving member, Constable Roach will receive a funeral with full RCMP honours and the superintendent has decided that the same should be offered to retired Sergeant Gilchrist. Sergeant Calloway will accompany me on these visits." That was news to Roxanne. He also had a meeting scheduled with the mayor and some members of the town council.

"I need you all to present a united and undaunted front to this town. We cannot allow the public to think that we are afraid. Be on guard at all times, but also be brave and assertive in your work, and we shall get results. I shall leave you to get acquainted." He indicated the two MCU officers. "Sergeant?" he beckoned to Roxanne and marched to the door. Roxanne did as she was told and followed in his wake.

"JULIE TEXTED. SHE's going to be late. She went to Winnipeg to drop off her daughter at the airport." Margo Wishart arranged cupcakes on a plate. They hadn't turned out as well as she had wanted. She had envisioned tall, swirly frosted toppings but hers had flattened out into white blobs. She had put a walnut on each in an attempt to make them look more presentable. Julie Gilchrist had a reputation as a fine cook and baker. Margo had hoped to impress.

"She's still going to do this project? Even though they think that her husband was murdered?" Roberta Axelsson was nursing a large mug of coffee.

"Seems so." Margo placed the plate on the table in front of her. "She says she's still interested. We have to have a quilter on board. There's so much of that going on in the Interlake and she is the best." That was not in any dispute. A specimen of Julie's work hung at the far end of the room, a smudge of purples and greens and browns rendered in torn applique, like it had been painted. Julie transformed the traditions of her craft into an art form.

"Maybe they won't suspect her of murder now that another cop's been killed." Roberta reached for one of the cakes.

"I wouldn't bet on it." Sasha Rosenberg was standing at the window, watching the dogs, hers and Margo's, barking at a squirrel up in a tree. Outside the sun was shining on puddles and on the lake. The trees dripped. "She could have had it in for him too."

"You think so?" Roberta bit a mouthful, chewed and swallowed. "These taste better than they look," she commented.

"I can't imagine Julie Gilchrist being capable of killing anyone." Margo fetched paper and pen, so she could get this meeting on track once Julie arrived. "She's so quiet. And well-mannered. You'd have to be in a blind rage to drive a person into a ditch. Or a creek. The car must have hit the fence hard for Constable Roach to have gone right through it."

"Not necessarily. It was pretty old and rickety. You should see the flowers that people are leaving there, along what's left of it. And teddy bears." Sasha had made a point of going to look on her way to Margo's. One of Janine Roach's friends had described Ken Roach as a "big bear of a man" on Facebook and the image had caught on. "Freya Halliday's there, complaining because people are ignoring the police tape, contaminating the crime scene."

"We still don't know why Julie took off to Kenora soon as she got back." Roberta rolled up an empty paper cup and reached for another cake. "Maybe we can find out when she gets here."

"I'm with Margo. I don't think it was her. Bet there's a loony on the loose." Sasha came to the table and reached for a bag at her feet. She'd brought along some sketches of an idea she had.

"Someone who's got it in for cops. Roxanne Calloway'd better watch out. And Izzy McBain. It could be one of them next."

FISKAR BAY'S REPUTATION as the Cop Killer Capital of Canada was now well established and that idea, like the one about Kenny Roach and the bears, had caught the collective imagination of the public. Tourist season was a mere six weeks away and the town relied on a thriving tourist trade. It was bad enough that spring thaw was late and the fields were still awash. At least the threat of flooding was waning. The mayor and his councillors expressed their concern.

"We can't get our boats in the water, either," complained a fisherman. "That chunk of ice is still floating out in the middle of the lake keeping the temperature down."

Roxanne had to hand it to Inspector Schultz. He was unfazed. His best men had been assigned to the job, he assured them. Constable Roach and ex-Sergeant Gilchrist had a long history together; the deaths were probably related to a past case and entirely the RCMP's concern, Schultz continued. He agreed that it seemed likely that both ex-Sergeant Gilchrist and Constable Roach had been killed, but the town need not worry. By the time the streets were cleaned up of all the winter's debris and the flower baskets were hanging from the light standards, that slab of ice on the water would have melted and the harbour would be full of pleasure boats, as usual. The public had a short memory and the tourists would come. Fiskar Bay would be safe. He was confident of that.

"My sister works for you. She's on your team." A fair-haired man in his thirties sat at the end of the table. Ed McBain was Izzy's brother, active in the surrounding farming community and representing the nearby rural municipality. He was earning a reputation for himself in local politics. And he liked to portray himself as being progressive. "You're saying that our local police, like her and Sergeant Calloway here, are not in danger?" He nodded in

Roxanne's direction, acknowledging her presence, and folded his arms, waiting for an answer.

Schultz rose to the challenge. "Members of the RCMP are trained to deal with difficult situations," he rumbled. "That comes with being a police officer. But, as I said, we consider that there must be a rational explanation for these deaths, a reason why these two officers have been targeted. When we find that reason we shall uncover the name of the killer."

"Lots of reasons why people might have it in for you guys," the large fisherman growled back at him. "There's druggies around here. That guy that lives with that Magnusson girl, for one. And plenty guys been growing weed out on their land forever. Way more than what's legal now. Folks like that don't need a reason. They go out of their minds and just get it into their heads to do something stupid." He stabbed a finger on the tabletop to emphasize his point.

"An investigation is underway, and no stone will be left unturned," Inspector Schultz intoned, resorting to words that were tried and true. He propped an elbow on the other side of the table and pointed right back. "Those two dead police officers worked together for many years. The deaths are connected, not random. We will find that connection and we will catch the perpetrator of this crime."

That was his story, and he was sticking to it. Roxanne hoped that he was right.

11

ROXANNE NEEDED TO drop Finn off at school around 8:30 on Monday morning, so by the time she got to the detachment, Mark Cappelli was already installed in the office upstairs. He was stylish, impeccable in dark greys and black, sleek as a seal, his hair neatly cut so it looked almost sculpted, a faint stubble on his chin, the edges shaved. He was seated at the central table, his attention focused on his computer screen.

Izzy and Jeff Riordan were lugging boxes full of old files upstairs. Kathy Isfeld believed in keeping a paper trail and she threw nothing out. Many of the files bulged. In her closet there were more, going all the way back to the days before Bill Gilchrist had taken command, thirteen years earlier. They piled them in a corner. It was going to be Izzy's task to sift through each and every one. She sighed. Talking to Kathy and listening to rumours was all right, her new boss had told her, but it was real evidence that was needed. There could be details in those files that a formal report might miss.

Kathy herself had shaken her head when she had been asked. "Could be anyone," she said. "Sometimes just a speeding ticket gets people riled up."

"What I don't get," said Izzy, straightening her back after dumping a particularly heavy box on the floor, "is why now? Why wait until Sergeant Bill retired? Why kill him soon as he got back from Arizona?"

"Because," Cappelli spoke without raising his head, "someone who just got out of jail might have done it. We're checking that out right now."

ROXANNE AND INSPECTOR Schultz had spent an hour or so with Janine Roach the day before. Her sister was driving down from Robson to help her, she had said. Her tears had dried for now. She was putting on a brave face. Her son was okay; he was with his friends, but her daughter was up in her room, refusing to go anywhere, talking on the phone all the time. Typical thirteen-year-old, but she had also been her dad's girl. She was taking this badly. Janine nodded when the inspector told her of the funeral plans. And when would that be, she asked? Not too long, Schultz reassured her. The autopsy was happening as they spoke. Janine had looked stricken at the thought. Tact wasn't Schultz's strong suit.

They had driven out to Heron Haven after, but Julie Gilchrist's house had been deserted. "Guess I'll have to leave that one to you," Schultz had said before he dropped Roxanne off back in Fiskar Bay, glad to be on his way back to the city.

"I've got to go talk to Julie," Roxanne now told the threesome in the MCU room. "This is as good a time as any. One of you should maybe come along."

Jeff Riordan had jumped at the offer, happy to leave the taciturn Cappelli at his computer. Izzy remained stuck in her corner, wading through the contents of the old files. Now, as Roxanne drove, Jeff stared out the car window at wet fields. His foot tapped on the floor of the car and his thumbs rubbed against the knuckles of his opposite hands, a restless kind of guy. A smattering of raindrops hit the windshield.

"Whaddaya do with yourself out here?" he asked. "I mean, summertime, there's stuff going on. But right now? It's kinda dead, isn't it?"

"It's okay." A pair of ducks paddled along the ditch beside the road. Mating season was beginning.

"Yeah. But you used to work with us, right? Schultz brags about you. Says you never gave up until the case was solved. Nose to the ground until you flushed the killer out. But then you quit and moved yourself out here?"

She had a family, a child to consider, she told him. The scar on her neck told part of another story. Riordan knew how that had happened, and more.

"You could have gone to Ottawa with Inspector Donohue, right? Transferred. Been right at the centre of things. Not stuck out here in the boonies."

Roxanne and Inspector Brian Donohue had been an item until he'd taken a job with CSIS, the Canadian Security Intelligence Service, and she had chosen not to go with him. It would have meant moving to the nation's capital, and she hadn't been ready for that big a commitment just yet. They'd tried to stay in touch but it hadn't worked out. That relationship was over.

"It's not really so quiet here," she replied. "Even in the winter, there's stuff going on. Tell me about Mark Cappelli." If Jeff Riordan knew most of the scuttlebutt around HQ, she might as well find out what he knew about his new team commander.

"Marco? Bet we'll hardly see him. He'll be back to town, soon as. He's busy trying to make an impression at HQ. Paper man. Computer whiz. Good at surveillance, stuff like that. Wants to be superintendent one of these days."

It had started to drizzle. Roxanne turned on the wipers.

"He wants to be the guy who solves this case. He thinks he'll do it from Winnipeg, that some felon Gilchrist and Roach locked up did it. Maybe he's right and we can get ourselves out of here real soon. How's the McBain chick to work with?"

She noticed a glint in his eye and the corner of his mouth twitch. Cheeky. She turned onto Heron Road before she set him right.

"Don't underestimate Izzy McBain," she told him. "She's wasted going through all those files. You could put Kathy Isfeld onto that job. She probably remembers half of what's in them anyway and it's quiet in the office right now as far as our regular work is concerned. Get Izzy out and about, asking questions in town. She grew up around here. She gets answers that none of us will because she's local."

"But if someone that lives around here really is the killer, they'll know that she's a cop. Doesn't that put her at risk if she has to work alone?"

"Izzy's a McBain. If anything happened to her, it wouldn't be us hunting down whoever did it. It would be her dad and her brothers and the whole town knows it. Nobody messes with the McBains around here. You need to watch out for yourself, though."

"Me? Nobody has a clue who I am."

He was right about that. Jeff Riordan was brand new to this area and his appearance was not memorable, unlike Sergeant Cappelli's. Jeff was muscular but of average height and had regular features. Dressed in jeans and a casual navy jacket, he would blend in easily.

It was raining in earnest now. Roxanne turned up the wipers.

"Don't you believe it," she said. "Fiskar Bay has eyes and ears. They'll have you pegged inside a week." They arrived at the Gilchrists' place. The Yukon was parked in the driveway, raindrops bouncing off the blue metalwork. It was coming down steadily. Riordan looked at the big new house. The lake was just visible behind it through the downpour, waves blowing in toward the shore.

"Will you look at that? Not bad on a retired sergeant's pension."

"That's what it gets you, out here in the country," Roxanne remarked and pulled her hat on. She ran for the shelter of the front porch. He loped after her, then stopped, looking at the front of the Yukon, his collar pulled up, water dripping off his head.

"Look at that. It's hit something," he called to her. Roxanne went back and took a quick look. There was a dent on the front.

"I'll talk about the funeral arrangements; you can ask Julie about that," she said and went to ring the doorbell.

Hazel Gilchrist had caught a plane back to Toronto the previous day. Julie had driven her daughter to the airport in Winnipeg; they had missed her. And Julie herself had had a meeting to attend in the afternoon.

"She's coming back soon," she said as she ushered them into the living room. "Her advisor at the university says it shouldn't be a problem. He heard about Bill's death on the news. Didn't know he was Hazel's father." Water streamed down the windows and waves were beginning to crash against the dock down at the shore. "He says she'll get extensions for the work she has due, no problem." She retreated behind the kitchen counter and began making coffee. "So she's got a ticket booked to fly back on Thursday."

They sat again on the big brown sofas. Julie turned on lights against the gloom. Roxanne explained the main reason for their visit.

"No, that won't do at all." Julie shook her head. She didn't want all that fuss, a parade, the speeches, a big crowd of Mounties in their red serge dress uniforms.

"The Force wants to honour your husband. It's only six months since he retired. Not long since he was a serving member." Roxanne remembered her own husband's funeral. She could understand Julie's point of view. Julie lived a private life. She would hate having to be on display as the widow of a fallen officer. But it was a tradition and the RCMP liked to observe those.

"Bill had left the RCMP," Julie insisted. "I'm planning a quiet cremation. Just me and the family. Then we'll invite people out here on a summer afternoon so they can come visit and remember him. We'll put his ashes into the lake."

"You and your girls?" asked Roxanne.

"Fern would like us to have a church service but neither Hazel nor I want that." So, she and her older daughter had been in touch.

"We could arrange for a joint memorial service, for Bill and Ken Roach," said Roxanne, still trying. "There could be a priest present, but it would still be mainly secular. It's about the Force paying its respects."

"Really?" Julie looked at her over the top of her coffee mug. "Do you think so, Sergeant? I don't think that's what it's all about at all. It's the RCMP burying its guilt." She laid the mug down on the table in front of them. "Because he wouldn't be dead if he hadn't belonged to the Force." There was no mistaking the anger in that bitter little voice. "He had retired. He wasn't in the RCMP anymore and you're not getting him back now that he's gone."

Julie Gilchrist might look mousy but when she wanted to, she could make her point. She frowned across the coffee table, then mustered a smile. She also knew when to remember her manners and be polite. "Tell your superiors, 'Thank you, but no.'"

"Mrs. Gilchrist," said Jeff Riordan, "how come there's a dent in the front of that big Yukon you're driving?"

Julie looked relieved at the change of topic, and not at all threatened by the question. "Oh, that," she said. "Bill dinged a post in the RV park. In Arizona, not long before we left."

"Did he report it?" he asked.

"To the insurance? No. It was his own fault, and the post was solid, it wasn't damaged. He was going to take the SUV to someone back here, someone he knows." Then her eyes rounded. So did her little mouth. "You think he was run down? By his own car?"

"Where were you this Saturday night?" asked Riordan.

"Here. With Hazel. I told you." This time, Julie made no attempt to hide the fact that the question annoyed her. "You think I might be responsible for Ken Roach's death? It was in the garage here all night."

Then they saw her realize that alibi might not work. Hazel might corroborate what she said, but would she be believed?

"What about how Bill died, Roxanne? I went to the Sunnywell Centre and then to Kenora. I wasn't here when it happened."

That was what she said, but it might not be true.

Julie mustered another polite smile and changed the subject. "Just so you know, before you hear it as gossip, I'm planning to sell this house and move to Kelowna where the weather's better in the winter."

"That's a quick decision," said Roxanne. Julie shook her curly head in response.

"No, it's not. Bill and I had decided already. The snowbird thing wasn't for us. We came back early from Arizona so we could get the house ready to put on the market in the spring and be in B.C. by the fall. My sister always said she would retire to B.C., so it makes sense that we share, now that Bill's gone. I want to sell as soon as I can. Are you going to have a problem with that?"

Julie wasn't high on the list of suspects so far, but Roxanne couldn't be sure. It wasn't her decision to make. "You'll be a long way away from your daughters," she said instead.

"Hazel loves the idea. She isn't tied to Manitoba. She moved away years ago."

"And Fern?"

"I haven't discussed it with her yet. But I will."

Shortly after, they took their leave. The rain had stopped and the sun was breaking through the clouds once more. Riordan took photos of the damage to the Yukon before they drove off.

"Do you believe her?" he asked as he got back into the car.

"I don't know," said Roxanne. "But I do wonder just how solid the Gilchrist marriage was. From everything I've heard, Bill loved that house and being in Arizona for the winter. Maybe it was just Julie who wanted to move to B.C."

"And her sister just happens to be ready to go there too. Bit of a coincidence, isn't it?" said Jeff, "Maybe she's only telling us what she wants us to know. Seems like a nice woman, but is she really?"

"Everyone seems to think she is. It's interesting that Fern is talking to her now that her father is dead. The story they tell around town is that since Fern joined the Wiebes' church, she won't have anything to do with her mother. Julie's into yoga and meditation and they're fundamentalist Christians. They don't approve. But maybe that's not true. Maybe it was her dad that Fern quarrelled with and now that he's gone, she feels like she can come back again. Izzy knows Fern. You should get her to find out about that."

12

MARK CAPPELLI HAD left by the time Roxanne and Jeff returned to the office.

"He got a message from Winnipeg. Didn't say what it was about," Izzy reported from her corner. "He said you should go interview the neighbours at Kuryk Road again, Jeff. The ones in the new house, that environmental thing, might have seen something. I'm to stay here and get all this done." She tapped the file in front of her.

"I need to call and get the Gilchrists' SUV towed in and examined first." Jeff took out his phone. "It's got a dent. Driver's side."

"It has? Oh, shit." Izzy looked up at him in dismay. "So it might have hit someone?"

"Maybe." Jeff turned away to make his call.

"Izzy, how about I take you out for lunch?" Roxanne asked.

"Sure!" Izzy needed a break from sitting reading and she was always ready to eat. "You buying?"

In the summer, the sidewalks close to the harbour and the beach were lined with small eateries. Some served fish, fresh from the lake. Fried walleye fillets, locally known as pickerel, were a speciality. Right now, the owners were still sprucing things up, ready for opening. The season hadn't begun yet and their kitchens were still closed. The restaurant at the hotel, however, stayed open all year.

They got a table overlooking the lake. Rain clouds still hung to the east, but the sun shone, a hint of the summer to come. The harbour wall jutted out into the water. The only boat berthed there was large vessel, the *Becky,* built to withstand the pressure of ice during the long winter, now used as a research boat to monitor the health of that vast expanse of fresh water.

"I'm having a burger." Izzy barely glanced at the menu. She knew what she liked. "And fries, they do great ones here. With mayo and ketchup. So, what's up?" Roxanne was still figuring out what to order. Izzy placed her menu on the plate beside her. "You didn't ask me here so we could just hang out together. We're here to talk, out of the office, right?"

The server approached. Roxanne ordered a salad, oil and vinegar dressing and coffee and waited until the woman had gone,

"It's about Julie Gilchrist. We never saw her around the detachment last year, when I was working the Magnusson case, did we? I don't think I ever met her, back then."

"Julie? She didn't come around much. Kept herself to herself. Why are you asking?" Izzy looked mystified. "Cappelli's chasing up an entirely different lead. They're looking at someone that Sergeant Bill put away years ago. Julie never really was a suspect, was she? Isn't she too mild-mannered to do anything as vulgar as bumping off her old man? Is this about the dent in the front of the Yukon?"

"Not really. I'm just checking. For my own interest." The server returned with a coffee carafe. She filled their cups and walked away. "Julie was very different from Bill," Roxanne continued once the woman was out of earshot.

"Sure, she was." Izzy added sugar and cream to her cup and stirred. "But it worked for them. There's couples like that, right? He was sociable, she was quiet. He talked, she didn't. He was always out and about, she liked to stay home." Just like her and Matt Stavros with the genders reversed, Roxanne thought. Sometimes pairings of opposites worked just fine.

"They got along?" she asked.

"Far as I know." Izzy still looked puzzled as to why she was interested.

"Fern's talking to her mother again, now that Bill's dead," said Roxanne.

"She is? That's good." Izzy smiled. "About time."

"What I've been told is that it's Julie that Fern never visited. People say it's about religion. That Fern and the Wiebes are fundamentalist, and Julie believes in meditation and New Age stuff."

"Could be." Izzy looked out over the water. The ice slab, close to the horizon, had diminished; it was half the size it had been a couple of days ago. It would soon be gone. "Look," she said. "I'll tell you something. But it stays between you and me, okay?"

"Okay," said Roxanne. Their food arrived. Once again they waited until the server was gone.

"I almost got raped once," said Izzy matter-of-factly, as she squeezed ketchup onto her plate. Then she added a dollop of mayo and mixed them.

"You did?" Roxanne lost all interest in her salad. Izzy put down the mayo bottle.

"Happened in the basement of the Rec Centre here in Fiskar Bay. I'd just turned sixteen. My dad gave me an old Corolla for my birthday so I wouldn't need rides anymore, so I drove myself. I helped coach a ringette team back then and I'd stayed in the locker room to clean up. I was last to leave, stupid really.

"Two hockey guys came out of their changing room right behind me. In the hallway. One of them hauled me back, toward the door. I screamed like mad and swung my skates at him. He hit me so hard my head bounced off the wall and I landed on the floor. The other one grabbed me by the foot and started dragging me. I was too dizzy to fight back. But I got lucky." She picked up a french fry and dipped it in the pink goop she'd created. "One of the kids in my team had left a backpack behind and her dad came back to get it. He knew I was there; he'd seen my car. He came downstairs and turned the corner just before they closed the door on me. Those boys booted it out of there real fast. My head was still spinning. The dad and the rec manager called my folks to come get me." She popped the fry into her mouth, chewed and swallowed.

"My brothers played hockey, right? One was in the league above them. He found out when their next practice was. The guys that play with them let my brothers deal with those boys in the parking lot. They knew better than to interfere.

"The one who hit me was Cory Wiebe," she said. "He got his arm broken in the fight and ended up in the hospital.

"His dad complained to Sergeant Bill. Wanted to press charges. Said his boy had nothing to do with the attack on me. That I was lying when I said it was him. But Sergeant Bill didn't buy it. He told Papa Wiebe to drop it. And then he told my dad that it was done, and that was that. Until Fern started dating Cory.

"The Gilchrists tried to stop her from seeing him. Bill knew what Cory was like. But Fern was nuts about him. She wouldn't listen. Then she got pregnant and the Wiebes love babies. More souls for Jesus, right? She moved in with them before she'd finished school. Swore that they made her sleep in his sister's room until they got married, even though she was getting big. The wedding happened in their church. I was there. Her family didn't go. She walked down the aisle, white poufy dress, the veil, his sisters were bridesmaids. My friends thought it was so romantic. She's been at home dressed like a frump ever since, popping out babies. That's why they never see Fern."

Izzy had demolished most of the fries. Now she inspected the inside of her burger. The patty was already spread with ketchup, mustard and relish. And a pickle. She closed it, satisfied.

"The Wiebes and Bill Gilchrist hated each other and that's why," she continued. "It's not because Julie's interested in yoga and has a Buddha in her room. That's all bullshit." She bit into the burger. Roxanne had picked at the salad while she listened, stunned at what she was hearing. "That Cory sure punched me hard. The side of my face was all bruised up for a while and I had a lump on the back of my head. Concussion. I wonder if Fern's okay, living with him. Maybe she just keeps quiet. Like a good, obedient little wife."

"She's never complained to anyone?"

"Wouldn't know. I haven't heard much about her since school. And this has nothing to do with these murders. I'm not saying Cory might have wanted to kill Fern's dad. He could have done it years ago if he'd wanted to. Why wait until now? The whole Wiebe clan had moved away by the time the Roaches came here, too, so they'd never have met him. But that's not all."

She scooped up what was left of the mayo-ketchup mix with the last of the fries. "My second brother, Mike, taught me some moves that summer. Just some basic self-defence. But then I decided to become a Mountie." She formed finger quotes in the air. The RCMP never called themselves by that name, but her brothers probably did. "Said I'd need to be able to take care of myself for sure in the Force. He and my other brothers couldn't risk taking on guys in uniform if I needed helping out. He showed me how to fight real dirty if I have to."

"And have you?" asked Roxanne.

"Couple of times, when I was training, back of the Depot." Izzy smirked. She had obviously won those fights. "Only once, since I came back home."

"Roach?"

"Nah. Didn't have to lay a finger on him," said Izzy. "He started getting too close one day and I just told him to back off or I'd tell. Not Janine but her girlfriends, and then they would tell her. 'Janine's gonna love that,' I said. That was all it took. Roach wasn't as tough as he looked, y'know. He just faked it. Janine's always been the boss in that household.

"No, it was Sergeant Bill himself, one night when I was working the late shift in the office. First year on the job. I got him real good, right where it hurt. Could have gone totally wrong for me. I just reacted. But he behaved himself after that." The burger had almost disappeared. "He acted like he thought it was funny once he got his breath back. Never tried it again. But if he made a move on me, he could have done it with other people. And I wonder if Julie Gilchrist knew anything about that."

LUNCH WAS ALSO being eaten at Sasha Rosenberg's house in Cullen Village. She had provided coffee and buns bought that morning at the local grocery store. Margo had brought a tub of carrot and ginger soup to reheat and Roberta's hens had contributed egg salad. Lenny the basset hound lolled on the sofa; Bob sprawled at his feet. They'd both been walked earlier, in the rain, and now the smell of damp dog competed with that of the food.

"All those flowers!" Roberta had driven to the house via Marina Road, so she could look. "Have you seen the plastic Mountie? There's one of those out at Kuryk Road too." She had been at Mo Magnusson's earlier, to see the new pups. "If I didn't have so many cats, I'd take one of them," she said. By the time she had left, the rain had stopped and she had detoured round to the place where Bill Gilchrist's body had been found. She had brought a tub of blue hyacinths as her own contribution to the shrine.

"I got yelled at by that crabby old Stan Kuryk," she said. "He drove by in his truck. 'Don't put that there!' he yelled at me. I'd walked over onto the other side of the ditch. 'That's my property,' he said. 'Who's supposed to clean up all this mess?'

"There's lots of flowers. Loads of people must have been stopping by and some of them have put them over where I was standing. On his land, I suppose."

"Did you leave any flowers for Constable Roach?" Margo stood at the stove in Sasha's tiny kitchen nook stirring the soup.

"Not sure that I will. He was mean. Not that you'd know it on Facebook. He's some kind of hero, there. Someone's started a GoFundMe page to help provide for his kids."

Margo ladled soup into pottery bowls fired in Sasha's own kiln in the studio out back. Their lunches together were a regular thing, but she also had business to discuss.

"Julie Gilchrist called me this morning," she said once they had settled around the table in Sasha's cramped living room. "She wanted me to know that she's putting her house on the market. She's planning to move to B.C."

"Already?" Roberta's soup spoon stopped halfway to her mouth. "Bill Gilchrist isn't in his grave yet."

"She says she's not planning to leave until the fall. She wanted to know if we had set a date for our show yet."

"We should do that." Sasha split open a bun and reached for the bowl of egg salad. "How long do we need to get ready?" The initial plan had been to each present a separate piece, but Sasha had come up with an idea that intrigued them.

"There's an old story about the lake," she had said as she pulled out a sketchbook and opened it. "The fishermen tell it, but it might be Indigenous. That the waves are three sisters called Agnes and Mabel and Becky. Most of the time they're peaceful but they can get riled up and then they'll sometimes go for someone. They're the reason why the lake is so dangerous."

She showed them some drawings of giant metal frames with heads and hands to represent the sisters. Roberta thought she could drape them in knitted lace, to represent foam and weed. They hadn't begun yet, but September was more than four months away.

"Easy," Roberta replied to Sasha's question. "Plenty of time."

"Julie says there's a room that might work for us at the Sunnywell Centre. They rent it out. I'm going to go check it out later today and find out when it's available. Want to come with me?" Margo asked. They did.

13

STAN KURYK GRIMACED when he saw Jeff Riordan's ID. "RCMP? About time," he growled. "I need to talk to you."

Jeff was ushered in the front door, to the living room. An orange shag rug covered the floor. It matched the furniture, upholstered in yellows and reds and browns, the colours of fall. Wooden tables and chairs were polished and so was the glass that fronted a cabinet stuffed with painted china and memorabilia, much of it Ukrainian. The Kuryks had eaten lunch already but there was banana cream pie, Netta told him. Jeff had worked on rural cases before. He knew he'd best say yes. And he got his question in before Stan Kuryk could wade into his complaints.

Neither of them had seen anyone out on Kuryk Road the weekend before the snowstorm. "Told you guys that already," said Stan. He had been busy with his beasts. Netta had been getting things ready for Ukrainian Easter. She'd been over at Desna Church for a while helping clean it up. The other people who had come to help were from the Fiskar Bay end of the road. They hadn't driven this way. Could she give him a list, he asked? She supposed she could. Was he enjoying the pie? He was, he said, took the hint and ate a bite.

They hadn't met their new neighbours yet, the ones who had built the new house two blocks over, but they knew who they were.

"Call themselves Featherstone. City folk. Do-gooders. That place is supposed to run on solar." Kuryk had skipped the pie. He smoked instead. "Must have cost a cent or two to build. Never see them."

"They're never home," his wife agreed. "Jenn the Potter managed to catch them in. Took her three tries. She stopped by with a cake, to say welcome, y'know. Never got invited across the doorstep. You think it could be them that killed the sergeant?"

"I didn't say that." Jeff swallowed another slice of banana smothered in cream. "We just need to talk to them. Like I'm doing with you. How about the farmhouse, the one you can see from the end of Kuryk Road, where we found the body?"

"The McKenzie place? Used to be a family farm. Now the sons just use it for holidays and rent out the pasture." Stan took another drag on his cigarette. He tapped the ash into a glass ashtray on a stand placed conveniently close to his elbow.

"To you?"

"No way," snapped the farmer. "I don't need to pay them for their land. Got plenty of my own. Now, about that mess people are leaving, end of the road there. What are you going to do about it?"

Jeff washed down more cream and crumbs with coffee. "Can't stop people from paying their respects, Mr. Kuryk," he said.

"They're tramping all over my land," the farmer complained. "The ground's too soft for that right now. And they're messing up the road, big time. Don't know how to drive on gravel, most of them."

"It's a public road, sir." Jeff speared the last chunk of banana. "The ditch doesn't belong to you either, does it? It's municipal land."

"They wander onto my field," the old man insisted, unwilling to let up. "And your guys left yellow tape there. Hammered rebar into the ground so you could tie it up. When you gonna get rid of that?"

"All in good time, sir," said Jeff. His phone buzzed. Izzy. Could he check in? Good. That gave him an excuse to leave. Maybe if the lead in the city was working out, they'd make an arrest real soon and he could check out of Fiskar Bay. Get back to civilization. This might be an okay place in the summer but right now it was grey and drab and wet. Miserable. Just like the people who inhabited it, like Farmer Kuryk.

"They've taken a guy called Lex McKenzie in for questioning," Izzy announced, soon as he got back. "He was doing time for embezzling a bunch of people out here about five years ago but now he's on parole. Sergeant Bill put him away and he got time added on for assaulting Ken Roach when they had him locked up downstairs."

"McKenzie?" asked Riordan. "Stan Kuryk said the old farmhouse near Kuryk Road belongs to a family called that."

"Huh?" Izzy grabbed her phone. "Let me call my mom."

INSPECTOR SCHULTZ LISTENED to a recording of the interview. Lex McKenzie had sat quietly, seeming unperturbed by the questions that Mark Cappelli had directed at him

"He's a con man," Cappelli insisted. "Look at his record."

He had a point. Lex had spent twenty years talking his way into different jobs, often positions of trust, and betrayed them again and again. The embezzlement scheme he'd cooked up to relieve people of their cash in exchange for the promise of a house near Fiskar Bay, with a patch of beach, a dock and a lake view, wasn't his first. Lex wasn't a very successful crook, but he had charm. He was a small man. His mugshot showed wide blue eyes and fair hair that flopped over his forehead. And he had been a convincing liar. But he insisted he had changed, and the prison warden, the chaplain and the parole officer had all been persuaded to believe him.

One of the counsellors who visited the penitentiary studied Buddhism. There was a study group in Winnipeg. They met in a house in the West End. "What he said made total sense to me," Lex now declared. "So I've been taking instruction."

He meditated and studied whenever he could, in his room at the halfway house in Winnipeg where he was serving out his parole. He'd been given permission to attend a retreat at the Sunnywell Centre. The dharma study group had been kind enough to cover the fee. Two weeks, in residence, at the same time that Bill Gilchrist must have died. The counsellor had dropped him off on the Saturday and picked him up two weekends after. He'd been there the entire time, attended every session, every day. The teacher, Lama John, could vouch for him. Not everyone in the group knew his history. Perhaps they would be discreet if they were going to be asking questions, he asked politely.

When Ken Roach had fallen to his death, Lex had been in the halfway house. He meditated most evenings after supper. He maintained a benign smile on his face, emulating the Buddha whose teachings he said he now followed. "We do not kill. Anything. Not even a mosquito," he stated. And he held no grudges against Bill Gilchrist or Ken Roach for accusing him of assault, although he hadn't done it, he still insisted. "I have learned to forgive," he remarked. Once he had been considered brash. Now he was transformed into a quiet man with eyes that proclaimed his innocence and the shaved head of a serious student of the dharma. Without his floppy forelock he looked less boyish.

His parole officer had called Inspector Schultz already, annoyed at Lex's detention.

"He's done well," he said. "Total success story. He's going to go to university and study eastern religions. He's starting a work placement at a wellness centre and his local dharma group is going to give him a room to live in, in exchange for taking care of the house they use for their meetings, once his parole is over. There's no way he'd go on a killing spree and compromise that opportunity. And he's never been violent. I know he was convicted for assault, but I don't believe a word of it. He's avoided that kind of trouble all the years he's been in jail. If it goes on his record that he's a suspect for these murders it'll screw that plan right up."

That wasn't what had convinced Schultz that they'd better let the guy go. It was simply that they had no evidence against him. McKenzie had a decent alibi for the time that Bill Gilchrist had died. Schultz sat back his chair, tucked his bull head into his uniform collar and drummed his fingertips together while he thought.

This was a high-profile case, one that was generating a lot of interest. What else did they know? There had been some talk about Bill Gilchrist's wife having disappeared soon as they got back from the States. She might have had enough of Bill's company after spending five months cooped up with him in a trailer, but that didn't mean she'd have wanted to kill him. Roach's death nixed that angle, anyway. Why would Julie Gilchrist decide to do away with him? They had nothing much except this Lex McKenzie guy. This was not good.

"Keep checking," he told Cappelli. "Would anyone in that Buddhist crowd be soft enough to lend him a car? How far is it from the Sunnywell Centre to Kuryk Road? Must be less than an hour's drive, right? And did anyone actually see him the night that Roach was killed?"

Mark Cappelli was reassured. He didn't believe in Lex McKenzie's conversion for a second. Lex had lied before, and he was lying now. If Mark kept digging he'd find something, he was sure of it.

"What other options do you have?" Schultz was shuffling papers on his desk, preparing to end this meeting.

"We're going through the archived files at Fiskar Bay," Cappelli said. "Thoroughly."

"What does Roxanne Calloway think?" asked Schultz.

Sergeant Cappelli hadn't expected that question. "She's not with the Major Crimes Unit any longer, sir," he reminded his boss.

"Yeah." Schultz spoke offhand. His attention had shifted to the next task in front of him. "But she's uncovered some murderers in her time. Talk to her. See if she's got any ideas."

Mark Cappelli was dismissed. He trotted downstairs. He didn't need any help from Calloway. She'd just got lucky when she was in Major Crimes. Rose fast through the ranks because they needed to promote more women. She'd always had a guy to hide behind, like Jake Calloway. She'd met him in training at the Depot. Married him straight after, Cappelli had been told. Had him at her back until he died and even then being the widow of a serving officer had given her some kind of special status. Some city cop had saved her from getting into real trouble last year. And now she had Schultz twisted around her little finger? What was that about? Was that how she'd got herself shunted into the team commander job at Fiskar Bay? Figured.

THE FLOOD CRISIS had been resolved at the Sunnywell Centre. A channel had been opened through the ice pack so that the river could flow toward the lake once more. The wall of sandbags remained. A few had burst, spilling their contents onto the grassy riverbank.

"Those must go! So unsightly." Bea Benedict waved a hand in their direction as she passed a window. She conducted Margo Wishart and her friends toward the room that she thought might serve their purpose. Margo, Sasha and Roberta walked into a large rectangular space with white walls and a black floor. Sunlight streamed in through south-facing windows.

"Are these blinds any good?" Sasha twitched a cord.

"Absolutely, we have only the best." Bea stood inside the door while they looked. She wore a crimson jacket and skirt, shoes with medium heels, and folded her ringed hands over her ample belly. Sasha grunted, unconvinced. She'd heard that said before, in other places, on other projects. The light always managed to seep through.

"This might work for us." Margo was more optimistic. "I'm glad we found you. Julie Gilchrist recommended that I talk to you."

Bea sniffed. She knew exactly who that was. The wife of the ex-Mountie who had been found dead. The one who had stayed here for a day and then had taken off without telling anyone and caused a fuss. What was all that about?

A tall man, sandy-haired, stooped at the shoulders, passed the doorway.

"Steven!" said Margo Wishart. "What are you doing here?"

Steve Rice was married to Susan, the yoga instructor. He had an office at the centre, he said. He offered counselling services. But right now, he had to go into the city. One of his clients needed some help. He disappeared down the hallway.

"You live in Cullen Village too?" asked Bea.

"We all do. Well, I'm just outside. But Sasha lives right on Edgeware Creek, where that second cop went into the water," Roberta's voice rang out behind her.

"Really." Bea turned a gracious head. She'd paid no attention so far to this shabby little person, all decked out in hand-me-downs, wandering around in the middle of the room. Some of what she wore looked handmade.

"Margo's house is nearby too," Roberta continued, unperturbed. "Just along the road from Steve."

"Steven," Bea corrected her. "He's very well qualified. A PhD. In demand as a counsellor. And so kind."

"Margo's one of those, too," Roberta remarked casually. "A PhD. She teaches at the university."

"Really?" Bea turned an unctuous eye on Margo.

"I didn't know he worked here," Margo said. That kind of attention made her uncomfortable. "I thought he was at the substance abuse clinic in Winnipeg."

"Only one day a week. He has a private practice. You know he sometimes works at the provincial jail as well? Pro bono. So, about the room? Do you think it is suitable?"

Margo looked up at a high ceiling. There was a grid where they could attach lights. It would work for them, she thought. Sasha drew the blinds. Bea was right, they closed off every chink of light.

"Y'know—" Roberta peered up into the instant gloom. Bea strode to the wall, threw a switch and light flooded the room again.

"We could hang the three sisters up above us. Suspend gauzy, thin fabric," she said. "Parachute silk, maybe, draped like it's the surface of the water. Up near the ceiling. Shine lights through it. And make everything under it look like it's underwater."

Sasha looked up, picturing it in her head. "The sculptures would be like giant puppets," she said, warming to the idea. She walked over to join Roberta "Maybe we could hang some fish, too. Make the floor look like the lakebed. Can we paint it?"

"If you return it to black when you are done," Bea replied. "And you must use good quality paint." Margo nodded her head. They could do it. And the room was available when she wanted, the last couple of weeks in September. They walked back to the entrance hall. Bea gave her forms to fill out and Margo promised to drop them off with a deposit.

"I wonder, Dr. Wishart," said Bea Benedict before they took their leave, "if you could return some things to Julie Gilchrist since you'll be seeing her soon. She left them here and they haven't been picked up yet." She reached under the counter and produced a tote bag and a plastic bag containing clothing. "I was going to give it to Dr. Rice, but he's such a busy man and I don't know if she's still seeing him."

"She's a client of his?"

Bea had the grace to look embarrassed. She knew better than to reveal confidential information of that sort. "I thought you knew. Since she referred you to us. I shouldn't have said, do excuse me."

"Not a problem."

But Margo was already thinking. Julie must have gone to Steve Rice for counselling before she and Bill took off to the U.S. for the winter. Why had she needed his advice? They'd come back from Arizona sooner than expected and she'd taken off, right away, to do a meditation retreat, but then she'd gone to Kenora to visit her sister instead without telling anyone. And now her husband was dead, and she was planning a sudden move to B.C. to live with that same sister. Julie had assured her that she was okay, but was she, really? Maybe involving her in this project wasn't such a great idea after all. Margo wished she'd never mentioned it to her.

14

IZZY'S MOM REMEMBERED all about Lex McKenzie. It had been the talk of the Interlake for a couple of years before she got sick, and Izzy came back home to help take care of her. "That's why you don't know about it," she said. "It was just before then."

Izzy's mother was a breast cancer survivor. The illness had forced Izzy to come back to Fiskar Bay to work once she had graduated from RCMP training at the Depot in Regina. It hadn't been a good career move, but the Force had grudgingly allowed it. Sometimes family had to come first. Especially if you were a McBain.

"Lex scammed people out of their life savings," Izzy now told Corporal Riordan. "They thought they were buying a new house on the water with a dock. Didn't happen. He blew all their money in Costa Rica or something instead. He's full of big ideas. Can talk a mile a minute but you can't believe a word of it. Gift of the gab, my mom says.

"The parents are both dead. He has two brothers. None of them wanted to carry on the farm but they still own it. My brother Ed rents some land from them. He went to school with Lex. There's also an uncle called Al Melnychuk, their mother's brother, who fishes the lake. He's a big cheese on the town council."

The autopsy results were in. Bill Gilchrist had most likely died of exposure, but Dr. Farooq could not be sure of the time of death, given the state of the body and the fact that it had been frozen. The strata created by the snowpack in the ditch suggested that he had been there when the storm on Wednesday, April 4th, had dumped more than a foot of snow on top of him. Julie Gilchrist said she had seen him at their house the previous Saturday, before she left to go to the Sunnywell Centre, so he had died within that four-day window, April 1st to 4th, Sunday to Wednesday morning. That was as close as Abdur Farooq could get.

"Maybe he was killed on April Fool's Day? Geez," said Izzy.

The break to his right leg had been caused by a lateral blow to the outside of the knee. His opposite shoulder and hip had been bruised and he had received another hit to the back of his skull, most likely when he landed on ice on the road or in the ditch, half full of hard wet ice. But that was not what had killed him. The best hypothesis was that a vehicle had hit him hard enough to knock him off his feet and into the ditch. The ligaments in his knee were torn and so was the meniscus. The damage meant that the knee could not support his weight. He could have dragged himself along the ice to find a way to get up the side of the ditch but failed to do so. The point of impact suggested that he had made contact with the front of a mid- to large-size car or a small to medium truck.

"So, he must have died slowly outside at night? Couldn't crawl out of the ditch because his knee was blown out?" Jeff looked up from reading.

"Sounds like it, plus he'd landed on hard wet ice, slippery as hell," said Izzy. "He didn't have a phone, so he couldn't call for help."

"That phone's never shown up?"

It hadn't.

The evidence regarding Ken Roach's demise revealed more. He'd also been hit, hard, on the side of his body. His right back and hip were bruised from being slammed into the wooden fence hard enough to shatter the rail where it joined an upright post. It hadn't taken much force to break it. The fence was old, beginning to rot. It would have given way quite easily. He had landed in the fast-moving creek below. The best scenario was that a moving vehicle, once again a mid- to large-size car or a small to medium-size truck, about twenty-four inches high at the point of contact, had hit him, forced him through the fence and into the rushing current. He hadn't had enough strength to get himself out of the creek because of his injuries and the force of the water had pushed his head into the mouth of the culvert which was full of water at the time. He had drowned quickly.

"Someone drove Bill and then Roach off the road and left them to die?" Izzy watched Jeff close the lid on his laptop.

He didn't reply for a moment. When he did, he said, "Better be careful, Isabel. Don't want it to be you next."

"Speak for yourself, Corporal," Izzy retorted. "Nobody's going to kill me out here. I'm a McBain, don't you know that? Nobody's going to risk laying a finger on me." Jeff Riordan raised a skeptical eyebrow. "'S true. You need to watch your own back." She grinned. He returned it.

"Nah," he replied. "They don't know who I am."

"Don't you believe it," said Izzy. She had a message from Matt. He'd taken a break from studying to search the web to find out more about the time the Gilchrists had lived in Robson, twenty years ago. A kid called Jeremy Featherstone had drowned in a waterhole where the local boys went to hang out and dive into the deep water. There had been an investigation. Bill Gilchrist, then an RCMP constable, had been involved. Kenneth Roach was one of the boys that had been questioned. The result had been a verdict of accidental death.

The couple who had built the new solar-powered house west of where Bill Gilchrist's body had been found were also called Featherstone. Matt had remembered that. He'd been introduced to the husband when he'd attended a meeting about lake conservation. James Featherstone had worked as a water resource engineer for the government in Winnipeg. Matt had tracked down a report from his retirement. It outlined his career and, yes, he'd been in Robson, late nineties. The family had left the year after Jeremy Featherstone had died.

"Guess I should go talk to them," Jeff said.

"I can come too, right? You don't want to be out there on your own-ee-o." Izzy jumped to her feet, not waiting to take no for an answer. She almost tripped over a couple of file boxes in her hurry. She pointed to one of them. "Do you think I'm done with having to go through these, now we've got some good leads? Have you seen how much stuff is in them? Going through them all is such a waste of time."

"Maybe." Jeff followed her downstairs. Ravi Anand was manning the front desk. The office was quiet. Kathy Isfeld tapped at her keyboard. Roxanne Calloway was out, called to her regular job, attending a meeting with some of the town council. Something about quads. As soon as the snow was gone, the winter sledders traded their skidoos for ATVs. They were always looking for places where they could roar along, tearing up the ground in their wake. Groomed, designated trails were the answer but many people did not welcome the noise they brought, or the exhaust fumes.

"How are you doing with my files?" asked Kathy.

"Boy," said Jeff. "There's way too much stuff in them. Most of what's in them could be shredded. You're retiring soon, right? Maybe you could clean them up before you go."

Kathy inspected him over the top of her screen. "Those," she said in a serious little voice, "are the history of this detachment. In detail."

"You're telling me!" Jeff laughed. The corners of Kathy's mouth turned down.

"They're great, Kathy," Izzy reassured her. She leaned forward and hissed in his ear: "Outside, right now, Corporal."

Jeff Riordan did as he was told. "I was just saying," he protested, spreading his hands. "You said they had way too much stuff in them yourself."

"But not to Kathy! You do not piss her off." Izzy unlocked the car.

"The civvy?"

"Kathy matters. Back when Bill Gilchrist was the boss, it was Kathy you went to if you wanted to get things done. She pretty well ran that office until Roxanne took over. Y'know what? Go buy her a coffee and an apple fritter—she likes those—when we get back. Get into her good books. It'll be worth it, I'm telling you."

JULIE GILCHRIST WATCHED the Yukon being towed out of her driveway on its way to Winnipeg for scrutiny by the Ident team. She wished she'd had time to take it to the car wash. It was still covered in grime from the long haul north from Arizona and the inside was a mess. Having the police probe even further into her family's lives was worrying and so unfair since they already had Bill's death to cope with. She'd phone her sister tonight and have a long chat about it.

Meantime, she was going upstairs to her sewing loft to unpack all the goodies she'd bought in the U.S. Not that she needed more stuff now that she knew for sure she was going to leave. She and Sherry had narrowed their choices to a couple of houses in Kelowna. Sherry was thinking about flying out there to look at each of them and maybe make an offer. She, Julie, couldn't go. She'd been told by the police to stay close to home while this awful business was going on.

Hazel was coming back on Thursday. She was good at organizing things. She liked being in charge, just like her dad. Julie would leave all the funeral arrangements and further dealings with the police to her. And Hazel could take care of all Bill's things, his clothes, his papers. Julie couldn't bring herself to touch them. Fern had called. There was talk of getting together. Maybe she'd get to see her grandkids. Even spend some time with them.

She opened her inbox to find a message from Margo Wishart. Margo had Julie's things from the Sunnywell Centre. Julie had forgotten all about them She sighed.

Come for tea, she emailed back. *Tomorrow afternoon is best.*

Meanwhile, she could finally escape into her world of fabric and thread, the magic of shape, texture, colour, the place where she could forget all these troubles, for a while at least.

ROXANNE SAT AT a table in the Fiskar Bay council office, in the presence of Al Melnychuk, uncle of Lex McKenzie, now one of their suspects. He was a tank of a man, muscular, strong-legged from keeping balance on a fishing boat, hands and arms equally solid from hauling in nets. He didn't mess around when it came to the issue of building more quad trails. Sure they should, he had said. He didn't give reasons. He just knew he was right and he expected that to be enough. Lots of local people had quad bikes and the council knew they backed him. He got his way. He cornered Roxanne on the way out.

"What's this about your guys taking our Lex in for questioning?" he demanded. "He's served his time. More than he should have if you ask me."

"He's helping us with our investigation," Roxanne replied blandly, looking past him to the exit.

"Bullshit!" He walled her in. "You're trying to pin these murders on him. Get yourselves off the hook. Close the case, double quick." He planted his feet squarely in front of her. He wasn't going anywhere until he'd had his say. "Lex couldn't have done it," he barked at her, inches from her face. "He's on parole. Was staying at some New Age-y place that almost got flooded last week. Around other folks. Wasn't here.

"And," he rumbled on, "Lex isn't the type to go around killing people. Hasn't got the guts. Too damned soft if you ask me. Not that that'll stop you from trying to hang this one on him, just like Kenny Roach did. He beat him up in a cell, then tried to say Lex attacked him. Got away with it, too. But this time it's murder. That could put Lex away for life. Not on, lady. Tell your lot to back off." He poked a finger right at her nose. "There's no way he did in Bill Gilchrist. And Kenny Roach was a mean bastard. Lex wasn't the only guy he fucked up. This whole town knows that. Go look for someone else."

He swung around and lumbered away down the hallway. The mayor's assistant stood at an office door. She watched as Melnychuk shoved the front door open with one hand and left, then gave Roxanne a nervous smile before she, too, disappeared from sight. No doubt the story of that confrontation would be circulating around Fiskar Bay in minutes. She headed back to the office.

Kathy Isfeld had got Ravi to retrieve the file boxes from upstairs and was directing him to stack them, in order, back in the closet.

"Sounds like they don't think they're useful," she sniffed. "So I'm putting them back where they belong."

Roxanne was surprised. She didn't think Izzy had gone through all of them already. Maybe they'd found something new; thought that Lex McKenzie really was their man, and the case was almost wrapped up. But that decision seemed premature. Roxanne wasn't at all sure that this case was over yet. Not at all.

15

JANE FEATHERSTONE WAS home when Izzy and Jeff reached her house. Her husband was not.

"He's gone into the city for a meeting about water conservation," she said as she ushered her two visitors inside. The room they entered was large—living room, dining room and kitchen combined, facing south. Big windows lined a wall with blinds half down. It was sparely furnished, the floor a glossy hardwood. Izzy had noticed solar panels on the roof and above the garage as she drove in. The windows were designed to trap light and store them in the sills. She took as much of it in as she could so she could tell her mother later.

"Crocuses?" She pointed out a window at purple heads that looked ready to burst open.

"They are." Jane brought a tray to a low table. On it were china teacups, a matching milk jug and a sugar bowl. "It's their first year. I planted lots of bulbs in the fall. I thought they'd drown with all that water we had. But some of them have survived."

"It's disappearing fast," said Izzy.

"I suppose the Interlake is always prone to flooding in the spring." Jane lifted a teapot and poured. "And it seems to be getting worse. Climate change." She had an accent. English. The tea was Earl Grey. It tasted soapy to Izzy, but she drank it anyway. There was a plate of cookies. Custard creams. Those were okay. Jeff sat down by her side.

"We've been trying to get hold of you," he explained. "To find out if you noticed anything unusual out near Kuryk Road three weekends ago. When there was that warm spell last month. Just before the big snowstorm."

"That was when the retired police officer died?" Jane's hand hesitated as she lifted her teacup. She was slim and simply dressed. A white shirt collar lay neatly above a grey sweater; her pants were a darker shade of the same colour. She must be in her sixties, Izzy figured, her hair almost white, cut short. Her skin was fair and rosy, which relieved the grey. She looked at them through rimless glasses.

"It was," said Jeff. "Ex-Sergeant Gilchrist of the RCMP."

They watched as the teacup was placed gently back on its saucer.

"We didn't see anything out of the ordinary. But we don't drive that way very often, officer," she told him, her eyes opaque behind their lenses. Their house was closer to another highway, over to the west. It led straight toward Winnipeg.

"You don't drive into Fiskar Bay?" asked Izzy. That route would take the Featherstones right past the end of Kuryk Road.

"Not often. We haven't had much reason this winter."

Izzy knew what that meant. She and her husband must fetch all their groceries and other supplies from the city. That wasn't unusual among people who moved to the country from Winnipeg, but it didn't endear them to the local tradespeople.

"Maybe in the summer," Jane continued. "James wants to buy a boat and join the yacht club at Fiskar Bay. And I hear there's a decent garden centre down near Cullen Village. I'm looking forward to getting out into the garden."

They had noticed a greenhouse out the back of the house and half a dozen raised beds.

"What brought you out here?" Izzy asked, continuing the polite chat. It didn't hurt to know, and she could pass the information on to her mother. She would love to know. This woman looked too much like a townie to have parked herself out here in the middle of farmland, miles from anyone else.

They'd been able to buy this piece of land, with an open southern view to catch the sunlight, Jane explained. To be out of the city, but still be close to it. And they wanted to live within reach of the lake. "James is taking an interest in its conservation," she added coolly.

Izzy had seen people like this move out here before. They didn't fit in. Probably didn't want to. They kept themselves aloof. It usually wasn't long before they got bored and moved back to Winnipeg or became snowbirds. Definitely not the neighbourly type.

"You used to live up in Robson?" Jeff said. Again, Jane hesitated before she replied.

"That was a very long time ago."

"Bill Gilchrist served in the RCMP up there. His wife, Julie, taught home economics at the high school. Did you know them?"

"I don't think so. Why would we?" Jane looked at him, her disdain unmistakeable.

"Just thought it was interesting that you both lived up there and then you retired here as well."

"I don't remember them."

"What were you doing in Robson?"

"My husband got a job there. He has a degree in water management and there's a lot of water in Canada," Jane said. "So, we emigrated."

She had studied mathematics. She'd taught in England before she and her husband emigrated to Canada but teaching opportunities had been scarce when they'd arrived. She'd taken a position at the bank instead.

"It wasn't the career I had planned but I did well. I was a branch manager when I retired last year."

"And your kids?" asked Izzy.

"Alison did environmental studies. She works for UNESCO. Out of New York," she said with pride.

"Other children?" Izzy asked.

"Alison is our only child." She looked away from them, toward the window.

Jeff looked at Izzy. She returned his gaze. She had noticed the evasion, too. Best to wait until they met the husband before they mentioned that they knew that there had been a son as well, who had died. She did not know when James would be back, Jane told them. He sometimes stayed in town and had dinner with a friend.

Izzy and Jeff took their leave. Jane led them to the back door, moving quietly. The glass from the greenhouse caught the sunlight.

"Have you met your neighbour, Netta Kuryk?" Izzy asked. "At the farm over there?" She pointed. "She gardens. Got some great seedlings coming along. Has one of those big Ukrainian vegetable plots."

"Really?" The woman asked with polite disdain again. "We grow ours organically."

"She's such a snot," said Izzy as she buckled her seat belt. "Can't stand folks like that, ones that move out here and think they know it all. Let's go look at the McKenzie house now, okay?"

The old farmhouse was locked, curtains drawn. It was being maintained, just. The windows had been replaced; the woodwork was painted. That was about all.

"There's got to be a key," said Izzy, reaching up to the top of the lintel. It wasn't there.

"Nah, best wait." Jeff walked toward the back of the house. "Someone's had a fire going." The firepit had ash in it.

Izzy made her way to a window in a large outbuilding. "There's a truck in there," she said. "You sure we can't go inside and look?"

"Better check with Cappelli first," said the corporal. "He'll maybe want Ident to check it out."

Izzy pointed toward the corner of Kuryk Road, just visible from where they stood.

"That looks like Stan Kuryk, poking around," she said. "Let's go see what he's up to."

A truck was parked at the roadside. Stan Kuryk stood beside it, glaring at them as they pulled up, his worn dungaree bottoms tucked into his muddy boots and his arms incongruously full of flowers, bunches lifted from the makeshift memorial to the dead RCMP Sergeant.

"What's he doing with those?" Jeff asked.

"Let me talk to him." Izzy hopped out. "Whatya doing, Mr. Kuryk?"

"Netta said to go fetch them," he said unabashed, opening the cab of his truck and putting the bouquets inside. "She's going to take them over to the hospital this afternoon. She's on the ladies' auxiliary. What did ya think? That I was stealing them?"

"Just asking. That's cute." Izzy squatted down to get a closer look at the plastic figure of a Mountie standing with its arm raised in a salute. RIP SGT GILCHRIST was painted in crude letters on a wooden cross beside it.

Jeff had wandered off along the ditch, peering down. There was still a lot of water in it, and a few inches of murky ice at the bottom.

"Are you taking the teddy bears too?" Izzy asked. There were four of those.

"Best leave one, I guess. And some flowers. They'll get trashed, lying out here in all weathers," Kuryk muttered. "And then guess who'll have to clean it up? Netta said if there's lots, she might take some to Harbourfront." That was a care home for the elderly at Fiskar Bay. He looked past Izzy at Jeff who was kicking at clumps of dead grass. "What's he think he's doing?"

"Looking for a phone. You haven't seen one, have you?"

He hadn't. But he'd be sure to let her know if he did, he told her. He could just let her dad know, right?

"Sure thing," Izzy replied. If Kuryk preferred to deal with her as the McBain girl that was fine with her.

"Look at these." Stan picked up a green plastic pot containing hyacinths, blue ones, just opening, the ones Roberta Axelsson had left earlier. "I'm not leaving these to die out here. They'll make some old biddy happy." He laid them carefully on the floor of his cab. "Not going to do Bill Gilchrist any good where he's gone, are they? People are stupid." He slammed the door shut, climbed aboard and drove off toward his house.

Jeff rejoined her. "It's a grim place to die," he said

"I dunno." Izzy raised her face to the April sun. She could feel warmth. On the other side of the road, sticky buds were emerging on the poplar trees. "This is one of those years when spring will happen overnight. Someday soon it'll be hot, all the leaves'll sprout and it will be summer." She got back into her car. "Changes everything. You'll see!"

"With a bit of luck, I'll be long gone by then."

MARGO WISHART GOT home just in time to see the school bus offload the Rices' two children. They ran up the path and Susan opened the door for them. Margo didn't hesitate.

"Susan!" she called. "Do you have a moment?"

She described the lake project while Susan poured glasses of almond milk for her son and daughter. "I asked Julie Gilchrist to join us. She's such an amazing quilter, but now I'm worried. I've just heard from her. The police have towed Bill's car away for examination. No one knows who killed him yet."

"Or that other Mountie. He was called Roach, right? Do you like green tea?" Susan reached for a canister.

"Julie's planning to move away from here." Margo leaned against the counter. "Did you know about that?"

Susan did. She poured boiling water into a teapot. It had a wooden handle and Japanese lettering on the side.

"Her daughter Hazel is coming here to help take care of things, and Julie says she'll be able to work with us, but I'm not at all sure that's true," Margo continued. "She seems so, well, oblivious. I'm not here to gossip, but I do need to know if I can rely on her, and you seem to know her better than most. I've got other artists involved in the project and I can't let it fail because someone is, well, unstable."

Susan pushed a strand of long dark hair behind her ears. "Let's go through next door and talk." She picked up the teapot with one hand and two small bowls in the other.

Margo found herself seated in one of the squishy chairs. The children had gone upstairs. They knew how to amuse themselves and were very well-behaved. Susan put a small table in front of the sofa, then folded herself down onto a cushion on the floor opposite.

"I'm glad you asked," she said. "Steve and I were discussing this just last night. He's very concerned about Julie, but of course a lot of what he knows is confidential. However, she and I are friends and she has told me quite a bit." She poured tea into the little bowls. "She is managing right now. She knows breathing techniques in case she feels panicky, and she does take antidepressants. That might be why she's staying so calm."

"Does she suffer from depression?"

"Sometimes," said Susan. "But the meds she takes seem to work well for her."

"Has she been taking them for long?"

"Oh, years I would think." Susan slid a teacup across the table

"She seems optimistic about the move to Kelowna." Margo reached out of the cushiony depths for her tea.

"She's been looking forward to that for a while."

"It's not a sudden decision?"

"No, it's not. She's been planning it since Christmas. She's been calling me, on and off all winter," Susan explained, "Just to chat.

"You see," she tucked her feet into a perfect lotus, "she and Bill have not been getting along for some time. She managed to cope here while he was working. He was out all the time so she had days to herself. And some evenings. But then he retired and he was home a lot more. It was his idea to go south for the winter. She didn't want to go at all."

"Couldn't she have said no?" asked Margo.

"Bill had a forceful personality." Margo watched Susan choose her words carefully. "He was used to being the person in charge. To getting his own way. So she went along with it. Bill loved it in Arizona, but when he wasn't golfing he was under her feet, in the trailer, talking all the time. Julie's very quiet." Susan lifted big eyes, soft with compassion. "Bill liked to go places. Car trips. And socialize. There were lots of parties at the trailer park. Happy hour. Barbecues. Not Julie's thing at all. She needs time and space to herself and she just wasn't getting it.

"He'd just turned sixty. She's younger than him by a couple of years. She said she saw the next twenty years or more stretching in front of her in the same fashion and all she felt was dread. So she had made up her mind that she had to leave him."

"She had? They've been together a long time." Margo remembered her own divorce and how calamitous it had felt.

"Almost thirty years." Susan took a thoughtful sip of her tea, then continued:

"The other person she talked to a lot was her sister. They're very close. The plan to move to Kelowna has been in place for a while. She told Bill she wanted a divorce about a month ago. He was furious. He refused to believe it, but the funny thing about Julie is that she can be quite tenacious when she has to be. She seems gentle, but, actually, once her mind is made up, there's no budging her. She called me the day that they got back. Said that the trip was a nightmare. She needed to get away from him right away. Needed a break. That's when Steve suggested the retreat. You know that she didn't stay? She went off to visit her sister the next day?"

Margo slowly nodded.

"What worries both of us," Susan continued, "is that the police don't know much of this, but we also believe that if they did, they would suspect that Julie had something to do with Bill's death."

"They might have thought that before," Margo reassured her, "but surely not now. Not when Constable Roach has been killed.

Those deaths must be related to something that happened in the RCMP."

"I thought that too," Susan said. "But they are examining their car."

"It may have nothing to do with Julie. If it's his big SUV that they've taken in." Margo suppressed a moment's unease.

"I don't think you need to worry about your project." Susan smiled and switched to a more positive note. "I think it's great that you've given Julie something creative to think about. I know that she is thrilled that you asked her. She told me so. And I'm sure she'll come through for you. She takes her commitments very seriously."

"She was ready to end her marriage," Margo reminded her.

"Well." Susan unwrapped her legs. "She put up with him for all that time."

"Was he violent?" The question hung in the air before Susan answered.

"Physically? I don't think so." She pushed herself upright from her feet in one smooth motion. Margo struggled up from the chair. "He was just, well, vocal." Susan reached down to pick up the teapot and the empty bowls. "She said she had gone along with what he wanted all those years, just to keep him happy. That house at Heron Haven was his idea. She's going to be so glad to get rid of it."

16

THE FOLLOWING MORNING fog engulfed the Interlake. Mark Cappelli drove north from the city to Fiskar Bay again. He'd called a meeting for ten, but he'd had to reduce his speed. He'd be lucky to make it in time. He clicked his tongue. He did not like to be late.

Matt Stavros drove in the opposite direction, toward Winnipeg. He had a presentation to make for a university class, one that counted toward his final mark for the year. He had gone to Mo Magnusson's first. Joseph was going to spend the day at doggie daycare, Mo's latest enterprise.

She'd met him at the door, without her usual makeup, her pink hair all mussed up. "I've got another couple of dogs coming. They can play together."

She charged twenty bucks a day, to help buy more food for the rescue. Matt had been worried that Joseph would think he'd been abandoned once more, dumped back at the kennel.

"Nah." Mo took the leash. "I'll keep him in the house when he's not in the yard." She hunkered down beside the dog and rubbed his ears. "Go now. He's fine."

Matt tried not to feel guilty as he walked away. He could hear Keenan, Mo's boyfriend, playing the piano somewhere inside the house, the same phrase, over and over again.

Izzy had been lazing around, still in pyjamas, talking to her mom on the phone, when he'd left home, something about the people who lived in the new ergonomic house near Desna Church, close to where Bill Gilchrist had died. She didn't have to be at work until ten, she had said. She had to be at a meeting with Sergeant Cappelli.

But when ten came, there was no sign of Izzy McBain at the Fiskar Bay detachment.

"She'll show up." Roxanne had gone upstairs to join the same meeting. Her thumbs tapped out a message on her phone while she spoke.

Cappelli had finally picked up speed and arrived just in time. He, Roxanne, and Jeff waited around the table. The fog had lifted as the sun rose. Roxanne laid her phone beside her on the table. No answer. "She's probably at the doughnut shop picking up jam busters."

But still Izzy did not appear. Jeff had called her too, just before Roxanne arrived, and got no answer. Mark sat with one ankle across his knee. He tapped his fingernails on the tabletop in irritation.

"Does she make a habit of this?" he asked.

"Not usually. Hope she's okay," Jeff replied. "She's out there, driving, alone. She thinks she's safe here. Maybe she isn't."

"She's not in danger," Cappelli declared. "McKenzie did it, course he did. We just need the evidence. That's what I'm here to do. Make sure we get it." He turned his elegantly trimmed head toward Roxanne. The shadow that covered his chin was even and symmetrical. One hand rested on his ankle. Roxanne noticed that the fingernails were perfectly shaped, too.

"I'm going to get my guys to keep an eye open for Izzy." She stood. "Just in case." And she went down to the front office.

Consternation registered on Ravi Anand's face. "She didn't say where she was going?" Izzy hadn't. He reached for his phone. "I'll call the house."

"I've done that already," said Roxanne. "No one's answering."

"She'll be all right," Kathy Isfeld murmured from her desk. "She'll show up. Don't worry." They both looked at her. "She always does." Kathy continued to type, unperturbed.

Aimee Vermette and Sam Mendes were out patrolling the roads. "Get them to keep an eye open for her car, Ravi," said Roxanne. "And keep checking."

She went back upstairs, in time to hear Jeff say, "Izzy and I dropped by the Featherstone house yesterday to have a word with the mother of that boy who drowned up in Robson. She told us she never knew the Gilchrists, but they did live there at the same time."

"That's a long shot," Mark Cappelli remarked, unconvinced. "And it was long ago."

"But they're here, now, living in the same neighbourhood," Roxanne said. He might not be curious, but she was.

"Coincidence." Mark Cappelli put his foot back on the floor and sat up straighter.

"I don't believe in those," she countered.

Jeff recognized the beginnings of a disagreement. Cappelli was his boss. He decided he'd best side with him.

"There's something else," he said. "Lex McKenzie and his brothers own a farm not far from there." That played into Cappelli's hand. He listened closely as Jeff told them about the ash in the firepit. "Someone's been out there this spring. We didn't go inside. Thought you might want Ident to do a thorough search."

He was interrupted by feet banging up the stairs. Izzy bounced into view, cheeks pink from hurrying, ponytail swinging.

"Where have you been?" Cappelli demanded. "It's 10:15."

"Janine Roach's!" Izzy announced. She unzipped her jacket, not one bit apologetic. "Did you know she's leaving town? Driving up to Robson? Today? With the kids? To go stay with her mom?"

"Roach's wife?" asked Jeff Riordan.

"Yup!" Izzy dragged out a chair. It scraped on the floor. Cappelli winced.

"She needs to be told about the autopsy results before she goes," said Roxanne.

"No problem. I did it." Izzy plopped down onto the chair and leaned forward, eager to tell more. "She'd have been gone if you'd waited. My mom told me she was leaving, on the phone, this morning. So I booted over there. Just as well I did, right?"

"She's from Robson too?" Cappelli's eyes narrowed. He leaned back, folded his arms, prepared to listen this time.

"Sure she is. She and Kenny met way back in high school. She knew the Featherstone kid. Didn't any of you think to pick up doughnuts?" Izzy looked around. "I skipped breakfast so I would catch her in time."

"And?" Cappelli prompted.

"She wasn't going to tell me anything," said Izzy. "But her sister was there. She still lives in Robson. She'd driven all the way down to help her pack. You know they're going to bury Kenny up there? In the Robson family plot? After the big memorial service in Winnipeg?

"Anyway, Janine was busy with one of the kids, she was acting up, doesn't want to leave all her friends here, so I went to help the sister load up the van and we got talking. Got the whole story." She grinned, pleased with herself. "Turns out the sister didn't like Kenny any more than we did. Says he was always full of himself, even when he was a kid. He was one of the jocks in school and Janine was on the cheerleading team. They were part of the in-crowd; you know the type.

"The Featherstone kid, on the other hand, was a bit of a nerd. English, had an accent. Got picked on a lot. He went out one Saturday by himself and never came home. They found his body floating in a pool in the river. There was a rocky outcrop. Kids used to dive off it. The coroner thought he'd jumped and hit himself on a rock and drowned. Nobody else had been around to see it happen. Kenny and the other kids swore they'd never been there that day. The boys had gone fishing further upstream. Stayed late, the girls came by, they cooked up the fish and drank some beer, got home after dark. The verdict was accidental death. But there was talk."

"Always is," Mark Cappelli commented. "You can't always believe it."

"Yeah." Izzy grinned at him and carried on undeterred. "But people wanted to know what he was doing there, all by himself. His clothes were found high up on the rock. He wasn't wearing a thing when they found him. He wasn't a good swimmer and he wasn't the type to go skinny-dipping. Why would he jump off a rock face way up high? Some folks thought he'd killed himself. That the coroner brought in a verdict of accidental death to spare the parents the embarrassment. But Janine's sister's a nurse. She'd just started work at the hospital when it happened. She heard the other staff talking about how the body was covered in bruises. And that information never made it into the inquest.

"So, she says people thought that it might not have been an accident or suicide. Someone might have forced Jeremy Featherstone to take his clothes off and jump off that rock face. Then made sure he didn't get out of the water."

"How long ago was it?" Cappelli asked.

"Twenty-one years," said Izzy. "And now the Featherstones have moved here. Their house is a two-minute drive from where Sergeant Bill was killed."

"Okay," Cappelli got to his feet. "It's all circumstantial, but we should question them, thoroughly this time. What's the Featherstones' first names?" He wrote them on the whiteboard. They were called Jane and James, like they were twins. Then he tapped his marker on the photo of Lex McKenzie. "He's still our main suspect," he said. "And now it looks like he's been visiting the family farmhouse. It's close to where Bill Gilchrist died too."

"No," Izzy countered. "My brother Ed knows all about that. Lex has a brother, Marvin, likes to come out from the city on the weekends to icefish. He keeps a shack near his uncle's out on the ice other side of the harbour wall. The uncle's Al Melnychuk, the town councillor."

"I met him yesterday," said Roxanne. "He seems to think Roach framed Lex on that assault charge years ago."

"Really? There's our motive." Cappelli smiled, satisfied, and sat again.

"Marvin's a big guy, like his uncle," said Izzy. "My brother Mike played hockey with him when they were in school. Marvin was their enforcer. So he's tough. Maybe he's got something to do with this."

"The brother is taking revenge?" Jeff asked. "On behalf of Lex? Why wait until now?"

"I think we're looking for someone who's less likely to use their fists," Roxanne remarked. "Think about the means of death. Using a car as a weapon. That tells us it could be someone physically weaker."

"Yeah. Like Lex McKenzie," Mark insisted.

"Or a woman. Like Julie Gilchrist." Roxanne got up, lifted a marker and underscored Julie's name on the whiteboard. "She could have killed either of them. She says she drove straight from the Sunnywell Centre to Kenora that Sunday, but we've only got her word for it.

"She could have come up here, had a row with Bill and killed him, then taken off to her sister's in Kenora because she needed to get as far away as possible. She left some things at the Sunnywell Centre, right? She meant to go back but then she changed her mind. Why did she do that unless something unexpected had happened? And she was at home the weekend that Ken Roach died. Her daughter Hazel will say she was there, but she would, wouldn't she? She doesn't really have an alibi.

"How long will it be until you get the results on the search of Bill Gilchrist's Yukon?" she asked. "Maybe it's the murder weapon."

She didn't wait for an answer. She drew other lines under the Featherstones' names. "Then there's them. That story about their son's death needs checking out." She wrote down another name. Janine Roach.

"Really?" asked Izzy. "You think so?"

Cappelli watched his meeting take off in an entirely different direction from the one he had planned. Roxanne had the floor.

"She's leaving here real fast," she said. "Pulling her kids out of school. She's lived here for years, she's got friends. They're helping her. Why the hurry? What's happening with the house? Is she going to sell it? How long is it since she and Roach moved away from Robson? Sure, they're going to do the family burial up there but why is she not sticking around, at least until the big service in Winnipeg happens? Why the need to run away from here, now? How well did she and Roach really get along? What do we know about her?"

"Stays home. Keeps it clean. You've seen it. House beautiful. She sells cleaning liquids on the side. Organizes house parties. Makes money at it," said Izzy. "I didn't talk to her much. She was never my type. We should ask Kathy. There's your chance to get back in her good books, Jeff." She nudged the corporal beside her. "Go suck up."

"You annoyed Kathy?" Roxanne looked at Jeff. He shrugged. She shook her head at him. "Not a good idea," she said.

"I'll get Ident to come out and look at the McKenzie farmhouse," Cappelli said, loud enough to regain their attention. "And I'd better meet the Gilchrist woman. I'll go tell her about the autopsy results."

"Let me come with you," said Roxanne. "It's really my job too, right? Since Bill was the previous boss here and he died on my watch."

He suppressed a sigh. She had a point. He could hardly refuse.

17

MARK CAPPELLI INSISTED on driving. From his side of the car, he could see the red scar that ran under Roxanne Calloway's jaw. He'd been told that most of her ear had been lopped off in a violent incident last year, one that had almost cost her her life, but it was covered by her hair. He'd asked around HQ, been told that she'd lost her nerve afterwards and opted for a safe job at Fiskar Bay. It wasn't working out that way, not if someone was hunting down members of her detachment. She could be targeted herself.

The fields they drove past were now mostly black earth, still puddled with some water, but the grass along the side of the road was turning green. The ditches were half full, no longer overflowing. The fog had entirely dissipated, the sky was blue, the lake shimmered all the way to the horizon. He wore sunshades against the dazzle.

He knew that she'd doubled up her team. They were not to venture out alone. She was playing it safe. And now she was arguing a case for getting Constable McBain out of the office. "Izzy's local. She knows the town and the farmers around here. She hears the talk."

"Gossip isn't evidence," he countered. They passed a road sign that led toward a summer camp for kids founded by a Ukrainian church group. There were others, up and down the lakeshore, of different faiths and ethnicities. One was Jewish, another Unitarian. He'd attended one like that himself when he was a kid, a Catholic one.

"Yes," she agreed, "but sometimes there's some truth in it."
She remembered how she had once ignored an old man who had
wanted to talk to her. If she had listened, fewer people might have
died in the Magnusson case, two winters ago. "Turn next right,"
she directed.

A little Toyota was parked in the driveway of the Gilchrist house.
A rental. Hazel Gilchrist was unloading a bag from the trunk.

"Sergeant Cappelli's heading up the team that's investigating
your father's death," Roxanne introduced him.

"Really." Hazel slammed the trunk lid down and shook
Cappelli's hand but didn't smile. "Perhaps you can tell me," she
said, "why someone from your department came out here on
Tuesday, towed my father's car away and didn't leave a replacement? I had to rent this one. This is costing me."

Julie Gilchrist appeared in the doorway of the house. "It
maybe wasn't his fault, Hazel." She stepped onto the front porch.
"I didn't think to ask him for a replacement. And he knew I had
my own car."

"He should have offered." Hazel folded her arms and confronted the two sergeants. "You take a car; you leave a car. Don't you?"

"I can pay for the rental." Julie fidgeted with her cuffs.

"You shouldn't have to," Hazel informed her, not taking her
eyes off Roxanne and the tall, dark-haired officer at her side.

"You've got the receipt?" Roxanne swung into damage control.
"I'll call and see what I can do."

Julie smiled. She visibly relaxed and opened the door to her
house. "Come in, come in," she said. "I've just taken a pizza out the
oven. Have you eaten?"

Hazel looked mildly exasperated hearing her mother issue the
invitation. She dragged a suitcase up the driveway behind the two
RCMP officers and refused any help lifting it up the steps. Inside,
the house was sunny and warm, smelling of baking. Hazel depos-
ited the cases in the hallway and went back to the car to retrieve
the paperwork for the rental. Roxanne called Ident.

"You can keep the Toyota and they'll cover the cost," she told Hazel, who looked mildly mollified. Now was as good a time as any to tell Julie and her daughter how Bill Gilchrist had died. Julie stood still in the middle of her kitchen and breathed deeply when she heard. Hazel wrapped an arm around her.

"At least we know now," she whispered in her mother's ear.

"Ken Roach is going to be buried in Robson," said Roxanne. "But the formal RCMP funeral is going to happen in Winnipeg. Are you sure you don't want the same for Bill?" Julie turned away and slid a pizza onto a large plate. She cut through melted cheese, sausage, vegetables and her own homemade crust.

"No," she said, her back to Roxanne. "He wasn't a member of the Force any longer. Let us know when the funeral home can pick up his remains." She picked up the plate and nodded. "Let's go over to that table. Bring over the salad, please, Hazel. I think we've got enough for four."

They sat in the sunny corner. Through the windows, grass stretched all the way to the lakeshore. There was a dock at the water's edge, seagulls perched on a rail.

"You have a boat?" Roxanne asked.

"Dad's." Hazel fetched more cutlery from the kitchen counter. She passed around forks and knives. "He had it stored for the winter in a warehouse at the edge of town. I guess it'll have to be sold."

"We should check with Fern," said her mother. "She might want it."

"She's been talking to you?"

Roxanne watched a smile brighten Julie's face. When she was young, she must have been pretty.

"She's coming to visit this weekend; bringing the grandkids," Julie said. She passed the salad bowl. Cappelli was picking at a wedge of pizza. "She wants them to sing at Bill's cremation service. The two oldest have lovely voices."

"You lived up in Robson once," Cappelli stated.

Julie looked surprised at the change of subject. "We did. When the girls were little."

"You taught high school?"

Julie put down her fork, puzzled. "Home economics. A neighbour ran a daycare, so I was able to get back to work when the girls were still small."

Hazel had also stopped eating. "What has this got to do with anything, Sergeant?" she asked.

"A kid died. Drowned. Called Jeremy Featherstone."

Roxanne was glad for once that it wasn't her job to ask questions like that. It seemed inappropriate, sitting here in this sunny spot, enjoying Julie Gilchrist's good food.

"That was years ago," Julie said slowly, still looking mystified.

"Did you know him? Or his parents?"

"I remember Jeremy," she said. "But I never saw either of them. They didn't come near me at parent-teacher nights. Bill might have spoken to them. There was an investigation. An inquest. What does this have to do with Bill's death?"

"You haven't met them recently?" Cappelli demanded.

Julie Gilchrist's face went blank. She appeared to have no idea what he was talking about. "Why would I?"

"They moved here." Roxanne decided that some explanation was in order. "Last fall. Before Bill retired and you both went off to Arizona."

Julie looked genuinely astonished. She said nothing.

"James Featherstone's involved with conservation of the lake," Roxanne continued. "They live out past Desna Church. They built a new solar-powered house there."

"You mean near where Bill died?" Julie's eyes widened in alarm as she began to realize where this conversation was leading. "I hadn't heard. Bill might have known they were there but if he did, he didn't say a thing."

"Ken and Janine Roach lived in Robson, too," said Cappelli. "Way back then. Didn't they?"

Julie laid her fork down gently on the table. She folded her hands in her lap and took another deep breath. Roxanne recognized that it was a calming technique.

"I knew Jeremy Featherstone quite well," she said quietly, looking out at the placid lake. "He was a sweet boy."

"Did he do home ec?" asked Roxanne.

"They all did back then," Julie explained, "while they were in grades seven to nine. It was compulsory, one class a week. We taught all grades in the high school, so I got them then. Those junior high boys were a handful, but they thought cooking was okay. I liked to keep them happy making pancakes and things like that."

Hazel poured coffee. She put sugar and cream in a cup, stirred it and passed it to Julie.

"Jeremy was different. He loved clothes." Julie sipped her coffee. "Some of the girls spent the lunch hour in the sewing room. He liked to hang out with them. He learned how to cut and sew. He was good at art too. He said he'd love to be a fashion designer, but his parents weren't in favour of that. They insisted he do sciences. He thought he might persuade his dad to let him do architecture. Something like that was as close as he would get to what he wanted to do.

"It was too bad," she continued. "He had real talent. He designed grad dresses for a couple of the girls and was helping make them. They were beautiful."

"Was Janine Roach one of the girls who hung out with him?" Cappelli asked.

"Janine? Goodness, no."

Hazel brought over a plate of cookies. No one touched them.

"She wasn't a Roach then, but she and Ken were in the same year. They belonged to an entirely different group. They had no time for a boy like Jeremy." She looked toward Roxanne. "The Featherstones arrived when Jeremy was in junior high, I think, and the boys bugged him at first but as they got older, they just ignored him.

"I don't know how Jeremy died," she added. "But I do know it wasn't suicide. Some people said it was, you know. When he was with the girls in the sewing room he could relax and be himself and he was happy. He was careful around boys like Ken Roach, the ones that were into sports," she said. "I don't know why he would have been up there, skinny-dipping in that watering hole. It was the place where Ken and his friends liked to hang out.

"Anyway." She looked bleakly out at the lake again. "The coroner decided it was an accident. I went to the funeral. That's the only time I ever saw his parents. His dad worked for the government. Someone said his mother was a teller in the bank. I don't think I'd recognize them if I saw them now."

"But you knew who the Roaches were when Ken got transferred here?"

"Not really. I only had them for those few classes in junior high. There were lots of kids like them, popular because they were athletic. I suppose it's not surprising that Ken ended up joining the police. He was big and strong and that still matters. I think Bill was quite happy to have him on his team. He knew his type. How to get along with him. I didn't see much of either of them. I ran into them when the staff got together at Christmas, that kind of thing. Janine tried to get me to host a party where she could sell cleaning materials, once, but I said no and after that she barely spoke to me."

That was all she could tell them. She hoped it would help but she was sorry if the Featherstones were involved in this murder inquiry. They'd had enough tragedy in their lives, she said. And of course she wouldn't mention this conversation to anyone. In the meantime, it was almost two, her friends would be arriving shortly.

Hazel got up from the table and began to clear the plates. Roxanne and Mark took the hint and rose to go.

Margo Wishart's Honda turned into the driveway just as they were leaving. She and her friends looked curiously at the tall, well-groomed man who strode to the driver's side of the car, not waiting to be introduced.

"Hello, Roxanne," said Margo. She hesitated, a box of cake in her hands, as if she had something else she wanted to say. Roberta Axelsson held out daffodils and tulips to Julie. Sasha had brought along a pottery vase to put them in.

"Thought these might cheer you up," she said.

"Thank you," said Julie. "Hazel and I miss Bill a lot."

Hazel wrapped a protective arm around her mother's shoulders. "It's hard on my mom. They were together thirty years and never a cross word," she said.

Roxanne watched a look of sheer incredulity pass over Margo Wishart's face, then disappear.

"Too bad that we didn't know about the Featherstone kid before," said Mark as they drove up the road toward the highway. "That Julie Gilchrist's for real, right?"

"I think what she told us is true," said Roxanne.

"She's pretty nervous. Did she really teach junior high boys home ec?"

"Must have done. She might be tougher than she seems."

Mark picked up speed. All this was interesting enough, but it was historical. He was still more interested in Lex McKenzie and his family. He'd drop Calloway off back at her office and go see if he could find the uncle. He might have a look around the McKenzie farmhouse as well before he drove home. Ident were going to get there, but they were taking their time. Meantime he'd get as much done on his own as he could while he was anonymous and in no danger of being attacked.

18

"IF WE USE something gauzy for the water surface, high up above people's heads, we can shine light right through and stitch blue lace onto it, so it looks like algae."

Roberta was still the person who had the clearest idea of what they intended to do for the Lake Fibre Arts Show. It was a good suggestion. The lake sometimes became choked with blue algae on warm summer days and part of their mission was to highlight how precarious and precious that fresh water was.

"And like I said, we could hang some of it off the three sisters."

The structure of those was Sasha's responsibility, but they needed to be clothed in weed and something to represent flowing water. "I could knit some, maybe," Sasha said.

"I learned to tat lace once." Julie Gilchrist had barely spoken so far. Margo wasn't surprised since the police had just visited. They seldom brought good news. But at this suggestion, Julie began to thaw. She pulled a bale of fabric off a shelf, sheer blue-green with a bit of a shimmer. "This might do for the water," she said. Her face lost the pinched look it had had when they arrived.

"It would!" Roberta enthused. "Could you show me how to tat?"

"I could!" Julie's smile lit up the room and the tension Margo had felt since they arrived evaporated. "And maybe I could make quilted mats in irregular shapes to put on the floor, to look like the lakebed. People can walk around them."

"Are you sure? Don't you have a lot to do, getting ready for the move?" Margo asked.

"I would love to do it. And I've got Hazel staying with me now. She's taking care of selling the house and organizing the move for me. I can use material like this." Julie walked to another shelf and pulled off more bales, browns and greens this time. "Sand, stone and weed growing on it?"

When Julie got enthused, she became quite animated, took on an intense, quiet energy. Her blue eyes shone. She moved quickly around her room, knowing where to find everything she needed. She and Roberta soon had their heads together over a table littered with swatches and threads. There was talk of quilted fish. Sasha got involved. Bugs made of wire and fabric were mentioned, and shellfish built from clay and felted wool. The project was taking on a life of its own, exactly as Margo had wished it would. She just hoped that the RCMP wouldn't focus their attention on Julie again and stop her from participating. Why had they been visiting this house? She had noticed the space in the garage where Bill Gilchrist's big SUV was usually parked. Had that something to do with their investigation? Was Julie still a suspect? She should say something to Roxanne about how Julie had planned to leave her husband, but she really did not want to.

Hazel brought the plate of uneaten cookies upstairs to their eyrie. Margo unwrapped the cake, chocolate, frosted with a dark ganache, made by a neighbour who baked. The tulips were opening in Sasha's blue pottery vase and the daffodils smelled of spring.

"Where is your SUV, the Yukon?" asked Margo.

"In the shop," said Julie. Her daughter did not correct the lie. "Hazel's driving a rental meantime. She's going to go arrange to get Bill's boat out of storage. Fern's bringing the kids for a visit on Saturday. They're saying it's going to get warm out. Maybe we'll be able to go for a boat ride and have a picnic."

"And get arrangements made for Dad's cremation," Hazel reminded her. "The police have done the autopsy so we should be able to set a date soon."

That must have been why Roxanne had been visiting. She must have been telling Julie about the autopsy results. Margo would have liked to know what they were, but for now she sliced the cake and kept quiet.

JAMES FEATHERSTONE ALSO had a date with a boat, the *Becky*, the research vessel maintained year round in the harbour at Fiskar Bay by the conservation group. His committee was due there at three, to see what refurbishments were needed before it voyaged out again. He asked Jeff Riordan if this would take long.

Like his wife, Featherstone wore grey. Jeff noticed how alike they were. His hair was similarly white, neatly trimmed. He was lean, medium height, quietly spoken, not a man to draw attention to himself. Even the glasses he wore were the same shape as hers. He admitted Jeff into their pristine house. Izzy waited outside while his wife carried a gardening fork to a shed. She had been turning over the soil in her raised beds when they arrived. A plastic-covered bale of peat moss and a bag full of dried manure sat, half used. Jane had been to the garden centre.

"I've talked with you already, Constable," she said to Izzy in her precise English voice as she took off her gardening gloves and laid them on a shelf. Everything inside the shed was tidily arranged. Tools hung on one wall, smaller ones lay on shelves, pots and boxes were stacked in corners, everything in its place.

"You didn't tell me about your son, Jeremy." Izzy stood in the doorway. A bare lightbulb glowed overhead, illuminating Jane Featherstone's face. For a second, she looked like she'd been slapped.

"He's been gone for over twenty years," she said.

"Did you know," Izzy continued, undeterred, leaning her shoulder against the door jamb, "that Bill Gilchrist, who died out there on Kuryk Road" —she nodded her head in the road's direction— "was a member of the Robson RCMP when they investigated your son's death?"

"I did not." Jane Featherstone wiped all expression from her face. "As I told you already, I did not know him. If you don't mind, I'd like to go and wash my hands."

Izzy stepped aside and let her pass. Jane walked to a rain trough at the side of the house and dipped her hands into the cold water.

"Ken Roach, who died last weekend, too, comes from Robson. He went to school with your son."

Jane stood still for a second, then shook out her hands. Droplets of water flew from them. She had not known him, she said.

"Where were you last Sunday evening?" Izzy asked.

Inside, Jeff was asking her husband the same question.

"Here," James Featherstone replied. "I was with my wife."

The weekend that Bill Gilchrist had died, they had driven to Winnipeg. They had season tickets for the Prairie Theatre Centre. Saturday matinee. They'd had dinner in town after. Then they had driven home. They were here all the next day and had talked with their daughter and their grandchild via Skype on Sunday afternoon. They did that weekly.

"Jeremy's death was accidental," he remarked. "That was proven at the inquest."

"Did you expect that verdict?"

"What else would it be, officer?" James said, silhouetted against one of his big, sunny windows. Jeff could not see his face for the light. "Jeremy was doing well at school. He had a bright future ahead of him. I know there was talk but he certainly did not kill himself." He had met Sergeant Gilchrist once, maybe twice, back in the fall, here at Fiskar Bay. There had been meetings regarding the lake. Gilchrist had said nothing about ever living in Robson. "I didn't make the connection," Featherstone remarked drily. "And I didn't remember his name from the inquiry. It was so long ago. Why would I?"

They asked to see the Featherstones' cars. Both were hybrids, one a Volvo, silver in colour, the other a Honda, charcoal grey. They were spotless and appeared to be damage free.

"Are you planning any travel soon?" asked Jeff, as they took their leave. No further than Winnipeg, they said. "Good. We need you to stick around for now."

"Cool house," Jeff said as they drove away. Izzy waved goodbye out the car window. The Featherstones stood side by side on their doorstep watching them go. "It can't just be a coincidence that they've come to live here. Can it?"

"No such thing, is there?" Izzy echoed Roxanne as she turned the car toward Fiskar Bay.

They got back to the office to be told what Julie Gilchrist had said about the Featherstones' son and the Roaches.

"Too bad we didn't know all that beforehand," Jeff said, shaking his head.

"Janine'll be way up the road by now, dammit. Do I get to go up to Robson and interview her?" asked Izzy.

Mark Cappelli replied with a withering look. "We've got enough people up there already that can do that, Constable," he said. He was still intent on pursuing the McKenzie lead. Where was the farmhouse? And where might he find Lex's uncle?

"Go ask Kathy," said Izzy.

Kathy knew. "He'll be at the harbour," she said, peering up at the sergeant from her seat and pushing her glasses onto the bridge of her nose. "They're putting the fishing boats into the water this afternoon."

The boats of the Fiskar Bay commercial fleet were steel-hulled and had wintered on the wharf, propped on upended oil drums. They were being loaded, in turn, onto a boat trailer. From there, they were backed down a ramp into the water. The launching was a tricky process and Al Melnychuk was directing it. He was not pleased to be interrupted.

"Fuck's sake," he said. "Can't it wait?"

"Leave this to me, Dad," said his son, who was as sturdy and seemed as capable as his father.

Cappelli had parked at the end of the parking lot where he could view the whole operation. Al pulled his large bulk into the passenger seat, reluctant to take his eyes away from the manoeuvres in front of him. He yanked the door shut.

"Lex McKenzie has cousins?" Cappelli reached inside his jacket, took out a small paper notebook and unclipped a pen from it.

"'Course he has. Lots of them. What's your problem with him this time? I told that Calloway woman to back off already."

Four men stood beside one of the boats. Al's son reversed a truck and began to edge its trailer under the hull. Their precision caught Cappelli's interest.

"Lex is an idiot but he's no killer." Al's big finger pushed the window button. "He's got nothing to do with these murders and neither do any of my boys." He reached an arm out the window and waved. His big, grey head followed. "To the right, to the right!" he hollered. One of the men waved back and called to the son. The truck stopped, moved forward and backed up again.

"Lex and his brother own a house near where Bill Gilchrist died," said Cappelli.

"Sure they do. Grew up there," Al barked. "Marvin stays there sometimes on the weekend when he's out here fishing. Lex hasn't been near it in years."

A couple of men walked past. They nodded at Al in recognition. He tapped a finger to his head in acknowledgement. They made their way toward the *Becky*, berthed at the other side of the harbour near the seawall. "See them?" Another thick finger pointed as the men approached the gangplank of the big blue boat. "Those guys think they're experts. Try to tell us we're overfishing the lake," he growled. "Problem is the government listens to them. Think they know better. As if we don't know this water. Been fishing it all my life."

"Is one of them called Featherstone?"

"He's the worst. The one in the coat," he sneered. "Look at him. Dresses like he's still in the city." Al had noticed Mark's neatly fitting pants, the perfect cut of his jacket. Those weren't proper working clothes, in his mind. He glared as James Featherstone disappeared inside the *Becky*. A man who'd probably never caught a fish in his life was supposed to know more about them than someone who'd been doing it for close on forty years?

Mark Cappelli watched too. James Featherstone looked exactly as Riordan and McBain had described.

"Was Marvin at the McKenzie farmhouse three weekends ago?"

Melnychuk swung back to face Cappelli, dark brown eyes in his square head narrowing with suspicion. "Don't think so." Each drum had been rolled out from under the boat. It now sat on the trailer and was being dragged forward, inch by inch. "What are you lot thinking now? Marvin's a good guy. Never been a problem."

"But Lex has been."

"Lex is doing okay," said his uncle. "Got religion or something these days. Staying out of trouble."

"He's unreliable. A liar. A con man," said the sergeant.

Al watched his son back the trailer, the boat's big hull high above it, to the top of the launch ramp.

"Sure," Melnychuk agreed for once. "Kinda crazy if you ask me. Has been since he was a kid." He puffed air out between narrow downturned lips. "Thing is, he really believes half the crap he says. When he conned all that money out of those city folks he was sure that idea he had would work. That's how he was able to convince them to cough up the cash."

"He spent it," said Mark Cappelli.

"Yeah, well, easy come, easy go." The boat was slowly backing down into the water. "Their stupid fault for giving it to them, wasn't it? Lex is a talker. That's what I don't get about this Buddhist thing he's got into now. Aren't they supposed to sit on a cushion and shut up for hours on end? How's Lex going to do that?" The boat was floating free on the water and his son was dragging the trailer out from under it. "Gotta go." He opened the car door and stuck one rubber-booted foot outside.

"Y'know what?" Melnychuk turned back to face Cappelli. "Lex might be an idiot, but he isn't what I'd call a fighter." He lifted his big bulk out of the car, then leaned on the door to look back inside. "Have you seen him? He's not a big guy. And did you ever see Kenny Roach? Not a chance Lex would go for him. Kenny was always quick with his fists. All the guys around here knew that and Gilchrist let him get away with it. Not just once. So, Lex got extra time for something he didn't do back then. And now you Mounties are trying to stick more of your dirt onto him. We done here?"

"We need to check out that farmhouse," said Mark Cappelli.

"Go ahead. Waste your time. Key's under a pot at the back door." Melnychuk slammed the door shut.

"Hey, guys, looks good," he yelled as he strode toward the truck. The boat's engine fired up and it chugged toward a mooring, water surging in its wake. Al's son drove toward the next boat. Mark watched. A big truck like that would bowl a person over, no trouble at all. Did Lex have access to it, or one like it? Was his uncle telling the truth when he said only Marvin visited their old family home?

A small green Toyota drove past him as he left the wharf and drew up at the harbourmaster's office. Hazel Gilchrist had arrived to book a time when she could get her dad's boat into the water.

19

JULIE GILCHRIST AND Hazel were seated on their deck eating breakfast when Roxanne arrived at their house early Friday morning. They had eaten scrambled eggs. Now they were enjoying toast and strawberry jam, made by Julie last summer. The sun hung high above the lake and it was warm. Not a particle of snow or ice remained to remind them of winter. This might be Friday the thirteenth, in April, but it was a beautiful, summery day.

Hazel had opened the door wearing shorts and a T-shirt. Her hair was tucked up into a ball cap, the visor pulled low to shade her eyes.

"Oh, it's you," she'd said when she saw Roxanne. "What brings you out here this time?"

Roxanne had driven straight to Heron Haven once she had dropped Finn off at school. She had called Margo Wishart at home the night before and learned what Margo had heard about state of the Gilchrist marriage. She could have gone into the office and passed the information to Mark Cappelli, but she thought a quiet word with Julie might yield better results than an official interrogation. Roxanne could do that herself and be back at her desk by ten at the latest. And this was a beautiful morning for a drive.

Julie was more welcoming than her daughter.

"We should have put the umbrella up," she said, squinting out over the water. "Have you seen the pelicans? They are back."

Above them, a flock of large birds sailed the thermals like winged galleons. Hazel cleared away the remains of their breakfast.

She had work she needed to get to, she said, but she'd fetch some coffee first. She disappeared into the house. Roxanne wished she'd left her uniform jacket in the car. This was a day for short sleeves.

"I need to get to work too," said Julie. "I'm starting a new project. Is this going to take long?" She sat in a padded wicker chair. Roxanne took the one vacated by Hazel.

"I've been told," she said, "that you and Bill were not getting along. That you wanted to leave him."

Julie Gilchrist's face tightened. "Well," she commented quietly but precisely. "Someone has been gossiping."

"It's been said that's why you needed to go and talk to your sister. To make arrangements to leave here."

"That is not true!" Hazel interrupted. She stood in the doorway, a mug in each hand. "My parents always got along. They'd been together forever."

"I think you've been misinformed," Julie assured Roxanne while Hazel put the mugs on the glass-topped table.

Was that true? Roxanne could not think of a reason why Susan Rice, the yoga teacher at Cullen Village, would want to lie about it. Or her friend, Margo Wishart.

"It's less than a month since Bill died," Roxanne persisted, "you've already decided to sell this house and move to B.C., to live there with your sister. You even know that you want to live in Kelowna and what kind of house you want to buy. Hasn't that all happened bit fast?"

"My sister Sherry had decided to go there already. And I've always liked the idea of moving to a warmer climate. I went along with what she'd decided." Julie stirred milk into her coffee. "And we had several days together to look at houses online."

"So, it's true that you didn't want to stay in Fiskar Bay when Bill retired? To do the snowbird thing and winter in Arizona? Did you go along with that because it was what he wanted?"

"Don't say any more, Mom." Hazel was still in the doorway, listening. "I know where you're going with this." She pointed a finger at Roxanne. "You're about to say that it was very convenient for my mother that Dad died when he did. That it freed her to do what she'd wanted to do all along. But it wasn't like that, was it, Mom?" She didn't look at her mother. Her attention stayed focused on Roxanne. "You'll be saying next that she had a good reason to want him dead."

"Hazel," her mother intervened in a gentle but determined little voice. "Go do the work you need to do before you go to pick up the boat at the harbour. I want to tell Roxanne something." Her daughter opened her mouth in protest. "It's got nothing to do with me moving or your father's death," Julie assured her.

Hazel grudgingly did as she was told. She disappeared into the house. Her mother rose and slid the glass door shut, then sat once more.

"Bill and I had our disagreements," she said, so softly that Roxanne had to lean in to hear her. "But what married couple doesn't? Adjusting to retirement was a challenge, I have to admit, but Bill and I were figuring it out. I did not have anything to do with his death, Roxanne.

"But there's something else I am going to tell you, because I think you should know about it. Something I was told, in Robson, way back when Jeremy Featherstone died."

Roxanne lifted the coffee mug and sat back to listen. She wasn't sure if she believed Julie when she said she hadn't planned to leave Bill Gilchrist. Was this an attempt to distract her from that line of questioning?

"Bill always said that Jeremy's death was an accident," said Julie. "But the girls that came to my classroom at lunchtime talked while they sewed. I think they sometimes forgot I was there. They told an entirely different story. That the other girls, the cheerleading crowd, the ones who hung out with Ken Roach and his friends, were responsible. That they were going along the riverbank on their way to where the boys were fishing one day and they came across Jeremy, walking alone.

"They liked to torment him when they could, the girls said, thought it was a joke that he was sewing and making dresses. Said that maybe he'd like to dress like a girl himself. And they decided it would be fun to make him take his clothes off and dress him in some of theirs.

"He wouldn't so they swarmed him. They tore off his clothes and he struggled, then they got mad at him and they pushed him into the waterhole. Jeremy wasn't much of a swimmer but they wouldn't let him get out. They threw stones at him. When he stopped moving they thought he was maybe pretending. They left his clothes up at the top of the rock where he would find them. Or so it would look like he'd taken them off himself. Then they went and found the other boys and partied like nothing had happened."

"They didn't go back to check up on him?"

Julie shook her head.

"It was a bullying that got out of hand?"

"It sounded like it. It happens sometimes, doesn't it?"

They each remembered a well-publicized case that had happened in B.C. a few years earlier where a girl had been attacked by a group of peers and left to die.

"Janine Roach was one of those girls?"

"I don't know for sure." Julie was rubbing her knuckles, anxious once more. "But she was always with that group, so I'd assume she was."

"And would the boys that they went to party with have known what they'd done? Would Ken Roach?"

"If the girls that sewed knew, most of the senior high kids must have been talking about it."

"Did you tell Bill?"

"I did." Julie's blue eyes met Roxanne's. "But nothing came of it. The inquest had already started by the time I heard the story. It was never mentioned. I asked him about it one day and he said it was just girls talking. There was no proof. The verdict came down shortly after. I don't know if any of the other kids told their parents."

"Didn't Jeremy Featherstone have a sister? Was she a student at the same time?"

"Alison. She was in junior high at the time."

"She might have heard?"

"I don't know, Roxanne." Julie reached for her coffee once more. "All I know is that the whole town seemed to be so relieved when the inquest was over and the coroner said it was an accident. No one was blamed and everyone carried on as if nothing had happened. If you're asking me if Jeremy's parents ever heard that story, I couldn't tell you. You'd have to ask them yourself."

MARGO WISHART HAD a class to teach at the university. She'd left home early so she could stop by the Sunnywell Centre on the way. Bea Benedict professed to be thrilled to have the booking for the lake project confirmed and to receive a deposit, but she hesitated when Margo asked if she could look at the room again and take some quick measurements. There was a list of questions in Margo's hand. Bea simply didn't have the time; workmen would be arriving shortly to remove those unsightly sandbags from the river's edge and a group had booked the room for later that morning. It simply wasn't convenient.

"However, there is a solution." She crossed to the office door behind her. "Lex will assist you."

Lex was a man about the same height as Margo; he had a shaved head and wore a loose cotton shirt and grey slacks. There were leather sandals on his feet and he had a string of brown wooden beads wrapped around his wrist. He smiled broadly, shook Margo's hand with a firm grasp, took the list and read her questions. She needed to know about power outlets, the lighting available, the voltage, the size of the doors. What kind of paint did they recommend that they use to paint the floor? He'd have answers for her later today, he assured her. What was her email? And could he call her if he had any questions of his own? What was the project about? She explained briefly.

"It sounds interesting" he said. "Too bad my work placement ends in July. I could have helped you set it up."

He must be in his forties, Margo thought, a bit old to be on a work training grant. She assumed that was why he was at the centre for only a few months. She exchanged details with him and left. He walked her to the door and shook her hand once more. Over by the river, Bea was giving orders to some men with a truck. Margo drove away, glad to know that her group's needs were going to be addressed by this pleasantly obliging man.

NETTA KURYK WATERED the plants in her porch, found a pair of shoes in her closet that she hadn't put on since last October, and went for a walk on this beautiful sunny day. Her dogs loped beside her down the driveway but stopped when she reached the gate. They were trained to stay in the farmyard. She strode down the middle of the road where hardly any gravel was left; it was dry enough not to be muddy anymore. The ditches were barely a third full of water. Some geese were swimming in a pool on a field but there were fewer puddles now. She could almost see the grass stretching up, greedy for sunlight. Leaves were bursting open on the poplars. She saw a paper cup, a bottle, a soggy pizza box strewn in the ditch. Some people were filthy, didn't care what they threw out their car windows. She'd have to come out with rubber gloves and a garbage bag and clean up later.

She'd go once around the block, see if any more flowers had been left at the roadside. There wouldn't be many. Stan had brought back several bunches yesterday. There were three or four old people at Harbourfront House, where she'd gone yesterday, who never saw a visitor. She's been at the hospital first, so she hadn't had much left, just a tub of spring bulbs she'd saved for one of them, an old woman, ninety years old, with dementia. She didn't remember who her kids were but she sure recognized the smell of hyacinths.

Netta turned the corner onto Kuryk Road. A car was parked at the far end, one she didn't recognize. There had been plenty of those stopping by lately. Someone must be visiting Bill Gilchrist's shrine. She hoped they'd be gone before she got there. She couldn't take flowers away if people were still around. Maybe they'd have brought some fresh daffs. Those would brighten up the day for some old soul.

She couldn't see anyone moving about as she got closer. A pair of crows flew over her head, cawing loudly. She reached the car. Silver. An SUV. Her son had one that looked like it. She still couldn't see anyone. Maybe, like her, they'd gone for a walk in the sunshine. It was really warm out. She took off her sweater and tied the sleeves around her waist.

She walked past the silver car and stopped. She could see black leather boots lying up on the road, just above the culvert opening. She walked cautiously up to the corner. A body lay stretched out in front of her. A man, not anyone she recognized. Tall, dark-haired, black jacket. He had fallen backwards. His head had landed among the flowers but from the waist down he lay on the gravel road surface. His arms were stretched out either side of his body. Above his shoulder, the cross daubed with RIP SGT GILCHRIST was skewed to one side and the plastic toy Mountie that someone had left lay beside his outstretched hand with pink tulips scattered around it.

Netta could see how he had died. Tire tracks ran across his jacket, right at the belly. And his feet lay at odd angles. There were similar marks on the black pants that covered his shins.

Netta didn't own a cellphone. She half ran, half trotted, past the silver car, back to her own house. The dogs ran to greet her but she ignored them. Stan was nowhere to be seen, didn't come when she mustered enough breath to call out to him. She staggered up the steps, banged the door open, ran through her sunny green porch and into the kitchen. She unhooked the phone from its place on the wall by the door and called 911.

20

POLICE VEHICLES CONVERGED on the corner where Sergeant Mark Cappelli's body had been found. It was obvious that he had been run over. Wheels had rolled across his body at the middle of his torso and the shins of both legs had been crushed. It appeared that a vehicle had struck him from one direction, turned, come back and hit him again. Or reversed back over him. The tire tracks on the front of his jacket were dusty but clear. The forensic unit could probably discover their type and make from the tread marks, but otherwise they knew little. Cappelli had last been seen yesterday at the harbour. Given that and the state of the body, he must have been killed sometime late afternoon or evening the previous day. Izzy and Jeff went in search of Al Melnychuk, the last person they knew to have seen him alive.

Word that another cop was dead in the Interlake had got out fast. Ravi Anand was fielding calls from the press when Roxanne left her office and drove out to Kuryk Road to have a look.

"Another one." Dave Novak shook his head. "Same method. That's three men down. You and your guys are in real danger, Roxanne."

"I've got them partnered up already," she told him.

"And yourself?"

"Me? I'm stuck in the office safe and sound." She shrugged.

"Yeah. Like right now."

"People watched me get into the car from the office window. And you're here. I'm not alone," Roxanne explained. "All the murders have occurred out in the open, on empty roads. As long as my highway crews aren't out there working solo, they should be fine." She hoped that was true.

A black Buick came into view and pulled in behind the Ident van. Inspector Schultz stepped briskly out of the passenger side, his hat squarely on his head. He planted himself on the roadway, feet astride, at the feet of Cappelli's prostrate body. A member of the communications team, his designated driver, hovered behind him.

"Run down?" he said. "Isn't that what happened to the other two?" He addressed Novak, then spotted Roxanne. "You here, Calloway?"

"Checking things out, sir." Roxanne joined him. "Since this has happened on my turf."

Schultz looked around. This place was bleak. Empty fields were dotted with pools of water. Trees were brown skeletons, just sprouting leaves, and the roads, edged with scrubby grass, stretched straight to the horizon. "Shitty place to die," he commented. "Friday the thirteenth," he added morosely. "Just our luck."

Roxanne pointed toward the distant farmhouse. "Lex McKenzie and his brothers own that place," she told him. "Lex was Mark's main suspect. And another couple that might be involved lives in that direction." She swung her arm in the direction of the Featherstone house. "There's a farm just behind those trees." She pointed to the Kuryk place. "The woman who found the body lives there. This area's not as empty as it looks, sir."

"That so? You'd best fill me in back at the detachment. First, I've got to go meet the press. At the harbour, at two. Maybe you should be there as well." And he strode off back to the car.

"What's he doing here?" asked Dave. "He never shows up at the scene of a crime. Why isn't he sending out another sergeant to replace Cappelli right away?"

"Who'd want the job," said one of his technicians kneeling beside the body, camera in hand, "when someone's going to try to kill you?"

DOWN CAME THE RAIN

"I'd best get back," said Roxanne. This was an unusual case and its profile would be even higher now that another member of the Force had been killed. It was possible that Schultz had come out because he was planning to command the investigation himself. Or he might want to assess the situation on site before he assigned another officer to the case. Maybe this trip was simply a PR venture. Meantime, Izzy, Jeff and the members of her detachment needed to know that the inspector was in town.

Not long after, she watched Schultz stand before a scenic backdrop of fishing boats and the sea wall surrounded by mics and television cameras.

"Every resource will be brought to bear," he declared, "so we can uncover the person or persons responsible. One retired RCMP officer and two serving ones have been killed in a cowardly manner. Not one more," his voice rumbled up from his belly, "shall die."

Roxanne hoped he was right.

"Someone has it in for the RCMP?" a reporter called out.

"We are pursuing several leads," was the evasive reply. Soon Schultz hoped to be able to tell them that they had discovered who was involved. "We shall bring him or her to justice." A crowd had gathered to listen. He was big on reassurance but short on facts.

"Six weeks until tourist season," Roxanne overheard the mayor remark. The town depended on the revenue that its summer visitors brought in. Being described as a place with a cop killer on the loose wasn't good for business.

When he got back to the detachment, Schultz took over the MCU room upstairs. He sat at the table directing operations like he was commanding a war room. Izzy and Jeff were questioned. Al Melnychuk had told them that Cappelli had said he was going to look at the old McKenzie farmhouse. He must have gone to the place where Bill Gilchrist had died, before or after he had been there. Had Al told anyone that the person he'd been talking to was an RCMP sergeant, they had asked him.

"Sure," he had replied. "They all wanted to know."

"Go look," growled Schultz at both of them. "And talk to that Featherstone couple while you're at it. Stay together," he barked as their backs disappeared down the stairs.

Roxanne was summoned next. She found Schultz talking on the phone with Dr. Abdur Farooq from the provincial medical examiner's office. The body was being transported to Winnipeg, but there was little doubt about what had happened. He had been maimed when the car ran across his legs, but he had died when the driver took a second swing at him, driving across his torso. The killing had been deliberate.

"So." The inspector indicated the chair opposite and put down his phone. "Tell me what you think is going on here."

"Well, sir," she said, "you know about Lex McKenzie."

Schultz already knew about the embezzlement case, but he needed to be reminded about the controversy regarding the incident in the cell at Fiskar Bay. He frowned when he heard that Al Melnychuk, Lex's uncle, still believed that Constable Roach had beat up his nephew, then blamed him. News that could cast a dark light on RCMP operations was never welcome.

"Whoever killed Sergeant Cappelli knew where to find him yesterday and the only person he told was Al Melnychuk." Roxanne continued. "He told his son and his friends who Mark was, and the news could have spread from there. It seems that one of the McKenzie brothers visits the farmhouse regularly, to ice fish, and they're a close-knit family. We can't rule them out.

"Then we've discovered that the Featherstones, the couple that live near where Cappelli and Gilchrist died, knew both Ken Roach and Bill Gilchrist." She told him about the Robson connection, then she added what Julie Gilchrist had told her that morning.

"She's saying that Roach's wife and a gang of girls killed the Featherstones' kid? Years ago, up in Robson? That they swarmed him? Threw stones at him and left him for dead? Do you believe her?"

"It's hard to say," Roxanne replied. "I think she's probably telling the truth about what she heard, but maybe Gilchrist was right when he said that the girls were just spreading gossip. It could just have been a bad rumour, but it should have been investigated at the time."

"Hmm." Schultz frowned.

"The Melnychuk uncle says that James Featherstone was on the wharf yesterday when Cappelli was talking to him. He could have found out who Mark was, easy."

"Shit," muttered Schultz under his breath. "If that old case needs to be reopened it'll be more bad press."

"There were bruises on the boy's body that were apparently never explained at the inquest," added Roxanne.

Schultz's brows lowered further. He didn't need to hear that either.

"Even if that story's not true, the Featherstones might have heard it," Roxanne continued. "That gives them a reason for wanting both Gilchrist and Roach dead. But it doesn't tell us why James Featherstone would want to kill Sergeant Cappelli."

"McBain and Riordan are on their way to the Featherstone place to talk to them again. They'd best bring them in instead." He picked up his phone. She waited while he made the call. "Anything else?"

There was. Julie Gilchrist denied anything was wrong with her marriage, but Roxanne thought she was lying. It was possible that Bill Gilchrist had died as the result of a marital row but there seemed no reason for her to want to kill Ken Roach or Mark Cappelli.

"And there's always the possibility that there's just a crazy out there," Inspector Schultz added. It was an option that neither of them wanted to believe. "Someone that holds a grudge because of some minor misdemeanor. Someone suffering from some kind of mental disorder. And that person is picking off our members at random." He tapped the tabletop with his fingers. "People like that talk. We'll hear, sooner or later.

"We've got a forensic search underway, checking the records for every person who has been charged for anything at all, a traffic offence, a petty crime. You know about that?"

Roxanne nodded.

"Has anyone local been complaining?"

"There's always those," she said. "But nothing that jumps out. Sir, who will be leading the investigation now that Mark Cappelli is gone?"

"Good question." The inspector sat back in his chair and tucked his chin into his collar. "No one's all that keen to put their life at risk. I might have to twist someone's arm. Like yours." He lasered a look across the table. "You could rejoin the Major Crimes Unit. It would be a temporary secondment. Things are quiet in this town right now, apart from this business, right? That corporal you've got on your team could manage the detachment for now. If you haven't solved the case by the time tourist season hits, we'd need to revisit that situation, but we could sure use someone like you who's got experience."

"I quit the Major Crimes Unit, sir," she reminded him.

"That's right. Came out here to live a quiet life with the kid, didn't you? But it hasn't worked out like that, has it?" He smiled, a rare occurrence unless he was on the golf course. "Your whole team is in harm's way out here until we find the killer. You owe it to them to help, Sergeant. You've as good a track record as any when it comes to investigating murders. You know this town and you're up to speed on the investigation so far. You knew all three victims, Gilchrist and Roach, and you'd met Mark Cappelli. You need to help bring their killer to justice. So, how's about it?"

"What do I get in the way of support?" asked Roxanne Calloway.

"Two new constables. One to replace Roach in the detachment and another to work with the MCU. Someone who can do the work of a file coordinator and free up Riordan and McBain to get out there as joint investigators, since we don't want either of them being clobbered next. Forensics, communications will all be told this case has priority. You on board?"

She was. She could hardly suppress the glee she felt at being back in charge of a murder case. She hadn't realized how much she'd missed the job, the sense of urgency, the hunt. She couldn't wait for Schultz to go so she could get to work in her new role.

"Do I tell my guys or do you?" she said.

"Send Corporal Robinson up here. I'll leave the rest to you."

Kathy Isfeld peered curiously up over her computer as she watched Pete go upstairs. She figured out what was happening right away.

"I'll tell Sigrid," she said. "You'll need her to look after Finn after school if you're taking this job on."

"Maybe not," said Roxanne. Matt would probably offer. She liked how happy Finn was around him. It was good for him to have a man in his life, and the dog helped too. "Who else is here right now?"

"They're in the lunchroom eating," Kathy turned her attention back to her screen. She herself had a half-eaten apple fritter and a fresh takeout coffee cup beside her. At the front desk Aimee Vermette was chewing on a cruller. Roxanne found Jeff and Izzy in the lunchroom with Schultz's driver. He got to his feet when he saw her and reached for a napkin to wipe sugar off his fingers.

"He done?" he asked.

"Not yet. Relax and finish your coffee." Roxanne sat. She looked in the doughnut box and tore one in half. It was chocolate. She didn't usually eat food like this, but she felt like celebrating.

"We've got the Featherstones waiting in the interview room," said Izzy. "Who's going to talk to them?"

"I am," said Roxanne and bit off a sugary mouthful. Izzy stared at her for a second, then it dawned.

"You're going to be the boss of us?" she asked. "Okay!"

Corporal Robinson was suitably pleased at his temporary promotion. Once he'd trotted back downstairs, Inspector Schultz reached for his phone once more and called the superintendent.

"Done," he said. "It was a slam dunk. Barely had to twist her arm. Told you she'd go for it. Be back in the office, soon as."

He hung up, put his hat back on and went to find his driver.

21

PETE ROBINSON WAS happy to move into Roxanne's old office. He was shooting for his sergeant stripes and being in temporary charge of the detachment was useful experience. Roxanne moved upstairs to where she'd worked the year before as primary investigator on the Magnusson case, this time as team commander for the MCU.

Matt Stavros dropped by the detachment soon as he heard that she'd be leading the investigation. He sat back in the MCU office, where he had worked when he, too, had been a member of the RCMP, and folded his arms. His stubborn look, Izzy called it.

"You shouldn't be living by yourself," he reasoned. "I can borrow spare beds from Izzy's family. You and Finn could move in with us. Just until you get this job done."

It was tempting, but Roxanne declined. She still didn't consider that living in her own house in Fiskar Bay was a risk. The killer worked out on quiet country roads, she said, not for the first time. Not in the middle of town.

"Not so. Ken Roach died at the end of a street in Cullen Village, and at night Fiskar Bay is just as deserted." Matt seemed genuinely concerned. "Mark Cappelli had the job that you have now and look what happened to him."

"I know not to stand at the side of a road all by myself," said Roxanne. "And I'm not going to have this town think I'm running scared. But I could use some help taking care of Finn, for now. If you're going to be around."

"Not a problem." Matt grinned. "He can come hang out with me and Joseph." He looked at his phone to check the time. "School will be out soon. Let them know I'll be the person that picks him up, okay?'

Kathy Isfeld was checking for available accommodation so that their new recruits could bunk up. Rental cabins and apartments were at a premium during tourist season, but Kathy had contacts and it was early enough to find some space.

"Tell Sigrid not to worry about Finn for now," Roxanne told her. "Matt's going to be looking after him. But what about you, Kathy? You work for us, and you live alone."

Kathy walked from work every day along the back lane from the detachment to her house, which was across the street from Roxanne's.

"I'm not RCMP. And no one is going to stop me walking around my own hometown," Kathy replied. "But I'll ask Sigrid to come stay for a while if that'll keep you happy. She'll have time if you don't need her." She sounded peeved. The new arrangement for Finn would cost Sigrid some babysitting income. Roxanne hadn't thought about that.

"It won't be for long. Just until we get this sorted out," she assured Kathy. She went back upstairs to get her own new work-space organized. Izzy trotted up behind her.

"So, I really think I should go up to Robson and talk to Janine Roach," she said.

Roxanne shook her head. "Don't think so. That's an old case, if it's even that. The Robson detachment will ask some questions and then if they decide it's worth opening again a new team will go in. We need you here."

ROXANNE HAD INTERVIEWED each of the Featherstones separately. The husband remained cool and distant throughout. His son had died accidentally. That had been determined at the inquest and he had no reason to doubt it. Yes, he'd been told that the man in the car at the harbour the previous afternoon was from the RCMP, but he had no way of knowing where the sergeant was going next.

"You'd have recognized him if you saw him after. You could have driven past him on the way home, at the side of the road where people have been leaving flowers for Bill Gilchrist. What time did you go home?" Roxanne had prodded.

The meeting had ended at four, he told her, He'd taken the other road, the one past the farm. It was more direct. He'd had no reason to detour.

He and his wife had driven to the detachment in his Volvo. Jeff Riordan had gone outside to photograph the tires. Jane Featherstone's Honda would need to be checked as well.

Jane herself was a little more forthcoming. Of course, she'd heard rumours about her son's death. People thought he had killed himself, but she was sure he had not.

"He was bullied at school?"

She didn't deny it. "That was earlier, when we first arrived in Robson," she said. "They mocked his accent. He and his sister soon learned to speak like Canadians," she added dryly, as polite as always.

"Your daughter was two years younger?"

Jane Featherstone nodded.

"If there was talk at school about something that might have happened, she might have heard something?"

"If she did, she said nothing to me." Jane frowned, obviously puzzled.

"How can I reach her?" asked Roxanne.

"You think it might not have been an accident?" Jane's face became pinker. "That some of those awful children were involved?"

"Awful children?"

"Well." She sat back and smoothed her pant legs. "You know how they are. Teenagers. When they get together."

"Who were Jeremy's friends?"

"He didn't have many," she answered slowly. "Do you think someone killed him?" She said each word carefully, as if she didn't believe them.

"We're just asking questions." Roxanne had not intended to arouse that suspicion, but at least she now knew that Jeremy Featherstone's mother had not heard the story that her son might have died because a group of teenage girls tormented him.

"One thing we can do is talk to Julie Gilchrist and find out if she remembers the names of the girls that talked in her sewing room," Roxanne said now to Izzy. Sunlight shone through the window of the upstairs office. "Some of them might still be living in Robson."

"I'll do it."

"You need to take Riordan with you."

"Guess I do," said Izzy.

She drove Jeff Riordan through town before they hit the road to Julie Gilchrist's house.

"The grand tour," she told him. "So you get to know the lie of the land." The sun still shone in a flawless blue sky and road cleaners were sweeping up the dirt left by the melting snowbanks. The town used a lot of sand on intersections during the winter months. It all needed to be carted away. Next, the roads would be washed clean, ready for the tourists to arrive.

All the fishing boats were moored in the harbour. They couldn't get out on the water just yet; fishing season was regulated by the government, but the crews could check their gear and tackle. Al Melnychuk was standing on the wharf, talking to other fishermen. He nodded as Izzy drove by. She could see him eyeballing Jeff sitting beside her.

"You know everybody around here?" asked Riordan.

"Just about. The locals anyway. And they all know me."

"Guess they know the sarge too."

"Sure they do."

"Word is that she came here for a quiet life and brought trouble with her."

Izzy knew about that talk. She'd heard it herself. It was common gossip and people loved to have someone to blame. She drove up the straight road toward Heron Haven, lake water sparking on their right.

"People forget that the first time she came here Stella Magnusson had just been killed," she said. "And she solved that murder. They were happy enough about that. This place can be a pain." She turned the corner onto Heron Road. "Talk, talk, talk. And always finger pointing."

"Thought you liked it here?"

"Me?" said Izzy. "I'm stuck. Forever, it looks like. First my mom got cancer, just as I was almost done training at the Depot, and I had to come home and help look after her. Not my choice at all. And now Matt has this house so we're back here living in the Interlake again. Tell you, once Fiskar Bay gets its hooks into you, it doesn't let you go."

She pulled into the Gilchrists' driveway behind a big van. Fern Wiebe had driven up already with her brood.

"Izzy McBain? What brings you here?" Fern opened the door to them with the toddler attached to her leg. Two of her kids were out on the grass, other side of the house, and the oldest boy was down at the dock, helping his Aunt Hazel with the boat.

"You're here for the weekend?" asked Izzy.

"Just a sleepover tonight. We'll be back home before Sunday. But we're going out on the boat tomorrow.

Julie was slicing up apples. An empty pie crust stood ready. There was a plate half full of cookies behind her and used drink glasses. She looked alarmed to see Izzy and another member of the police force walk into her kitchen once more. Jeff said he'd go talk to Hazel and left Izzy with Julie and Fern.

"I heard another police sergeant has died," Julie said. She had heard the news on the CBC. "A new one? Just out from the city? So first it was Bill, then Roach, now someone else? Someone is running down people like you?"

"Maybe," said Izzy, face deadpan. She explained the reason for the visit.

Julie couldn't remember the names of any of the girls from her sewing room all those years ago, but she had photos, she said, upstairs in her loft. She was sure she had an album from her days at Robson High. She'd go look. She trotted off down the hallway. A small hand reached up toward a plate of cookies.

"No more!" said Fern.

"You haven't been out here much these past few years," said Izzy. Fern hoisted her child onto her hip and went to the sink. She pulled a paper towel off a rack and wet it under the tap.

"No," she said. "But it's just Mom that's living here now. And she wanted to see the kids."

"You're okay with that?"

"Why wouldn't I be?" The child was swinging his head from side to side to avoid having his face wiped. Fern put him down and squatted so she could use both hands.

"The story around Fiskar Bay is that you don't speak to your mom anymore because she's into some funny New Age stuff and Cory's folks don't approve," Izzy said.

"Everybody says wrong!" Fern stood back up. "Honestly, this town!"

"If it's not your mom, how come you've never been back? It's been years." Izzy leaned against the countertop. She tried to relax into their old friendly way of talking, as if she wasn't a cop. The child trotted off toward the glass doors. A girl who looked about the same age as Finn came and took his hand. Fern opened the door under the sink and dropped the paper towel into a waste bin.

"Well," she said, stretching her back. "Dad wasn't the easiest."

"That's not what your sister says."

They both glanced across to the window. It looked like Hazel was showing Jeff around the boat.

"Well, she would." Fern took her mother's place opposite and reached for another apple. "Hazel was always Dad's girl," she said ruefully. "She did everything right, exactly as he wanted." She lifted a sharp knife and began slicing. "Not like me. He kicked me out, you know. Seventeen and pregnant. Told me not to come back, so I didn't. Cory's mother took me in. My parents didn't come to my wedding. Well, you know that. You were there. I wanted Hazel to be a bridesmaid, but she wasn't allowed to come either."

Izzy could tell that the memory was still bitter. But here was Fern, back visiting her mother soon as her father was dead and gone.

"We've been told that your mom was thinking about leaving him."

"She was?" Fern stopped slicing, the knife poised in mid-air. "Really? How about that!"

"They didn't get along?"

"They did as long she did what he wanted," she said. She looked out the window again. Her littlest son was trying to kick a ball. "Usually, she went along with it."

Julie appeared at the end of the hallway, a photograph album in her hand.

"I found it," she announced. "And look, I've got all of their names, written below them." She had staff photographs, too, with the names listed. Fern rolled her eyes at Izzy, glad that her mother appeared not to have heard what she had been saying.

"Good to see you again, Iz." Fern put down the knife and went outside to her children.

"You can borrow the album," said Julie Gilchrist.

Jeff returned from the dock. "Mind if I look at your car?" he asked.

Julie looked anxious but nodded. The Mazda was in the garage. It took Jeff seconds to photograph the tires and check for damage to the front end. He could see none. Soon he and Izzy were on their way again.

"Hazel Gilchrist was at the dock in town yesterday," he said as he fastened his seat belt. "She had to go book a time at the boat launch. Al Melnychuk was there telling everybody about the police picking on his family. Said he'd already talked to that useless woman that was running the RCMP out here these days. Told her they needed to back off on his family and picking on his boys. And now some new guy in fancy city clothes was poking his nose into their business."

"So, Hazel might have known that Mark Cappelli was going to look at the McKenzie farmhouse?"

"Says she didn't, but do we believe her?"

22

RICHARD PETERS, ROXANNE'S new file coordinator, a round-faced constable with black hair and a cherubic smile, arrived on Saturday morning. He wasted no time taking over the corner that Izzy had vacated. He took out a laptop and a phone and soon had his nose buried in a heap of printed spreadsheets.

"Hey, Rick," said Jeff Riordan. As members of the MCU they had met before.

"You know each other? Good," said Roxanne. "Because you are going to be bunking together. Kathy's found you a rental cottage beside the beach. She's gone over to turn on the heat and she's getting keys cut for you. But right now, we all need to get up to speed."

They gathered at the table in the centre of the room and ran through what they knew. None of it helped much. They had scraps of information, but nothing added up to a strong lead.

"Hazel could have known about Mark and that he'd been at the harbour talking to Melnychuk," Jeff said. "She might even have known that he'd gone to look at the house. We don't know if Mark stopped at the road shrine on the way to the McKenzie farmhouse or after. If he died later, Hazel might have had time to find him there."

"She was in Toronto when her dad died, and she got along with him." Izzy objected. "She couldn't have killed him."

Roxanne's phone buzzed.

"This is Bea Benedict, executive director of the Sunnywell Centre," a loud voice boomed in her ear. Bea was calling to protest the RCMP's handling of her employee yesterday. "Very brusque," she declaimed. "Quite unnecessary. Mr. McKenzie was being cooperative." Lex had been placed in the back of a police car and driven off, as if already convicted. "Again," she added pointedly.

"He has been released," Roxanne assured her. "He's free to be back at work."

"And so he should be!" was the sharp response. "I want you to know, Sergeant, that Lex McKenzie has earned my deepest respect. He may have been guilty of a misdemeanor in the past, but his work here has been exemplary and he is moving on in life. He needs encouragement and support and that is not what he is receiving from the RCMP."

Bea continued with the character reference. Lex was efficient, pleasant to work with and, in Bea's opinion, trustworthy. "He has learned his lesson, Sergeant, and paid his dues."

"Thank you for the information," Roxanne said, as Mrs. Benedict reached the end of her spiel.

Lex's alibi had been checked already. He had worked an eight-hour shift at the Sunnywell Centre on Thursday and got a ride back to the halfway house in Winnipeg, helped cook supper and then went upstairs to his room. So it didn't look like he'd have been in the Interlake on Thursday night.

"What about his brother, Marvin?" asked Izzy.

"I talked to him," said Rick Peters. "This morning, before I drove out here." He looked eager to have something concrete to contribute to the discussion.

"He's a good man. Thorough. Shows potential," Inspector Schultz had informed Roxanne when he called to tell her that Peters had been assigned to the case. Now was Rick's chance to live up to that recommendation.

"He's a big guy," Rick continued. "Cooperative. A car mechanic. He works in town and didn't finish until six on Thursday, then he went home and was there all evening. So his only alibi is that his wife corroborates what he's saying. He lives in the North End of Winnipeg." That was less than an hour's drive from Fiskar Bay. "So, we can't rule out the possibility that he drove here. I've got a photo of him. I'll send it to you right now."

He pulled out his phone and clicked. Marvin McKenzie's face popped up on Roxanne's laptop. He resembled his uncle, the fisherman Al Melnychuk. She clicked and the printer whirred into life.

The photo album Julie Gilchrist had loaned them lay on the table. The photos were covered with plastic film, ordered by class year, a label below each one. Julie had put a red dot beside the girls she remembered hanging around her sewing room.

"It sounds like Sergeant Bill played favourites in his family. He was really hard on Fern but was great with Hazel." Izzy carried the album over to the printer as she spoke, ready to make copies. "I guess she did what he wanted her to do, like Julie did, until now."

She lifted the photo of Marvin McKenzie from the printer tray and looked out the window. "Kathy Isfeld's just turned the corner. It looks like she's coming here. And Al Melnychuk's pulled up too."

ROXANNE BARELY MADE it downstairs before Melnychuk slammed inside. She opened the door to an interview room.

"No need for that," he bellowed. "I'll say what I've got to say right here."

He planted his big boots in the centre of the room and thrust an accusing finger in Roxanne's direction.

"I told you," he continued shouting, "to back off on Lex and what do you do? Send one of your guys to haul him out of work, just when he's got started in a new job. Take him to the cop shop and ask him the same old bunch of questions. I tell you, I thought it was Gilchrist that had it in for him, that he was covering up for that jerk Roach."

The door opened and Kathy Isfeld walked in.

"Not supposed to speak ill of the dead, right? But it's true and this whole town knows it. Lex got beat up in one of your cells by Roach, middle of the night, and he put the blame right on Lex. Then Gilchrist backed the bastard up. And now you're trying to nail Lex for killing the pair of them. That'll put him away for life, and he didn't do it. You Mounties just don't know when to quit, do you?"

Kathy closed the door quietly and crept behind him to her desk.

"So then you have a go at Marvin." Al's head lowered like a bull about to charge. "Like he's trouble, too? Marvin? He's a good guy, right, Kathy?"

He waved in Kathy's direction. Kathy opened her mouth to speak but didn't get a word out.

"Used to go fishing with me and your old man when he was a kid, that's right, eh?"

Kathy nodded slowly.

"Still comes out and fishes on the weekend when he can. But ice fishing's been over these past four weeks, and we had to come off the lake. This is what happens when some dumb city cop like you gets sent to run things in a place like this. Don't know nothing about anything."

He pulled back his arm and thrust his big hands deep into his pockets as if he needed to keep them from grabbing Roxanne.

"We won't get back out on the water until end of the month. Damned government regulations, telling us what to do. Marvin hasn't been out here fishing for weeks. Long before whoever it is started bumping your lot off.

"You've got it in for my family," he ranted on. "Maybe someone's been telling you wrong. Who is it? Stan Kuryk? Always wanted those boys out of their house so he could buy up their land. That's what he's up to. Asshole. Just causing more trouble. You want to be careful who you listen to around here. But you know what else I think? Maybe it's one of you cops that did it."

He swivelled his head, taking in all of them, Aimee and Kathy behind the front desk, Izzy and Rick at the foot of the stairs, Roxanne right in front of him.

"Think about it. Gilchrist. Roach. Now the new guy. He'd just arrived. Who else around here knew who he was except you guys, right here in this office? Someone's killing off the tough cops. Using a car to do it because they're too scared to take them on face to face."

He stepped closer, his face within inches of Roxanne's nose. "Someone weak. Someone who isn't strong enough to fight their own battles. I'm telling you once more—back right off. Leave my family be. Look to your own house, lady."

He swung around on his heels, yanked open the door, letting it bang shut behind him as he left.

"That's Marvin McKenzie's uncle? He looks just like him," said Rick.

"He's only on the attack because his family's under threat," said Roxanne. "Don't let what he said get to you." Having her team start to suspect one another was a development she did not need. "Did Stan Kuryk really want to buy the McKenzie farm, Kathy?"

"Oh, probably." Kathy took off her coat and hung it on a hook behind a cupboard door. "Stan owns chunks of land around here. He's always on the lookout for more. And the McKenzie fields are right beside his own."

Rick stepped forward, hand outstretched. "You must be Kathy Isfeld." He beamed and introduced himself. "I've been told all about you! How you know absolutely everything about this detachment." He seized her hand and shook it. Kathy looked surprised but pleased. "I have been told that you have files that just might contain exactly what we need to know."

"I have," Kathy responded. "I've kept everything. Do you want to see them?"

"Absolutely," said Rick. "I can't wait."

"You got keys cut? So Rick and Jeff can move into that apartment?" Roxanne reminded her.

"Of course. That's why I'm here. But first let me show Richard my file cupboard." Kathy was already turning toward the closet door.

Roxanne left them to it. If Rick and Kathy could discover something in those archival files, that was fine by her, but she didn't think they would. She went back upstairs. She needed to think about what Melnychuk had said. Was it possible that one of her own staff was responsible for these deaths? Who, among them, had worked with all three men who had died? Izzy had been gone from Fiskar Bay for a year, so she hadn't been here when her old boss had retired. She hadn't liked Roach; she said she got along well with Bill Gilchrist, but he had made a pass at her early in her career and she'd acted like nothing had happened. But Izzy couldn't possibly be involved. It was unthinkable. And besides, she'd barely known Mark Cappelli.

Sam Mendes had been stricken at the death of his best buddy, Ken Roach. Roxanne was sure he hadn't faked that. Pete Robinson? Pete was canny, unflappable. What reason would he have to dislike either Gilchrist or Roach, or Mark Cappelli? Aimee and Ravi were both young constables and had worked in Fiskar Bay for less than a year. Kathy, of course, had been present throughout but she wasn't an active member of the Force. She was about to retire, with a solid pension. Why would she risk that? Roxanne knew that Melnychuk was just stirring things up, being annoying, as usual. But what he had said was unsettling.

She had a new message from Ident: The tire tread marks that they had found on Mark Cappelli's jacket were made by Firestone. Winter tires, of a size used primarily for light trucks. Roxanne looked out the window into the parking lot. The detachment had two trucks, big Fords. Neither Mendes nor Robinson owned a pickup, nor did Aimee or Ravi, she was sure of that. Izzy and Matt had a Ford truck, but it was a big F-150 and she'd seen Kathy driving a plain white Chevy sedan. None of her team owned a small truck.

The Featherstones didn't drive a truck either, and the tire marks couldn't have been made by Julie Gilchrist's Mazda or her daughter's rental Toyota. This new evidence helped narrow their field of suspects right down and they finally had a solid piece of evidence. She forwarded the report to Izzy, Jeff and Rick.

"There's a truck in the outbuilding at the McKenzie farmhouse." Izzy ran upstairs, soon as she'd read it. "We should get a search warrant. And you know who's got a little red pickup? Stan Kuryk. That's who."

23

THERE WAS NO one home at the Kuryk farm. The dogs barked at first, then resorted to prowling, watchful and suspicious as Roxanne and Izzy checked the doors. The porch was unlocked, the plants watered earlier that day, but the door that led into the kitchen was locked. No one was in the outbuildings. Cows with calves grazed in a field across the road. The grass was growing, but not enough for them to eat yet. Stan Kuryk had laid out rows of hay for them.

The Toyota truck was easy to spot, parked outside the barn. It was a dirty red, but not old and in decent shape. Its doors were also locked.

"Summer tires," said Izzy. She had seen Stan load bunches of flowers into this same truck last time she saw him. "Doesn't mean anything. Stan could have changed them since Thursday. Bet he does the job himself. Wonder where he stores his winter ones?" She rattled the door handle of a shed. It was shut tight.

Roxanne walked to the other side of the barn. She pointed in the direction of the McKenzie house.

"Where do you think this property ends?" she asked. Izzy walked over to join her.

"Not sure. At the road where we found the bodies, maybe? Or the next road over? Then it'll be McKenzie land. You can see why Stan would have wanted to buy it. He could have rented it if Lex and his brothers wouldn't sell. Wonder why he didn't. Bet my dad'll know."

She went back to the farmhouse and sat on the steps in the sunshine while she made the call. Her dad was out but her mom was home.

"Stan doesn't rent. He doesn't need to. He owns parcels of land all over the area. He must have wanted that piece, but old man McKenzie and Stan didn't get along. That could have something to do with it," she said.

"Do you know what they fell out about?" Izzy asked.

"No, I don't. Must have been ages ago. Want me to find out?"

"Sure," said Izzy.

"I've heard your dad and your brother say Stan's obsessed when it comes to buying land. He can't get enough of it. The Kuryks have daughters and neither of them are going to want the farm. But that doesn't stop Stan from going after everything that comes up for sale. You know those city folks that built that fancy solar house west of him? Eighty-six acres and Stan held out for a cheaper price. They scooped it up meantime. Your dad said he was pretty pissed off about that. Why are you asking?"

"Just wondered," said Izzy. "Don't tell anyone it's me that wants to know, okay?"

"Not a word."

Roxanne leaned against the stair railing in the sunshine. "Bill Gilchrist could have come out here and got into some kind of argument with Stan the weekend that he died. Walked away for some reason and got run over and left to die in the ditch. He might have driven out here in that big SUV of his, then Netta could have helped Stan return it to the house at Heron Haven."

"What would Bill Gilchrist and Stan Kuryk have to argue about?" Izzy said dubiously. "Just after he'd got back from Arizona? He'd been gone for five months." The dogs lay beside the driveway, watching them.

"I have no idea." Roxanne walked back toward her car. The dogs stirred and rose on their haunches.

"I don't think Netta Kuryk would leave a man to die in a ditch next to where she lives. She's a good, God-fearing Christian." Izzy followed her.

"You're probably right. Maybe she's more likely than he is to tell the truth if we ask her, though."

"I wouldn't count on it," said Izzy. "Loyalty runs deep around here." They drove out of the yard, the dogs running at their back wheels until they were clear of the gate.

"Hey, look!" Izzy held her phone out. Matt had sent a photo of Finn sitting on a floor, a tiny newborn pup in each hand. "They must have gone over to Mo Magnusson's place."

Roxanne glanced at the picture of her smiling son. "Hope he doesn't think we're getting one of those," she said.

LEX MCKENZIE CALLED Margo Wishart to tell her he had the answers to all her questions. Now it was Saturday. He needed to apologize for being so late getting the information to her, but he had been unavoidably detained. He had just sent her an email, but he had wanted to tell her how sorry he was himself.

"Not a problem. So you have extra lights that we can use?" Margo scanned the answers he had supplied while she talked. "And the power to run all of them?"

They did. The Sunnywell Centre sometimes hosted concerts and small theatrical events. Lex could show her what they had if she wanted to drop by and have a look. She arranged to do so next week, on the way home after teaching her university class. Soon as she hung up, she called Roberta Axelsson. With those lights, Roberta's idea to make the room look like it was underwater could work.

"This nice man called Lex McKenzie is working there. He's being very helpful."

"Lex? McKenzie?" Roberta was at her kitchen sink washing eggs. She turned off a tap. "That's the guy they think might have murdered all those cops!"

"Can't be. He's working for Bea Benedict." Then Margo thought: a forty-something-year-old man on work placement. What was that all about?

"He embezzled a pile of money a few years back," Roberta was happy to inform her. "Went to jail for it. He's probably out by now. Sergeant Gilchrist and that constable that died were the ones that put him behind bars. That's why they think he did it."

"He's so pleasant," said Margo. "You sure it's him?"

"With a name like Lex? How many of those are there? But"—Margo could hear Roberta pull out a chair and sit, ready for a good chat—"they can't be sure that it's him that did it because Roxanne Calloway's just been over at the Kuryk farm snooping around. And she's asking questions about land deals."

Izzy McBain's mom had called, not long before. She and Roberta were old friends and neighbours. They told each other everything.

Margo hoped that Lex McKenzie wasn't involved in the murders. She prided herself on being a decent judge of character. Had she been wrong this time, taken in by a warm smile and a firm handshake? Bea Benedict had taken the man on board, given him a job. She must have been persuaded by him too. She must know that he had been in prison. That might be the reason for the work placement. But did she also know that he was suspected of murder?

ROXANNE AND IZZY drove straight from the farm to the old McKenzie place. They found the key under the pot at the back door. It opened the house but none of the outbuildings. They wandered from room to room inside. It was untidy, needed a good clean, had been slept in. Someone had drunk beer and eaten pizza, but that could have been weeks ago. Only the empty boxes and bottles remained. There was no sign that anything had been disturbed as recently as the day before. The furniture was old and shabby. There was framed needlework on the walls. Some old photos, taken outside this same house when it was new, showed a woman in a long skirt and an apron, a moustached man in shirt and overalls, and four children, the oldest no more than ten, the youngest a baby, held by the mother. The McKenzie family must have lived here for at least three generations.

The ashes in the firepit outside looked like the last fire must have happened since the snowstorm. Izzy stood on tiptoe, peering in the window of what had once been a stock barn and was now a storage shed. In the gloom she could just see the outline of the small truck inside.

"That's an old Ford Ranger," she said. "There's dozens of those around. That model's out of date but it's got an engine that goes on forever. Guys with small farms love them." She stepped back from the window and rubbed dirt off her fingers. "Marvin probably uses it for going out on the ice when he's fishing. Bet it's still got its winter tires on." She examined the door closely. "No sign that anyone's unlocked this and taken it out recently, though."

"Well," said Roxanne as they returned to her car. "We don't know if Marvin's been out here this month. But we do know that the Kuryks and the McKenzies both have the kind of truck we're looking for and the Featherstones and Julie Gilchrist don't. That helps."

Izzy stopped with her hand on the handle of the car door. "It's gone two," she said. "I'm hungry. Can we stop at the chip van in town?"

The van was a summer favourite at Fiskar Bay. The season might not have started yet but this was a weekend and it was open, first time this year. It was doing good trade, parked in its usual spot, an empty lot next to the liquor store. Several picnic tables sat under trees on the grass. It was sunny enough to sit outside and two of them were occupied. Roxanne found another, at a distance, so they would not be overheard while they talked, and Izzy went to fetch their order: french fries and a smokie on a bun for her, a burger and a diet Coke for Roxanne.

A couple walked by on the sidewalk. "Hi, Izzy," said the woman. "Sergeant Calloway." Fiskar Bay's residents noticed every move the RCMP made.

Izzy brought over their food. "Don't look now but the Kuryks have just pulled up behind you." She watched as Stan Kuryk clambered out of a big Silverado and went into the liquor store. Netta stayed in the passenger seat. She noticed Izzy and waved. Izzy smiled and raised a hand in response.

"We've been spotted," she said as she opened a package of fries. She doused them in ketchup. "Netta doesn't look worried. Or like she's guilty of anything."

"Does Stan drink?" Roxanne asked.

"Don't know. Let's wait and see what he brings out." Shortly after, Stan emerged with a large paper bag.

"Can't tell. Big bottles. Not beer. Spirits." The Kuryk truck passed close by them as it left the parking lot. Netta smiled and waved again. Izzy waved back. "They must have been in town for groceries. It looks like they're going back home. I wonder if he likes a shot of rye now and then."

"Kathy might still be at the detachment. She'll maybe know."

Kathy was not.

"She's taken the guys over to the cottage to make sure everything works," Aimee Vermette reported. "She'll be back. Rick has spreadsheets of all the past cases that Ident thought might be worth checking out. She wants to find out if they've missed anything."

"I need Jeff and Rick back here." Roxanne took out her phone and texted them. "I want the Kuryks brought in here for questioning. And you and I need to go back to the Gilchrist house, Izzy. Fern Wiebe is still in Fiskar Bay today, right?"

"Expect so," Izzy agreed. "She'll have to get back home before the stroke of midnight. They're not allowed to travel on the Lord's Day, right? They might not be at the house yet, though. They were going to go out a boat trip. They won't be back yet."

"I need to know if she and Cory Wiebe own a small pickup," said Roxanne. "And if she's been up here visiting before this. She still has friends here, right?"

"She does. And I know who she might have visited." Izzy walked toward the door. "Give me an hour and I'll go see what I can find out."

24

WHEN NETTA KURYK was displeased, she became still. Her features were etched into her broad, granite face, her mouth a grim line. She sat in the interview room, her hands folded on top of her belly, and studied the edge of the table in front of her. Occasionally, two slits the colour of a thundercloud rose to look at Roxanne, sitting opposite, with Jeff Riordan at her side. When she replied to a question she did so as briefly as possible.

Yes, she and Stan owned a Toyota pickup. She drove it sometimes; so did he. It used less gas than the Silverado. Often, he was out and about on his land. She didn't keep track of where he went. She couldn't say exactly where he was all of the weekend after the big snowstorm. That was Easter Sunday, regular Easter, not Ukrainian, so they'd gone into Winnipeg to see the grandkids. They'd had an Easter egg hunt. She'd gone to Desna Church after they got home, to help get it ready for real Easter, the Ukrainian one. She liked to keep the place tidy.

Did her husband know Sergeant Gilchrist? Probably. Gilchrist had been around for years. Had the sergeant visited the farm that weekend? Not that she knew of. Did her husband like a drink?

"A shot of rye. End of a long day. That's all." She looked from Roxanne to Jeff and back again, uneasy at the question.

Why did her husband and the McKenzies not get along? She paused before she answered. "Just because," she finally replied.

Had they disagreed about something? It went back, she said, to when Stan's dad and Peter McKenzie was alive. She didn't know what that was about. The two families didn't talk much. That was all.

Had Stan ever been in trouble with the police? "Never," she asserted, without any hesitation.

THAT WASN'T TRUE, Rick Peters told Roxanne once they emerged from the room. He'd checked back through the records to see if the Kuryk name showed up. Stanislav Kuryk had a temper. It had got him into trouble, way back, thirty, forty years ago. His favourite target had been Peter McKenzie. "Al Melnychuk's brother-in-law. Father of Marvin, Paul and Lex," said Rick, laying an old report in front of Roxanne.

Peter McKenzie had died of a heart attack at the age of sixty. He'd been a couple of years older than Stan. The fights had stopped as they grew older; there had been none for at least thirty years, so nothing like that had happened during Sergeant Bill Gilchrist's tenure in Fiskar Bay. There was no reason to link them to the murders.

Netta was moved to the front office and given a coffee to mollify her while she waited. Stan replaced her at the table in the interview room. He'd resisted coming to the detachment when Jeff and Rick asked him. He needed to get his beasts inside, he'd complained, pointing west, in the direction of darkening clouds. It was going to rain later, maybe thunder. But Jeff had insisted.

"Sooner we get this done, sooner you'll be back home," he'd said as he loaded Stan onto the back seat of the police car beside his wife. The Kuryks had said nothing during the drive to Fiskar Bay, just looked out of each window in opposite directions. Stan was still riled up. Unlike his wife, he had plenty to say and he'd had to wait; they had talked to his wife first. That irked him.

Of course he had a pickup. So did most guys that farmed around here. No, he hadn't seen anything of Gilchrist. He'd heard that he'd taken off south for the winter and didn't know that he was back. Why would he? So someone had run the old cop down and left him in a ditch next to his field? Didn't mean that it was him that did it.

"Don't think you can pin this murder on me." He banged the tabletop. The knuckles on his hand were enlarged. Roxanne wondered if he suffered from arthritis and if pain fuelled his bad temper. "That's what you do, right? Pick someone that could have done it, then make sure it looks like they get the blame. I've been told. Well, forget it. I keep myself to myself. Stay out of trouble."

He pulled the hand away and tucked it and its partner under his armpits. Above them, his brown, weather-beaten face looked as impassive as his wife's. All the creases on it turned downward. Stanislav Kuryk was not given to smiling.

"You used to get into fights," Roxanne remarked.

"Not in a long time," he responded, gritting his teeth.

"Not since Peter McKenzie was alive?"

"What's Gilchrist's murder got to do with him?" The hands emerged again and smoothed the legs of his jeans. They were clean. He must have changed out of his usual coveralls to go shopping in town. "Peter's long gone."

Twenty-two years, to be exact. Rick Peters had found out that McKenzie's widow had stayed on in the farmhouse for ten years after her husband's death, then she'd moved to Winnipeg, into an apartment for seniors not far from where Marvin and his wife lived.

"Bad lot, those McKenzies. Well, Marvin's not so bad. And Paul's never around. But Alexander, him they call Lex, he's always been a loose cannon. Takes after his dad. Big mouth. Don't know when to shut up, either of them." Stan spat the words out like they were dirt he needed to get out of his system. "Always been like that. Think they're something because their family got here first, from the old country, more than a hundred years ago. Think they own the place."

"My dad" —he banged the table again—"got here later, in the forties, after that big war in Europe ended. He ended up in a camp for DPs. A displaced person. Had nothing and nowhere to go. Got shipped out here, came from Kiev, didn't know a thing about

RAYE ANDERSON

farming but he learned. And he met my mother. See that land we live on, me and Netta? My grandfather on my mother's side gave them it as a wedding present. Helped my dad a lot. Pissed the McKenzies right off because the land was next to theirs. They said that if my grandfather had wanted to get rid of it he should have said. They'd have paid real money for it.

"They didn't make life easy for my family. Never raised a finger to help. Not neighbourly. When I went to school, their son, Peter, picked on me. I was younger, but I learned to fight back." His hands balled into fists at the memory. "And came a day I got bigger. Started winning those fights." Two vertical folds appeared on his cheeks, as close as he got to a smile. "He learned to leave me alone. I've got more land than the McKenzies now." He nodded his head in satisfaction. "One of these days I'll buy what's left of theirs too."

He clasped both hands in front of him, like he was trying to get them under control, and leaned in. Roxanne caught a whiff of alcohol on his breath. Stan must have downed a glass or two while his wife unloaded groceries in her kitchen.

"So," he said. "Since I didn't do it, maybe it was one of them that's your murderer?"

Roxanne had nothing more to ask him. Jeff and Rick drove the Kuryks back home. Kathy Isfeld sat beside Rick upstairs in the Major Crimes room, checking over his facts and figures.

"Don't know how Netta puts up with him," she said. She ran into Netta occasionally. They both served on the ladies' auxiliary at the hospital.

"How is it that all three of the McKenzie brothers inherited the farm equally?" Roxanne asked. "That it didn't go straight to Marvin? He's the oldest, right? And he seems to be sensible."

"The mother saw to that. Lovely old soul, she was. She knew Marvin wasn't going to farm it, nor was Paul, and she had a soft spot for Lex. Spoiled him rotten. Some people say that's his problem. So she made sure he got his share."

"It's not usually like that in farming families though, is it. Like Izzy's. Her brother Ed will get the McBain farm, right?"

"Oh, well. Makes sense, doesn't it. You break it up it's not big enough to be a viable business anymore.'

"Izzy's not back yet?"

Izzy was not, but she had sent a text. AT ELISE EINARSON'S. MIGHT TAKE A WHILE.

MARGO WISHART WALKED her dog. It was warm out, but it wasn't going to stay like that. The clouds were gathering and rain was predicted. That wasn't a bad thing. It would settle the dust left by a winter's worth of debris and get the plants growing again. The few perennials around her house had sprouted and could do with a soak. Steve Rice was in his yard raking up dead leaves and grass and bagging them in large paper compostable bags.

"Got everything sorted out with Mrs. Benedict?" he remarked as she passed.

"I did," said Margo, glad of the opportunity to stop and talk to him. "Her assistant, Lex McKenzie, is being helpful. I believe you know who he is?"

"Ah, yes," said Steve, leaning on his rake.

"He seems very pleasant. But he's mismanaged finances in the past, I'm told." Margo's dog stood at her side. She rubbed his ear. "And it seems he is also a suspect in this murder investigation that's going on. Bea Benedict seems to trust him implicitly."

"Indeed she does." The neighbourly smile on Steve's face disappeared. "But Bea, like me, knows that Lex has put his past behind him. He has become a religious man and that has changed him entirely. Bea is helping him get back on his feet and we are all grateful for that. Men like Lex need all the help he can get, Dr. Wishart, and I would have thought a woman of your educational background would understand that. I'm surprised at you passing on malicious gossip."

He returned to his raking. Margo had been suitably chastised. That was what she got for interfering, she thought, and turned toward Sasha Rosenberg's house.

Sasha was in her studio, welding, sparks flying as she attached a piece of metal to a skeletal frame. She turned off her blowtorch and pulled off her protective goggles. "Look," she said. "Becky's beginning to get a face."

Margo could see a mask beginning to form, one that looked full of pent-up fury. The arms of the creature stretched out, ready for hands to be attached. She liked it. This project was going to work.

"Let's go outside," said Sasha, "and catch the last of the sun. It looks like we might have a storm brewing."

They sat on a bench overlooking the creek. Sasha brought out a couple of glasses and a plastic screw-top bottle of her homemade wine. "Way easier than bottling it," she said. "And I don't keep it that long." This one was white and was more palatable than most.

"I've just been told off by Steve Rice," said Margo, and told her the story.

"Why did you bring it up with him?" A couple of geese waddled around on the grassy bank opposite. They were building a nest nearby. Bob the dog and Lenny were off leash, but the water lay between them and the birds. It still flowed fast and deep. "He's bound to be on Lex's side. He works as a counsellor at the jail sometimes. It's probably him that got Lex the job."

"I liked Lex, too, first time I met him. Now I wonder if he's just too plausible. And I thought I'd sound Steve out, that was all."

"Wouldn't worry if I was you." Sasha stretched her legs. "Steve's always been a pious prick. Did you know that Susan sometimes talks about kicking him out? Says he's a control freak and she's had enough." There was a rumble from the west. The gathering clouds had formed thunderheads on the horizon, one bulging on top of the other, in varying shades of purple and grey.

"Drink up," said Sasha, "We're in for a doozy."

25

IZZY MCBAIN DROVE the road to Heron Haven alone. She'd had a good time catching up with Elise Einarson, sitting in her sunny backyard, enjoying being outside. She hadn't seen much of Elise lately. Izzy had gone to university in Winnipeg after school and Elise had headed to Brandon, in the west of the province. There was a good music program there, and Elise played the saxophone. She still did, in a jazz band sometimes, but her paying job was teaching band at their alma mater.

"Look at us, both back where we started." Elise had lounged in a deck chair, beer in hand.

"I thought the RCMP was my ticket out of here, but it didn't work out that way. I've got myself stuck." Izzy shrugged. She'd opted for a can of Coke. She was still on the job and driving. "Regina's as far as I ever got."

Elise was one of a few classmates who had kept in touch with Fern Gilchrist, now Wiebe. "Mainly on Facebook. She doesn't get much further than home with all those kids."

"So, she hasn't been up here at all visiting? Since before her father died?"

"Not that I know of. He wrote her off when she married Cory. Well, you know about that."

"I sure do. Remember the wedding? We were all just seventeen. And there was Fern, all decked out in that long white dress, belly bulging under her bouquet. No family of her own. That uncle of Cory's walking her down the aisle because her dad wasn't there.

Cory's sister as maid of honour. She didn't ask you or anyone else to be bridesmaids?"

"She really hoped Hazel would step up at the last minute, but she didn't."

"Hazel was only fourteen, maybe fifteen. She probably wasn't allowed."

"Guess so." Elise looked sideways at Izzy through her sunglasses. "There was a rumour, back in school, that Cory Wiebe cornered you after hockey practice one night."

"Him and a buddy." Izzy stretched out her legs in the sunshine, wishing she was wearing shorts like Elise. "We'd nail them for sexual assault if they tried that now."

"But not then."

"They got a talking to. That was it. You know how it was. 'Boys will be boys.' They'd probably have said that I was asking for it, back then. It was a different story, though, when Fern, Sergeant Bill's own daughter, got mixed up with him. Do you know if she's okay, living out there with Cory?"

"She doesn't say. She's pretty busy with the kids. Four already and another on the way."

"Really?" So Fern's fuller waist wasn't weight gain. It was another baby.

"She's pretty involved with Cory's family and the church. I don't think she sees anyone else much."

The sun had moved over to the west and the shadows were lengthening. Izzy could see storm clouds gathering. The Gilchrist family should be back from their boat trip by now.

"I should get going," she said.

Elise wagged her beer bottle. "I've got to get back to work too," she agreed. The music festival was coming up. She needed to figure out what the school choirs were going to sing.

So Izzy had set off, by herself. She'd never get Fern to talk with either of the guys sitting at her elbow. Or Roxanne Calloway. But as an old school friend, she might have a chance of wheedling something out of Fern. And she wasn't running any risk. Izzy didn't believe that Fern or her mother were any danger.

She cranked up the car radio. Saturday Afternoon at the Opera was a fixture on CBC. Izzy quite liked opera. Her dad listened to it most Saturdays. He sometimes played Wagner, full blast, while he combined in the fall. "The Ride of the Valkyries," as he took in the crop, row upon row. She recognized what was playing now. Turandot. The tenor launched into his big aria, "Nessun Dorma," and Izzy McBain sang along at the top of her lungs as she turned the car toward the Gilchrist house sun sparkling on the surface of the lake ahead of her and dark grey clouds piling up behind her.

MARGO WISHART ALSO liked to listen to the opera on a Saturday afternoon. When the phone rang in the middle of that famous song, she thought she might let the call go to voicemail, but she did glance at the name of the caller. SUNNYWELL CENTRE, it said. Reluctantly, she silenced the tenor as Bea Benedict's voice rang fruitily in her ear.

"Dr. Wishart! So glad I caught you. I must ask, you paid the deposit for the rental of the room here by cheque, did you not?"

Margo had. When she worked on a project, she liked to keep the finances separate, and to have a paper trail. "Is there a problem with it?" she asked, sure that she'd had enough cash in that account to cover it.

"Well…" Bea hesitated, unusual for her. "I'm afraid it has gone missing. It may have been misplaced, but I wonder if you could check to see if anyone has cashed it? You can do that, can't you?"

Margo opened her laptop so she could log into her bank account while they talked. "You don't think anyone has stolen it, do you?" she asked, remembering her conversations earlier this afternoon about Lex McKenzie, Bea's new temporary employee.

"Perhaps," was Bea's reluctant response.

"Has anything else gone missing?" Margo's account data came up on the screen.

"I'm afraid so," Bea admitted. "It was in a cash drawer in my office and the contents are all gone. Did Lex call you regarding those questions that you needed answering?"

"He did." Margo could see no sign of the cheque having been cashed. She'd have to contact the bank and put a hold on it. "Do you think he's the one responsible? That he's stolen it?" She watched a police car drive by her house slowly. She was too far from the window to see where it was going.

"He doesn't come in on the weekends," said Bea. "His meditation group meets on Sundays and he helps get the place ready on Saturdays. But I did call the house in Winnipeg where he is staying at present and it seems he left there yesterday after dinner and hasn't been seen since."

FERN WIEBE's VAN was still parked in the driveway of the Gilchrist house but Izzy had cut it too fine. Fern was planning to head off home with her brood. She was fastening her youngest child into his jacket. Her mother was helping the other children. There was no sign of her sister, Hazel.

"You can't stay a little while longer so we can talk?" Izzy asked. "I thought we could maybe visit for a while. Catch up."

"Sorry, can't." Fern straightened and rubbed her back. Izzy noticed the baby bump under the long skirt that she wore. How could she have missed that? "Once I get the kids all loaded into the van, I need to get going. It's going to rain. I'd as soon get home before it starts." The drive would take her through Winnipeg and beyond, two hours with four children in the back.

"I've asked her to stay. Just for another night, to make a weekend of it." Julie rubbed a round little cheek. "Maybe another time if Cory doesn't mind?"

"We've got church in the morning," Fern explained to Izzy. She looked back at the large comfortable house. Perhaps she was tempted, Izzy hoped, but then it seemed that Fern recovered her resolve. "I've got to go."

"When will you be back?" asked Izzy.

"Not sure. Soon. If Mom's selling, I'll come and help. And she'll have a chance to get to know her grandkids a bit before she takes off for B.C. Maybe we can get together then?" Julie Gilchrist brightened as Fern said this. Izzy decided to leave them to say goodbye together.

"Is Hazel around?" she asked.

"She's at the dock." Izzy walked through the house just as Hazel carried a cooler up to the back deck. She opened the glass door and stepped outside.

"Good boat ride?" The motorboat was at the dock, bobbing at its mooring.

"Those kids have never been out in a boat before." Hazel rested the cooler on the patio table. "It's too bad they've missed out on that. They loved being on the water." She was dressed for boating, in cropped jeans, a T-shirt, a visor to shade her eyes, flat-soled canvas shoes.

"You got a few minutes to talk?" Seagulls cackled overhead, close to land.

"The boat needs to be gassed up," said Hazel. "I was just going to run in to Fiskar Bay and fill up the tank before it starts to rain. It won't take long. Want to come along for the ride?"

ALL WAS PEACEFUL in the Fiskar Bay Detachment of the RCMP. Kathy Isfeld and Rick Peters were still upstairs in his corner, heads together, one dark, one fair. Kathy had a prodigious memory and Rick was busy making notes.

Pete Robinson had gone out with Sam Mendes to check on a domestic dispute at Cullen Village, leaving Aimee Vermette to take care of the front office. The town was quiet. It was late afternoon and a thunderstorm was predicted. Soon most of the local shops would close.

"It's time you two knocked off for the day," Roxanne said. "Go get stocked up on groceries and beer before it pours."

Jeff Riordan didn't need a second telling. "Coming, Rick?" he asked.

Rick lifted his head, fingers still at his keyboard. "Just a bit more." He and Kathy were almost done. That was okay, Kathy told him. She would come back later to look for things that mattered, now that she had an idea about which old cases interested him.

"I like that Richard," she whispered confidentially to Roxanne as Rick and Jeff disappeared downstairs. "He's got his head screwed on. And he's a good worker."

Roxanne's phone pinged. Izzy texted, ON BOAT W HAZEL G TALK LATER. That explained where Izzy had got to. She must have gone to visit Julie Gilchrist and her daughters on her own. It was typical of Izzy to act spontaneously, to use her initiative, but Roxanne felt uneasy. Why was Izzy going out on the water with a storm brewing?

CHECK BACK WITH ME SOON AS, Roxanne tapped in response. She went into the office that Pete Robinson now occupied, the one she had vacated when she was seconded into the MCU, and closed the door. She called Matt Stavros.

"How's my boy?" she asked. Just fine, Matt told her.

"Tell him I'll be over to pick him up in an hour or so."

"It's going to storm. If you get held up, let me know."

She'd barely hung up when Margo Wishart called.

"Roxanne," she said. "I've had a call from Bea Benedict. Are you aware that some money has gone missing at the Sunnywell Centre and that Lex McKenzie might be responsible? That he didn't go home to the house where he is staying last night? That he's gone missing?"

So, Lex had reverted to his old ways. Where might he have gone? Someone should go check the McKenzie house out near Kuryk Road to make sure he hadn't gone to ground there. Roxanne had planned to stick around the office until Pete Robinson got back from Cullen Village. She didn't want to leave Aimee alone.

She could call Jeff and Rick, but they were probably out in the grocery aisles.

"Kathy," she said. "I need to run out. I won't be long. Can you hold the fort with Aimee until Pete or I get back?"

"I'll be okay on my own." Aimee Vermette looked up from her desk. "There's nothing going on out there. It's quiet."

"No," Roxanne insisted. "We should have someone else here. I have to go look at something."

"By yourself?" Aimee asked. Lightning flashed just west of the town. The sky was getting darker.

"If I need help, I'll call in."

Thunder rumbled in the distance.

"You'd better be quick," said Aimee. "That's coming our way."

26

"I LOVE THIS old boat."

It took Hazel only ten minutes to cover the distance between her own dock and Fiskar Bay harbour. She sat up front, steering the *Julie Ann* with practised ease, Izzy at her side. Behind them was seating for four more people and a door that led down to a tiny galley and living quarters. The seats there folded down to make beds. Bill had bought the motorboat the first summer they had lived in Fiskar Bay. They had made family trips up and down the lake every year while Hazel was growing up. She'd liked being out on the water and hanging out on the dock with the other kids. Later, when she'd been in senior high, her dad had let her take the boat out herself. She'd invited a few friends along. That had been fun. But now the *Julie Ann* would have to go. Her mother planned to sell it along with the house.

"He named it for her," she said, rounding a point. "It's what he always called her." Now they faced the town, shining in the sunlight, banks of dark clouds rolling in behind it. "Mom never liked boating much, though, being stuck with all of us in close quarters. She always was glad to get home. So was Fern."

She reduced speed, brought the boat smoothly inside the harbour wall and steered it to the gas pump at the quay. There weren't many people around. Other boats were securely tied to their moorings. Fishing yawls lined one jetty and the larger fishing boats, including the one owned by Al Melnychuk, lay alongside another. The far side of the harbour had filled up with yachts, their masts pointing skyward. The harbourmaster himself manned the pump for her.

"Hazel!" he welcomed her. "Glad to see you out on the water." Then he noticed Izzy McBain.

"Just visiting," said Izzy. She didn't want word spreading that she was talking with members of the Gilchrist family. "Not many visitors hanging around, are there?" Often people walked the harbour and its seawall, sightseeing.

"They've gone home. Or to the pub. The yacht club's fairly busy. You don't want to be out there much longer today, Hazel. We're going to get a blow." A flicker of light lit up the purple clouds behind him, followed by a rumble. "Hear that?"

"Just going straight home. We'll make it okay," said Hazel as he unhooked the nozzle. She charged the cost of the gas. Her dad had set up the account years ago.

"I know someone who's interested in buying your boat," he said.

"I'll tell my mom and get back to you. Best be off right now." Hazel started up the motor again.

"You girls take care now." The harbourmaster waved them off. They heard another rumble as they chugged out of the shelter of the harbour. Izzy looked to the west. The thunderheads were moving closer to town.

"We'll beat it home," said Hazel. The sun still shone on the water. "I wish we didn't have to sell this boat. But I can't keep it."

"Fern won't want to have it?" asked Izzy.

"Don't think so. I don't think the Wiebes are much for boating. They're farming types."

They were almost at the end of a point. There was a cluster of houses along the shore. Some had lights on against the gathering gloom, but one family still sat on their dock, enjoying a beer. They were close enough to recognize the *Julie Ann*. Someone waved. Hazel waved back.

"I got along with your dad just fine when he was my boss," said Izzy.

"He was a good father, too."

"Fern didn't think so."

Izzy couldn't read Hazel's expression. Her face was shaded by her visor.

"Fern was an idiot." Hazel drove beyond the end of the point into open water. "Dad had put away money for both of us, to pay for university. She was smart at school. She didn't have to end up where she is, stuck out in the boonies, having one kid after another."

"Sounds like she didn't have much choice," said Izzy.

Hazel slowed the boat down so it bobbed on the water.

"Sure she did." She turned to face Izzy. "I heard them talking about it. Well, they were yelling. Dad and Fern. Couldn't help hearing them. She waited too long to tell them about the baby, so it was too late for her to get rid of it. But even then, she could have gone to Kenora, and had it there. Our aunt Sherry would have taken care of her. She offered. Fern could have put the kid up for adoption once she'd had it and gone off to university, like she'd always planned, but no. She was starry-eyed and all her friends thought it was so romantic. Seventeen and in love, what did she know?

"She was crazy about Cory and the Wiebes were all for it. She'd been to their church and she liked it, was hanging out with Cory's mom and his sisters. They convinced her that she shouldn't give it away. So she got married. They helped her sew her wedding dress. She asked me to be her bridesmaid. But Dad was adamant that we shouldn't go to the wedding. I'm not sure what all that was all about. But I did what I was told and I didn't go."

Izzy figured that the story about Cory attacking her hadn't reached Fern's younger sister. Hazel would have still been in junior high when that happened, in a different school. If she'd known that Cory had the potential to be violent she'd have said so.

A sudden gust rocked the boat. "Wind's turning." Hazel revved the engine. A mild southerly breeze had switched suddenly and now a strong wind from the northwest was whipping up the surface of the lake. The sun disappeared behind a bank of cloud and the air grew instantly colder. "This lake can turn mean on you. Let's get out of here."

FAT RAINDROPS SPLATTERED against Roxanne's windshield as she drove past Desna Church and the Kuryk farm. The sun had vanished into a growing mass of ominous clouds. A bolt of lightning lit the sky followed by a crack of thunder. It rumbled on as she reached the corner of Kuryk Road. She saw a few bouquets on the ground, the plastic Mountie standing at attention, the wooden cross propped up once more. They were going to get battered by this coming rain. It was already getting heavier. There was another flash of light and this time the thunder followed more quickly. The storm was getting closer, fast. She looked through the rain in the direction of the McKenzie farmhouse and saw a light at a window. Someone was there.

She shouldn't go banging on the door alone, she told herself. Not when she had insisted that her team should only investigate in pairs. But she could drive by and see if a car was in the driveway. The sky became dark, the gloom broken by the occasional flicker of lightning. The rain sheeted down, making it hard for her to see. She slowed the car to a crawl.

The house sat on a corner. Light forked across the sky and illuminated the scene enough for her to see a hatchback parked in the driveway. She crept past it, wishing she could turn on her headlights, but trying not to attract attention, glad that the noise of the storm would mask the sound of her car engine. On the north side, a stand of spruce trees sheltered the house. She reached the next corner, turned the car around, then drove back and stopped behind them. The rain battered down, but she could just see the light shining from a window. Someone was moving around inside.

Her phone buzzed. She took the call, still watching to see if she could identify the shadowy person inside.

"Julie Gilchrist just called," Aimee reported. "Izzy and her daughter, Hazel, went out on a boat. Now it's storming and they haven't made it back to Heron Haven. She hasn't heard from them, and she wondered if Izzy had been in touch."

"I got a text earlier saying they had gone out. Call the harbour-master and find out if they've docked there. Maybe we should alert the coast guard."

"I'll try," said Aimee. "Power's out in town."

"I'm on my way back. I'll go straight to the harbour and check it out." She bit her lip. She really wanted to know who was in that house. She drove slowly to the driveway and noted the number plate on the parked car as the lighting flashed again. She could contact Pete and Sam. See if they would check the number when they were done at Cullen Village. They were taking their time.

The rain was still teeming down when she reached Fiskar Bay. No one roamed the street or drove their cars in this deluge except her. Houses were lit within, some by flickering candles. The town's residents were tucked safely inside while the storm gathered force. The lights were on at the hospital. It had a generator. Ambulances stood in their bays, ready if needed. She glanced along the side road to the RCMP detachment as she passed. Lights glowed through the gloom. It had a generator too.

Roxanne's wipers were making hard work of it. She would nor-mally pull over in a torrent like this and wait for the thunderclouds to pass, but she drove steadily on down the street. She didn't have far to go now. A brilliant flash cracked its way across the sky. The thunder was incessant, the rain pounded on the roof of her car as the strength of the storm continued to mount. Roxanne hoped Izzy and Hazel Gilchrist were somewhere safe off the water. When she reached the lakeshore, she could see waves, whipped up by the wind, crashing high enough to surge over the top of the sea wall, built thick and strong to stand up to weather like this.

She crawled the car along the quay and parked it beside the harbourmaster's office. It was in darkness. She pushed her car door open and ran through the downpour to a portico. It didn't give much shelter. She tried the door. It was locked. The coast guard station sat nearby, beside a slipway down into the water of the harbour. A light shone through sheets of rain from above the doorway. They must have a power source too, but no one answered when she hammered on the door. She scurried back to the car, grateful to get back under cover, rubbed the rainwater from her face and called Izzy's number again. Still no answer.

Aimee answered her next call. She hadn't heard from Izzy either. She'd left a message for the harbourmaster, but he hadn't got back to her.

"Do you know what the Gilchrists' boat looks like?" Roxanne asked. Aimee did. She'd seen it last summer. The hull was blue and it was called the *Julie Ann*. Roxanne decided she'd check the boats in the harbour before she raised the alarm. There weren't many this early in the year. It wouldn't take long. Maybe the *Julie Ann* was rocking at its berth, and Hazel and Izzy were somewhere safe but, still, she was worried. Wouldn't Izzy have had the sense to let people know she was okay?

The rain still poured down. The next lightning flash was straight overhead. The storm would soon move out over the lake. The waves crashed, louder and higher. She jogged past the wharf where the fishing yawls were moored and out onto the next one where some motorboats were docked. Wooden slats clattered under her feet. She concentrated on keeping to the centre of the walkway, maintaining her balance as she read the name on each prow. There was no *Julie Ann*.

She picked her way back carefully. She was soaked and glad to get back onto firm ground. A wind had picked up. Rain battered her face. A few more boats of varying sizes were moored along the jetty that lined the seawall. She should go check them out.

Roxanne was still on the quay when she saw car lights coming from the town toward her. Someone else had ventured out in this storm. Two roads approached the harbour, one at each end. One led straight to the seawall. The vehicle was driving down it, fast, given the conditions. She expected it to slow. It didn't. It was coming toward her and it didn't reduce its speed. She realized it was coming straight for her.

She turned and ran out along the concrete jetty away from the oncoming lights. The car wasn't slowing. It was accelerating. The seawall formed a solid barricade on her left. The jetty ran ahead in a sweeping curve wide enough to take a vehicle. Roxanne raced on against the wind, feet slapping through puddles, rain blinding her. The driver behind her wasn't slowing down. The car lights shone through the streaming rain. Her moving shadow elongated as the vehicle closed in on her.

She could almost hear the engine through the raindrops battering the pavement, the waves crashing over the top of the seawall. She turned abruptly to her right. Two steps took her to the side of the jetty. She put one foot onto the low barricade that edged it, pushed off and jumped.

The water was deep and freezing cold. She sank down into the darkness, closing her eyes, trying to hold her breath, swallowing oily water despite herself. Then she bobbed up to the surface and spewed it out. Chilled, she needed to find a way out. She had landed between two boats, lucky not to have hit a deck hard. She brushed water from her eyes, spat out another mouthful of acrid water, and trod in place. She could see small red lights flickering on the jetty above her and heard a loud bang. The truck had backed up, maybe hit something. It didn't stop, though. It moved forward and backed up again. It was turning around. Would it drive off? Or would the driver come looking for her, searching to see if she came out of the water? She could try to make for one of the wharfs at the other side of the harbour and hope that whoever it was didn't see her. She couldn't stay where she was in this deadly cold. Her teeth were chattering.

A beam of light to her right cut through the grey miasma. Then another. She heard voices. Someone was shining a flashlight from the deck of the *Becky*, the big research vessel, berthed further along the jetty. "Over here!" she tried to yell. "I'm in the water." Her voice wavered she was so cold. Two beams of light met over the water like spotlights. A dark shadow moved on the gangplank to the boat. The truck drove away fast, back down the jetty to the quay and up the road into town. A lifebelt splashed to her right.

"Grab that!" a loud voice hollered. Roxanne mustered enough strength to paddle toward it. Within seconds she was hauled out of the ice-cold harbour. James Featherstone ran down the gangplank of the *Becky*, carrying a blanket. There were more voices. One of them was Al Melnychuk's. "It's Calloway? That woman cop?"

"How did you land up in there?" Featherstone asked as he wrapped the blanket around her. "Did you swallow much of that water?"

"Whack her on the back," said Melnychuk.

"You saw that truck? The one that drove away?" Roxanne gasped.

"Sure did," Al Melnychuk growled. "I'd just gone up on deck to check the weather. Saw the lights and watched you jump. It was a Ford Ranger, grey. Y'know who's got one just like it? That Kathy Isfeld that works for you. It belonged to her old man. Is it her that's out to get you?"

27

AL MELNYCHUK AND a couple of his friends from the Fishermen's Association had been aboard the *Becky* in earnest discussion with the lake conservationists when the storm struck.

"We'd as soon ride it out here as stuck in a house. And we could keep an eye on things in the harbour. Just as well we did and were able to fish you out, eh?" he said, brewing up a mug of cocoa. "Want a shot of rum in this? You look like you could use it."

Roxanne had stopped shivering. She was wrapped in blankets, a heater blasting warmth at her feet. There was a gym bag in the trunk of her car with clothes in it, she told them. Her car keys were still in the pocket of her sodden jacket. One of the fishermen had gone over to the quay to fetch the bag so she could change. He drove her car back to where the *Becky* was moored and deftly parked it so it faced back along the jetty.

"Not like that idiot that tried to run you down. Smacked a capstan real good trying to turn that truck around. The back end's got to be marked up."

Al had come up on deck to see how the storm was doing and heard a bang, seen the truck turning around in a hurry. He'd called down below to let the others know something was going on. They'd brought up flashlights and heard Roxanne holler. And they'd seen the red tail lights vanish off into town.

Her phone hadn't survived its immersion. She radioed from the boat while she sipped the boozy cocoa, instructed Jeff Riordan and Rick Peters to call round to Kathy Isfeld's house. It only took them minutes to get there. In the garage was a grey-coloured Ford

Ranger. It was old, had a few scratches and dents but the scrape marks on the back bumper were recent. And it was wet. Kathy had been playing cribbage with her granddaughter when they arrived. Sigrid had looked on in consternation as they tucked her grandmother into the back of the police car.

Pete Robinson had arrived back at the detachment. They had heard nothing yet from Izzy. She and Hazel could have got caught in a squall and pulled in somewhere to ride out the storm. She might be out of cellphone range. There were dead spots up and down the lakeshore where service didn't reach.

"I'll be right there," she told him. She downed the rest of the cocoa and went off to a cabin to change. She needed a shower, badly, to get rid of the oily feel that remained on her skin, but that would have to wait. She ran her fingers through her damp hair, emerged in a T-shirt and sweats, runners on her feet, thanked the men who had rescued her and got back to work.

KATHY ISFELD DENIED everything. She drooped in her chair, full of reproach. How could they imagine she would try to kill anyone, far less members of the RCMP, she who was almost one of them, who had worked all these years, long and hard on their behalf? Jeff Riordan sat beside Roxanne, taking notes. The recorder emitted a faint buzz. The room was grey, lit by harsh fluorescent strips bleaching colour from their faces.

"My son borrowed the truck earlier today." She spoke so quietly, her chin tucked down between her shoulders, that they could barely hear her. "He'd trimmed dead branches off a couple of trees. Needed to take them to the dump. He left the Ranger in the driveway when he was done. It got rained on before I put it away. I got wet too." She raised a hand and smoothed back her hair. She'd dented the back of the truck herself, not long ago, trying to back it into the garage.

"I'm not very good at driving backwards. I clipped the edge of the garage door." The truck had belonged to her husband. She'd kept it after he died, ten years ago. It was useful to have around. Her son used it sometimes, and one of the neighbours.

"You know what this town's like, Roxanne." She whimpered like a fretful little chipmunk. "It'll be all over the place that you've brought me in for questioning. They'll say I did it, even though I didn't. Mud sticks. They won't let me forget this. I'll never live this down."

Tears glistened on pale eyelashes magnified by her glasses. Jeff pushed a box of tissues toward her. She took the glasses off, dabbed at her eyes and blew her nose.

"You shouldn't be wasting time sitting here. You need to be out there, finding whoever it was that tried to kill you. And Bill."

"Let's take a break," said Roxanne. This was going nowhere. Either Kathy was completely innocent or she was an accomplished liar. Her truck had probably been involved in the attack on Roxanne, but had Kathy? They didn't have enough evidence to pin the murders on her, but they would hold her for now. Jeff led her to a cell.

"Do you really have to put me in there?" she protested as he led her down the corridor.

The cell next door was occupied. Steve Rice sat on the bunk, his hands clasped at his knees. He looked up balefully as they passed. Pete Robinson had locked him inside.

"He assaulted his wife. She's the one who called us."

"Really?" Roxanne stretched her arms above her head. She could smell the brackish water of the harbour when she moved. It brought back the memory of that freezing cold and made her shudder. "He's a counsellor. Supposed to help people. I wouldn't have thought he was the violent sort. You've charged him?"

"For now. You know what it's like. Sometimes wives change their minds. But we've also got him for theft."

The fight between the Rices had started because Susan had searched her husband's briefcase while he was out cutting grass before the storm hit. He'd bought a new iPad for himself. She had wondered where he was getting the money. He'd also ordered some books he wanted. They didn't have much cash to spare. Counselling and teaching yoga barely covered their costs. So she had been suspicious and she had gone looking. Snooping, her husband had called it. She had found an envelope with money and uncashed cheques in it. Margo Wishart had written one of them. Susan had called her. The cheque was for the Sunnywell Centre, Margo had said. She hadn't filled in the name because she'd been told they had a stamp and she was in a hurry.

When Steve came into the house, Susan had confronted him. The argument had escalated. He'd threatened her before, but he'd never actually hit her until now. The side of her face was still red when Pete had talked to her. Steve had backhanded her, hard.

"I'm not safe with him, officer," she had said, the rain pelting down outside, Sam Mendes guarding her husband at the doorway behind the hanging bead curtain, her children huddled on the sofa. They had heard every word, the sound of the hit and their mother yelling. Susan never yelled. She wanted him gone and a restraining order taken out against him.

"So, Lex McKenzie didn't steal that money," said Roxanne. "Someone needs to go check if it's him that's in their old farm-house. He needs to know about this." She'd already dispatched Rick to have a closer look at the back of Kathy Isfeld's truck. It was going to be picked up later by Ident, but she wanted to find out more about it now.

"Kathy?" Pete Robinson shook his head in disbelief. "Surely not. She's been here forever. We trust her. Don't we?"

Izzy McBain banged through the door. "You should have seen the waves out there! Freaky. Hazel pulled in at a dock. The cottage there was still closed up, but we waited out the storm inside the boat." She leaned against the front counter and chattered on, eager to tell what had happened to her, unaware of the new develop-ments. There had been no cellphone connection while she'd been stranded.

"Hazel says she thinks her dad was seeing someone on the side," she said. "We opened a bottle of gin and played rummy, down inside that boat. Gin's not my drink but Hazel sure likes it. She got pretty chatty. She says her dad often used to stay out late. It happened a lot on Wednesdays. He never said where he'd been and her mother seemed to be quite happy to spend the evening stitching and go off to bed with a book. I drove the boat back to their place after the storm passed because she'd drunk too much. That was fun."

Rick Peters radioed in from the car. The back bumper of Kathy's truck was equipped to take a trailer hitch. He'd found particles of paint on it that hadn't been washed away by the downpour. The particles were bright blue. Kathy's garage was painted a darker, duller shade. Her son had shown up, wanting to know what was going on. Said his daughter was upset. What was happening with his mother?

"Run by the harbour and have a look at the capstans," said Roxanne. "They're painted blue, aren't they?" They were. Royal blue, Izzy said. "Check the colour and see if there's marks on the one that's about halfway between the quay and the *Becky*."

"Y'know what? Kathy and Bill Gilchrist were real good pals," said Izzy, once she heard what had happened. "Do you think it was her that he was seeing?"

"Kathy? Seriously?"

"Sure. Why not? Her old man's been gone for years and she's never dated anybody else that I know of. Maybe Julie knows more than she's letting on."

"Let's go ask her," said Roxanne Calloway.

JULIE HAD FED her daughter hot soup and warm bread to try to sober her up and suggested she go to bed, but Roxanne and Izzy arriving on police business put paid to that.

"Come on, Mom," Hazel protested when Julie insisted that her husband could not possibly have been in a relationship with Kathy Isfeld. "She was soft on him. You said so yourself. I heard you talking to Dad when we were having a barbecue for all the cops. You told him you thought she was a bit smitten. Your words exactly." She wiggled a finger in the direction of her mother, still quite drunk.

"I don't think I ever said that!"

"You did. And he was always over at her place visiting."

"He went to see her husband. They needed help," Julie explained to the two policewomen sitting opposite. "Joe had cancer. He was sick for two years before he died. It was hard on Kathy. She did like Bill. I knew that, but he always said they were just good friends." She paused. "I never imagined he'd go for someone like Kathy. I thought it would be someone younger."

"You knew? That Dad was having an affair?" Hazel rested her hands on the table and dropped her head onto them. She sniggered.

"Well, it is possible." Julie avoided looking at her daughter. "Bill and I stopped having relations like that years ago. He reminded me now and then that he had 'needs' but I just wasn't interested anymore. I wanted us to sleep in separate beds. Sometimes I made up a bed for myself in the studio. I told him I needed to get away from his snoring."

"This is more than I need to know," commented Hazel. She was getting groggy but was still too interested to doze off.

"Funny thing is," Julie addressed Roxanne, ignoring her drunken daughter, "we'd got together again. Back in Arizona. I guess all that time in a trailer by ourselves did it. We were back to being a couple, and now he's dead." She took in a very deep breath and let it out slowly.

"You still needed to get away from him, soon as you got back here," Roxanne pointed out.

"Well, yes." She shrugged. "But we would probably have stayed together."

"Do you know if there was anyone else he might have been seeing, before then, back here in the Interlake?"

Julie shook her head. "No," she said. "I never asked. Never wanted to know. There was a girl constable once. I thought he was interested in her but she's long gone. Maybe there wasn't just one. Maybe there were several."

"You've no idea who they might be?"

"No," said Julie. "And I still don't want to know."

ROXANNE DROVE THE now familiar road to the highway and turned toward Fiskar Bay. It had grown dark.

"I just thought it was a power thing, to do with work, when Sergeant Bill made that move on me," said Izzy. "I didn't take it seriously. Maybe I should have." The car lights lit a road sign at the entrance to the Ukrainian summer camp. "You know that Kathy Isfeld isn't Icelandic?" she asked. "She's Ukrainian."

"She looks like she's an Icelander. Her hair's blonde. Blue eyes. Those even features."

"Sure," said Izzy. "And she might have some Icelandic in her. But she married an Isfeld, that's how she got the name. Before she was married, her name was Hnatiuk. So was Netta Kuryk's. They're cousins. Bet they both went to Desna Church when they were kids. Maybe Kathy still goes out there sometimes and helps. Want me to go talk to Netta and find out?"

Roxanne looked at the time on the dash. It was too late for that tonight. "I need to go to your place and pick up Finn. Maybe tomorrow we'll nail this case."

28

IT WAS SUNDAY morning and the sun shone once more on Fiskar Bay. Day trippers were beginning to straggle in, and the merchants of the town were preparing to welcome them. Store windows had been shined and by the afternoon the doors would be open. It was no day of rest for them.

Nor was it for the RCMP. Kathy Isfeld's son showed up at the detachment first thing, demanding to know if his mother had been charged with anything. If not, they should let her go.

"We can hold her for twenty-four hours," Jeff Riordan had informed him. John Isfeld was taller than he, blond and solid, a clean-shaven Viking. He faced Jeff across the counter, grim-faced.

"Right," he said. "I'm gonna go find us a lawyer. You don't talk to her again until after he's seen her."

Now Kathy was back in the grey, harshly lit interview room with the humming lights. Jeff was at Roxanne's side once more. Izzy was off to a McBain family christening. One of her brother's kids was being baptized and her mother wasn't taking no for an answer.

"What's with that job of yours that you can't have a Sunday off?" she had asked.

"It's a murder investigation," Izzy had protested.

"So Sergeant Calloway can manage without you for a change!"

Matt had gone too, and said he'd take Finn with him. "There'll be other kids there that he can play with afterwards," he had said. He planned to stick around. He liked family events, he said.

"I have to go the ceremony, but then I'll duck out," Izzy had grouched to Roxanne on the phone, annoyed at missing out, just as the case seemed to be moving toward a conclusion.

Derek McVicar had been the go-to lawyer in Fiskar Bay most of his professional life. He did wills, house sales, divorces. Occasionally he was brought in to support an accused client, but that was rare. He had certainly never been asked to advise someone suspected of multiple murders. And he seldom worked on weekends. His was a nine-to-five weekday practice, and this case was taking him away from a meeting at the yacht club to discuss the first regatta of the season. One of the sailboats in the harbour was his. He was in his sixties, approaching retirement, once a tall man, now beginning to shrink, and he'd lost his hair years ago.

"If in doubt, say nothing," he had advised his client. Roxanne suspected he was seriously out of his depth.

When did Kathy go home yesterday afternoon? She had left the detachment just after Roxanne had spoken to Aimee Vermette about Izzy being out on a boat in that storm. She'd intended to stay and work some more but she needed to get home and make sure everything was shut and tied down; she would run along the lane before the rain got worse. Aimee had said she'd be okay on her own. Pete Robinson had been in touch and would be back before long. The power had been out. Sigrid had come right over to keep her company. Kathy had said that she would be okay by herself: she had candles and her phone was charged, but Sigrid had said no, she was staying anyway. She was a good girl, Sigrid. Kathy looked at her lawyer for assurance. He smiled blandly back.

There were traces of blue paint on the back bumper of her Ford Ranger truck. They didn't match the paint on her garage, but it was exactly like the colour of the capstans at the seawall jetty. And one of those was scratched. How had the paint got there?

Kathy didn't know. Other people borrowed the truck. Like her neighbour. He was one of those guys that liked to sit at the seawall with a rod and line and fish away an afternoon. Maybe he'd banged one of those capstans.

"Do you ever attend services at Desna Church?" asked Roxanne.

She did, she'd been going there since she was a little girl. She had sung in the choir, back when they had one. Roxanne wondered if Kathy's singing voice had been any louder than the one she spoke with. It was still hard to hear what she was saying. Kathy's father had helped build that church, she said with some pride. Her parents were buried in the churchyard nearby.

"You were there on the Sunday, April 1st?"

"April Fool's Day?" Kathy remarked without a hint of humour. She had been at the church that afternoon. She'd helped polish the pews and wash the windows.

"And then?" asked Roxanne.

"And then what?" Kathy whispered. "I went home. I took dishes with me that needed washing. Heating up water at the church takes forever."

"How well did you know Bill Gilchrist?"

Kathy blinked, not once but twice. Her lawyer looked puzzled. "I worked alongside him. And he was a friend."

"How good a friend?"

"What are you trying to say, Roxanne Calloway?"

"Were you and Bill Gilchrist more than friends? Were you in a relationship?"

"I don't know who's put that idea into your head," Kathy protested. "I'm surprised at you, Roxanne. I thought better of you than that, listening to bad gossip." She sat back in her chair. "Do I need to answer any more of these questions?" she demanded of Derck McVicar.

He sighed, any hope of making it to the yacht club rapidly evaporating. He needed to consult with his client, he said. Perhaps someone could provide them with some coffee?

"how's it going?" said Pete Robinson.

"She's stubborn." But Roxanne had noted how quickly Kathy had shut down the interview when the topic of her relationship with Bill Gilchrist had come up.

Pete had let Steve Rice go. He'd have a date in court and he'd promised to attend. He'd been warned not to approach his wife. She had emergency numbers to call, just in case, but this was the weekend, when shelters for battered women filled up fast. Pete thought she'd be okay, though. She had relatives in town and friends in the area. And he believed that Steve Rice would keep his distance.

Lex had not been at the McKenzie house. The third brother, Paul, had been staying there, taking a weekend break with his wife and kids. She had been bustling around, tutting about the state the house was in. No one knew where Lex had gone. He must have known that some money had been stolen from the Sunnywell Centre, that he'd be suspected of taking it, and he'd done a runner. He was innocent of the theft, but he had broken his parole. That was too bad.

Izzy showed up, dressed in an unfamiliar skirt and jacket, her hair fastened at the back of her head. She wore high heels. They made her taller than Roxanne. "What have I missed?" she asked.

"Nothing much," Roxanne replied. "It almost certainly was Kathy's Ranger that was used to chase me down last night, but it might not have been her driving. And she's saying nothing about her and Bill Gilchrist being in a relationship. Her granddaughter, Sigrid, was with her last night. She might know something. Maybe we should go ask her."

She and Izzy walked along the back lane behind the detachment toward Kathy Isfeld's house. Her son lived across the road, the next street from Roxanne's own house. Izzy had swapped her heels for a pair of white sneakers. With the skirt, she managed to look sporty, as if she belonged on the golf course. Buds had opened on the trees after last night's downpour; the grass was a fresh green, and the birds were singing. Large brown paper bags full of garden debris were beginning to pile up behind some garages ready for garbage pickup the following day. Spring cleanup was well under way.

John Isfeld and his wife, Melanie, had bought their house almost twenty years ago and made extensive renovations. It looked spanking new.

"What are you here for?" John asked the instant he opened the door.

"We need to ask your daughter a few questions."

"What about?"

"We just need her help. Is she home?"

"You're not talking to her without me and her mother present." He blocked the doorway, not inviting them in.

"We could go and do this at the detachment," Roxanne said. "But it doesn't need to be formal. Just a chat."

He grudgingly opened the door wider. "Well, then," he said, then called out, "Mel, Sigrid, we've got company."

The three Isfelds sat in a row on a large leather sofa, Sigrid in the middle, guarded by a parent on either side. A long coffee table separated them from the straight-backed chairs that had been provided for Roxanne and Izzy. Sigrid, Roxanne's one-time babysitter, avoided looking at her. She had long blonde hair, straight as a die, high cheekbones set in a wide face with slightly almond-shaped eyes. Roxanne glanced at Izzy: Sigrid's face was thinner, more like Kathy's, but Izzy would have looked a bit like this when she was seventeen. They were of the same ethnic mix, Icelandic with a dash of Ukrainian. Interlakers, born and bred.

"You're close to your grandmother, Sigrid?" Roxanne began.

"My amma? Sure I am."

"You spend a lot of time at her house?"

"John's mother took care of Sigrid after school." Melanie interrupted before Sigrid could reply. "I work at the hotel. I'm often there at nights." She managed the restaurant, had done so for years. Sigrid had gone to an after-school program, the same one that Finn attended, when she was younger, and Kathy had picked her up after work. For a couple of years, when her husband had been sick, Kathy had worked part-time, so she'd been home more. Then, she'd been available to pick her granddaughter up as soon as school was out. Later, Sigrid had walked over to Kathy's house by herself. Since junior high she'd had a key so she could let herself in.

"Did Sergeant Gilchrist visit the house often?"

"Of course he did. Lots of people dropped by." Melanie answered again.

"Bill Gilchrist helped my parents a lot when my dad was sick," John explained. "I was commuting in and out of Winnipeg. Mel had her job to get to. It was a hard time for everyone. He became a good friend. To us all. Why are you asking Sigrid about this?"

"I need Sigrid to answer for herself," Roxanne replied.

Sigrid still avoided catching her eye, but now she flashed Roxanne a resentful look, unfamiliarly cold. "It's all right, Dad, let me speak to her. I can't believe you've got Amma locked up." Roxanne was used to Sigrid being pleasant, always smiling and accommodating. She'd never seen her resentful. "She's worked for the RCMP for years. Way longer than you have. You know that she's a good person. She couldn't have killed Sergeant Gilchrist. He'd been her friend as well as her boss for years."

"How often did Sergeant Gilchrist visit your grandmother?"

"He dropped round sometimes, just to see how she was doing. Wednesdays, usually. That's all."

"They were close?"

"Nothing like that!" Sigrid responded, screwing up her nose in scorn. "She just kind of depended on him to help her out. Mom and dad were so busy."

Roxanne had noticed how well-maintained the house was. It gleamed. It was dusted, vacuumed and polished. A large TV screen dominated one wall. Two shiny SUVs were parked outside. The clothes the family wore were new and of good quality. The Isfeld parents must work hard to provide this well for themselves. They probably needed both salaries. Earning them must have been a priority, even when John's father had suffered through a long illness and left Kathy a widow when she was barely fifty.

"They were just friends. What's wrong with that?" Sigrid asked, her voice rising in annoyance.

"She must have missed him when he went away to Arizona for the winter."

"You'll have to ask her that yourself," Sigrid shot back.

"Do you ever drive your grandmother's truck?"

Three pairs of eyes stared across the low table. Three mouths opened to speak.

"Let Sigrid answer," Roxanne told them again.

Sigrid hesitated before she replied. "I know how. Amma thought I should be able to drive a stick shift. She taught me."

"Sigrid was here last night," John interjected quickly, anticipating the next question. "We all were. The storm broke, then Sigrid went across the back lane to her grandmother's. Kathy was home the whole time. She never went out. I put that old Ranger into the garage for her. In the rain. We were all here, right through that storm."

Roxanne wasn't surprised that John Isfeld knew that the RCMP was interested in his mother's truck. He must know that Rick Peters had examined it yesterday. But why did he think he, his daughter and his mother needed alibis?

Roxanne excused herself and Izzy, so they could talk. John Isfeld ushered them out the door.

"What do you think?" she asked Izzy. They'd closed the gate behind them and were standing in the lane.

"John and Mel know more than they're letting on. Maybe Sigrid too. That's why they keep jumping in and answering for her."

"So, what are they covering up?"

They turned down a street shaded with large old elms. Those wouldn't be with them much longer. Dutch elm disease was ravaging them, but for now they canopied the road.

"If Netta Kuryk is one of that family, too," Roxanne said, "she might have known if Kathy was driving the Ranger that Sunday when Bill may have died."

Izzy shook her head. "Why would Kathy not be driving her car? The Chevy? That's what she always drives. She's had that truck for years and I've never seen it. It sounds like it's only kept for jobs that need it, and those are usually done by her son. Or a neighbour."

"Sigrid knows how to drive it."

"Sure." Izzy nodded. "And having a set of wheels matters when you're seventeen. Maybe she uses it sometimes. But you don't think she's got something to do with this?"

"Not really. I'm just fishing around for an answer. Something is missing here."

They passed by the street where Roxanne lived and continued toward the lake. The sun was beating down and deck chairs were scattered on the beach. A few brave souls had ventured into the water. The air might be warm, but Roxanne knew first-hand just how close to freezing the lake was.

"So, we know that Sergeant Bill was out on Kuryk Road weekend of April 1st and was run down in a truck like the Ranger." Izzy strode along the wooden boardwalk, the rubber soles of her shoes slapping the planks.

"It's pretty evident that Kathy's Ranger is our murder weapon," Roxanne agreed, striding along beside her, glad of the exercise.

"And we know that Kathy was at Desna Church that afternoon." Izzy stopped suddenly. "We never did find out what happened to Sergeant Bill's phone, did we?"

"Good point," said Roxanne. "Let's go do some more asking."

29

NETTA KURYK WAS not at home, nor was her husband, but a red pickup was parked outside Desna Church. The side door to the building was unlocked and Netta was inside. She liked to visit on a Sunday, even when there wasn't a service, she said, putting a broom back in a closet. She tidied up a bit while she was here. Old places like this needed keeping up. The interior of the church showed evidence of her care. The pews were old and worn but they glowed with a soft patina. The altar was covered with an embroidered cloth and bore an ornate gilded cross and tall candlesticks with thick wax candles. Behind it was a table on which sat the tabernacle, made to look like a miniature church, complete with onion domes on each corner and a tall one in the middle. It was brightly painted and gilded, as was a three-panelled screen along the back wall.

"You were here the weekend before your Easter celebrations?" Roxanne asked, looking at the three icons displayed on the screen, Mary, Jesus and a saint she didn't recognize. They appeared dim in the light that filtered through the tall clean windows above, but their golden haloes glowed.

"I was." Netta walked to a large cast-iron wood stove. She touched its cold black surface. There wasn't a speck of ash to be seen. "I used to sit beside this when I was a little girl. It would get so hot my legs were scorched by the end of the service."

"Your cousin Kathy Isfeld was here too?"

"Sometimes. She used to sit beside me."

"Not then. The Sunday at the beginning of April."

Netta removed her hand from the old stove. "She wasn't here for long. Why are you asking about Kathy?"

So, any rumour about the incident at the harbour in Fiskar Bay the previous night and the RCMP taking Kathy in for questioning had not yet reached Netta.

"Do you remember exactly when she left that day?"

"Some time in the afternoon. She got here right after lunch. The dishes in the kitchen needed to be washed so we could use them Easter weekend. We always do a lunch after the service. We boxed them and loaded them into her truck. Heating water here is a hassle so she took them home so she could run them through her dishwasher."

"She was driving her truck? The Ford Ranger?"

"Sure," said Netta. "Her granddaughter, Sigrid, had borrowed her car so she could go into Winnipeg with a bunch of her friends. They were going shopping for grad stuff. Sigrid sometimes drives that old truck but that day she needed the extra seats."

Izzy stood at the doorway that led into a small kitchen. Behind her was a row of cupboards above a counter. Stacked white dishes were visible through their glass doors.

"When did Kathy bring the dishes back?" she asked.

Netta's jaw clamped shut.

"Was it later that day?" asked Roxanne. "And was Bill Gilchrist with her?"

Netta looked at the icons on the screen behind the altar. She focused her narrow eyes on the one at the centre, a portrait of Jesus, his fingers raised as if he were blessing her. Roxanne waited. Netta sat down on a side pew, one broad hand fingering the hem of the opposite sleeve.

"I always told her it wasn't right. That it would lead to trouble," she said after a moment. Her lips compressed once more, then she took a breath and looked from Roxanne to Izzy and back again.

"I was the only person still here. It was after five and I was waiting for her to bring the dishes back. I didn't expect her to show up with him. He carried the boxes in for her and I could see that she was pleased. They were acting like they were a real couple. But of course they weren't. He still had that wife of his at home. They were just pretending. Kathy was just fooling herself. Like always.

"They didn't stay long. Just left the boxes on the counter, then they drove off together like they had somewhere to go. I didn't watch them leave. I got busy putting the dishes away."

"You never asked her what had happened, after his body was found in your ditch?" Roxanne asked quietly.

"No, I did not. That's all that I can tell you." Netta rose to her feet and made to leave.

"Where's the phone, Netta?" Izzy remained in the doorway, blocking her way.

"What phone?"

"Did you find it? Lying out on the road?" Roxanne asked.

"I did not," she replied, enunciating each word.

"Then did Stan? Your husband?"

"You leave my Stan out of this."

"If you won't tell us, we will have to ask him."

Netta was stuck in the middle, Izzy on one side of her, Roxanne on the other. She blew air out between her teeth in a steady hiss, like a deflating balloon.

"All right, all right," she said. "I'll tell you. But don't you go bothering Stan." She looked back at the row of icons, like she was checking in with Jesus and Mary to make sure that what she was going to say was okay. Then she walked over and sat back down on the pew again.

"It was the Tuesday. Stan went for a drive around, just to make sure that everything was fine before that big snowstorm blew in. Came back pretty shook up and said that there was a dead body out on Kuryk Road. He knew who it was. And I knew Gilchrist had been with Kathy on the Sunday. I told Stan to leave things be for now, that the snow would cover him up soon, we might as

well wait and let nature take its course. Best keep our noses out
of trouble.

"I did go look, before it got dark. Gilchrist was long gone. The
ravens had taken out his eyes and the coyotes had been by. I'd
heard them, middle of the night before, yipping their heads off
and wondered what they'd found. I said a prayer for him. I did
do that." She looked up at the image of Mary, like she was letting
her know. "And I left him there. By morning he was buried deep
in snow. I didn't tell anyone. Except Kathy. I called her after Stan
had gone to sleep, so he wouldn't hear. She didn't tell me what had
happened and how Bill Gilchrist got there and I didn't ask her.
None of my business, was it? She asked me to leave things be and
I said I'd already done that, hadn't I. I didn't promise I wouldn't
tell, but I'd known about her and Gilchrist all these years and I'd
kept her secret, so I supposed she just assumed I'd do the same
this time. But it didn't sit well with me. Not that. Blood's blood
but there are limits."

"Did you or Stan find the phone?"

Netta shook her big head slowly, side to side.

"There was no phone," she said.

KATHY ISFELD READ through Netta's statement. The lawyer was
back at her side, any hope of making it to the yacht club in time
for the meeting gone. Kathy looked weary.

"I never thought Netta would tell," she said.

"She was at Desna Church," said Izzy.

"That would do it." Kathy lifted her eyes from the paper in her
hand. "She never did approve of me and Bill seeing each other like
that when he was still married. And she really believes in everything
the priest says. She wouldn't be able to tell a lie in front of Jesus." Her
eyes slid in Roxanne's direction. "You got lucky, finding her there at
the church. And again when those guys hauled you out of the water."

This time there was no mistaking the loathing in her voice.
Roxanne realized that Kathy Isfeld had wanted her dead. She was

shocked. She had never imagined that Kathy disliked her. "Tell us what happened," she said.

"Sure, you might as well know." Kathy sat back on the upright chair, averting her eyes from Roxanne and Izzy.

"We should have a word," her lawyer intervened, but she brushed him off.

"Let me be," she said. She told her story more to Izzy than to Roxanne. "Bill didn't call me. I knew they'd arrived back in Fiskar Bay that Friday. I thought I'd hear from him, that he'd be around that Saturday, but not a word. I waited for him. I thought he'd be dying to see me. We'd never been apart for so long before.

"I liked him right away, you know. Even when I was still married to Joe. We didn't do much about it at first. Behaved ourselves all that time that Joe was dying. It gave us time to get to know each other better. Well, I thought so. Maybe I got that wrong." The narrow line of her mouth twisted at a crooked angle.

"He didn't have much of a marriage. Not in the proper sense. But he couldn't leave Julie Ann. That was what he always called her, you know. Said he couldn't abandon her, that she needed him, that she couldn't cope on her own. She'd had to give up teaching because she couldn't handle it when those rowdy teenage boys started taking home ec. And he didn't mind if she didn't work. He got his sergeant stripes and paid for everything while she sat in her room and sewed. 'She's not strong like you, Kathy,' he told me.

"I thought I was the one that he really cared about. All those years. 'I'll stay in Fiskar Bay when I retire, Kathy,' he said, 'so I'll always be near you.' He told me it was Julie who really wanted to go south for the winter, but now I'm not so sure. Maybe I got that wrong, too.

"He stayed in touch by email when he was in Arizona, but it wasn't often. He said it was hard to get time alone. He sent a message just before they left saying he was on his way home. I thought that he meant back home to me.

"But it wasn't. It was late on Sunday afternoon before he showed up. I'd brought all the dishes back from Desna Church, the ones they'd need for a lunch the following week. They needed a good wash so I'd run them through the washer. I was loading them back into the truck when he finally appeared. I don't drive the Ranger often, but Sigrid had borrowed my car. I'd told Netta that I'd be back at the church by five to return the clean dishes before she locked up. I couldn't call her to let her know I'd be late. Netta doesn't have a cellphone. Stan's too cheap to pay for one.

"'That's okay. I'll come along for the ride and give you a hand,' Bill said. That made me happy. I thought it meant he didn't mind being seen out and about with me. That maybe we didn't need to keep things a secret anymore. The women who'd been helping us clean at the church had said that Julie had taken off on him soon as she got back to Fiskar Bay. I thought maybe that was why I hadn't heard from him yet. A lot must have been happening. They were finally splitting up and he was going to tell me that.

"He sat beside me in the truck while I drove and told me that Julie wanted to leave him. She knew about me. Well, she didn't know it was me, but she knew there was someone. And she'd hated Arizona. 'I don't get it,' he said. 'But I guess Julie Ann's not the sociable kind. And there's a lot of visiting goes on at the trailer park. She just couldn't hack it.'

"'So,' he said, 'she's got this idea in her head that she's going to take off on me. Go live with her sister in Kelowna.' And I thought, it's true! This is it. The marriage is over. He really has come back to me.

"We'd reached the church by then, and Netta came right out the door to say hello, so he stopped talking about it. I was so happy—there was Bill carrying those heavy boxes of china through to the kitchen for me. Netta saw me smiling. 'You're in a good mood,' she said. But she didn't look like she was pleased to see us together. 'Look at her, giving me the evil eye,' Bill said when we got back to the truck. We laughed about that.

"We were just driving out of the church gate when he said, 'I'm not letting Julie Ann leave me.' It was like I'd been stabbed with a shard of ice, one that freezes your heart, like in an old fairy tale. I kept driving, along past Stan and Netta's farm, in the opposite direction from home, so we'd have more time to talk. I needed to listen to what he had to say. I turned onto Kuryk Road and stopped driving so I could pay attention.

"He was going to tell Julie that he would move to B.C. with her, if that was what she wanted. That they'd sell the house at Heron Haven and the trailer in Arizona. Look for somewhere on Vancouver Island, if that was where she wanted to go. Or in the Interior. Somewhere with a room where she could have a studio so she could carry on making those quilts of hers and a golf course nearby so he could get out of her hair sometimes.

"He was going to leave me. Break his promise to always stay close, to always come back to me. And he sounded so damned pleased about it.

"'Get out,' I said to him. 'Get out of my truck.'

"'What, here?' He looked surprised; can you believe it? 'My car's back at your place,' he said.

"'You can walk,' I told him. 'I never want to see your face again.'

"And it was like he didn't care. That it didn't matter one little bit. 'Okay, Kathy,' he said, just like that, and he got out. Walked off along the road and took out his phone.

"I reached him before he had time to talk to anyone. He heard me coming. The engine must have been really loud. I pushed my foot right to the floor. He turned to look and I hit him so hard that he flew off the front of the truck toward the ditch. And I drove away. I didn't look back."

Derek McVicar drew in a breath and leaned forward, about to protest.

"Where were you the night Ken Roach died?" Roxanne asked before he could speak.

Kathy paused for a moment before she responded. "Ken Roach was one of the worst," she said in a matter-of-fact little voice. He talked about me like I was a thing around the office to be ordered around. Ms. Fixit, he called me behind my back. Know-it-all Kathy. I knew he had no respect. Bill told him off sometimes. No one who worked in that office respected me except Bill. And in the end it turned out he didn't either.

"That Mark Cappelli, he was another one. Just as bad. Took all my work for granted. Couldn't believe someone like me could do the job right. Thought I was just a civvie, past her best, ready for the retirement scrapheap. Spoke to me like I was some kind of idiot. Nobody in that office appreciated what I did for them, keeping things in order. Making sure that they all had everything they needed. They didn't care.

"You, too, Roxanne." She turned her head to look directly at Roxanne. "At first, I thought you'd be better, but you used me as well. And Sigrid. You used her too. She worked hard for you. Took care of that little boy of yours whenever you asked. Then soon as Matt Stavros offered to help, you didn't need her anymore and you dropped her like it didn't matter. She'd been offered other jobs, you know, and she'd turned them down so she could babysit for you, and there she was, left without anything. I guess that's what they teach you when you join the force. To think of people as things. To take us for granted."

Roxanne suppressed a desire to protest. She did her best. She acted on the public's behalf. She kept people safe. She tried to be a good cop—that was all she'd wanted to be when she started in this career. She tried to be a good mother as well. It was too bad that she had laid Sigrid off from her babysitting job but was that such a big deal? She had done nothing that justified this loathing, or the crimes that had occurred. The woman in front of her was telling her she was responsible for the death of two serving members of the Force as well as retired Sergeant Bill.

"Was that a good reason to try to kill me?" she asked.

Kathy shifted in her chair and looked uncomfortable.
"I'm not saying anything else to them," she told her lawyer.

30

SIGRID ISFELD'S PARENTS sat on either side of her once more, but this time in the confines of the interview room. With Derek McVicar also present the room was quite crowded

"Bill Gilchrist left his Yukon SUV parked at Kathy Isfeld's place on Sunday, April 1st," Roxanne said. "Which of you helped move it back to Heron Haven?"

Melanie shrugged. "Don't know."

"I did," John said.

"No, you didn't, Dad," Sigrid countered. "It was my idea."

"Did she tell you why it was at her house?"

"Amma said he had visited her, then he'd been called away. Someone came to pick him up. She'd told him she would take the car back to his house for him." Sigrid didn't blink. Roxanne thought she was probably lying.

"Why would he not take his car with him? Wherever it was he was going?" she asked.

Sigrid's mouth opened and closed as she groped for an answer.

"You're not telling the truth. It was still there because something had happened to him. And if you didn't know exactly what, you must have realized when we found his body."

All three Isfelds sat silent. The lawyer coughed discreetly, giving them a moment to think. Sigrid was first to respond:

"I got back from Winnipeg and went straight to my amma's house." She sat up, her back ramrod straight, her hands grasping the seat of her chair on either side of her. "She was in a state. Shaking, she was so angry. I'd never seen her like that before. I got Dad to come over and she told us the whole story. How that man, that Bill Gilchrist, that she'd been seeing for years, had let her down and how she'd been so upset that she'd run the car at him and he'd fallen.

"Dad said that he would probably be okay, he had a phone with him, right? And Amma said yes, he'd been talking to someone when she hit him. So, we thought he'd be fine, that someone would go help him and take him to the hospital. And maybe he wouldn't tell that it was Amma that hit him because he wouldn't want people to know about the two of them being…well, you know what.

"But his SUV was sitting right outside Amma's house. She knew his wife wasn't home, she'd gone away somewhere, and none of the neighbours out there had moved back yet for the summer, so nobody would be around. We took it back. Dad drove it and I followed in Amma's car so I could bring him home. The SUV had a garage door opener on the visor so Dad drove it straight in. We wiped it all down, just in case there was any trouble, Dad said."

"How did you get the car keys?"

Sigrid fell silent again.

"And what happened to his phone? We haven't found it. We've searched, thoroughly. Dredged the ditch. It isn't there. Where is it, Sigrid?"

John turned toward Roxanne, eyebrows lowered, chin jutting in her direction.

"Leave her be," he said. "I took it. I went back, soon as my mother told us that she'd run the bastard over. All that stuff that Sigrid's saying about him maybe phoning for help and being okay didn't happen. I went to check on him and there he was, lying at the edge of the ditch. The phone was in the snow beside him. I picked it up, just in case there was anything on it that would incriminate my mom. Then I went into his jacket pocket and took his keys. He wasn't moving. It looked like he was already dead. I pushed him into the ditch with my foot, so he'd be out of sight if anyone drove past. I didn't want anyone finding him real soon and figuring out that my mother had something to do with it. Served him right. He was a jerk. Used my mother all those years. She worked her butt off for him. He kept stringing her along, like he was going to do anything about it? Ditch that wife of his? Of course, he wasn't. So I left him there. And I made sure that Sigrid and Mel here didn't tell. You can let them go."

"You didn't check his pulse? To see if he was still breathing?"

John shook his head.

"Where is the phone now?"

"In my sock drawer," he said. "Back home." He looked apologetically toward his wife. Melanie did not seem surprised to hear it. Had she known about this all the time, Roxanne wondered.

"Did you kill Ken Roach?"

"Huh? The cop? Don't know anything about that, lady. And don't go saying it was my mom's Ranger that hit him. Loads of guys drive those things. Could have been anybody."

"I don't think so. Your mother's truck has traces of paint on the back hitch from the capstan at the harbour. The truck that tried to run me down hit it. I saw it happen. It was storming that night, and the truck was back in the garage, wet from the rain, less than an hour after I was attacked. So one of your family had to be driving. Either it was your mother or it was one of you."

All three Isfelds clammed up once more. Roxanne pushed her chair back, frustrated.

"Okay," she said. "I'll go talk to Kathy again."

She had almost reached the door when Sigrid's voice stopped her. "It wasn't Amma who tried to kill you," she said. "And it wasn't my dad either. It was me."

"Be quiet, Sigrid!" Melanie grasped her daughter's arm.

"Shut up, now!" her dad hissed between his teeth. Sigrid pulled her hand away from her mother. Derek McVicar raised a hand to intervene but she ignored him.

"You think you're so good, but you're not, are you, Sergeant Calloway. You're as bad as all the rest. Worse, even, because you pretend to be nice. But you're not. All you really care about is your job. Amma told me all about you. How you got to be the boss here, at Fiskar Bay, after you'd worked in Major Crimes, and you asked her to stay on, kept telling her she was such an asset to the detachment, bringing her coffee and apple fritters, all that stuff, but you were just using her like everybody else.

"You thought she was a bit of a joke, didn't you? Amma knew that. You were just being nice to her face but behind her back it was a different story. And you were dangerous. She got worried when they put you in charge of the murders, because you used to track down killers. 'She always finds out,' she said. 'I've seen her do it. Just keeps digging away until she finds out what really happened. They call her Foxy, you know, because that's what she's like. Nose to the ground, sniffing. If anyone's going to figure out what's happened here, it'll be her.'

"So, I was over at Amma's house during that big rain and she said you were looking for Izzy McBain down by the harbour, that Izzy was out in a boat in that thunder and lightning. I said I'd put the Ranger away. It was sitting in the driveway outside in the rain. And I decided I'd go drive down to the harbour and have a look. I almost got you." The corners of her mouth twitched in a half smile. "Too bad those guys were up on that big old boat and saw you and pulled you out of the harbour."

"Say no more, Sigrid," said the lawyer, but she wasn't done.

"I'm so sorry for that little kid of yours," she sneered. "You're so busy with your big important job. You'll dump him off on anyone who'll take care of him. First me and now that Stavros guy."

Those words hit home, but Roxanne didn't have time to dwell on them. Sigrid rocked back and forth on the seat of her chair. Suddenly, she leaned forward and turned her head toward her father. A veil of blonde hair fell over her shoulder. "Amma thought it was you, Dad, who had killed those cops. The Roach guy and that sergeant they sent up from the city. She told me. Amma used to talk to me about everything. She was worried that Sergeant Calloway here was going to arrest you one of these days."

"She didn't say anything to me."

"Well, she wouldn't. And you thought it was her that had done it, right? That she was the Cop Killer."

John slowly nodded, like he was trying to understand.

"So, you both kept quiet to protect the other. And it was neither of you. I thought that was kind of funny."

"It was you who killed them?" Roxanne stepped forward to grasp the back of her chair.

Sigrid looked up at her and swept the loose hair back behind her ear.

"I didn't set out to," she said. "But I knew how Constable Roach behaved around Amma. He called her names. Acted like she was some kind of dinosaur. An antique. A has-been. It just happened. I'd been sandbagging with my hockey team out at that creek in Cullen Village, that weekend when it almost flooded and Roach was there bossing everybody about. I had Amma's truck and I drove a friend home afterwards. I came back by Marina Road and there he was, all by himself, rolling up police tape. I don't know what got into me, really. It was super easy. I just drove straight at him, like Amma had done with the Gilchrist guy, and he crashed right though the fence. I thought I'd just given him a scare. That he might be hurt a bit, nothing more. He was a big, tough kind of guy, right? I didn't think he'd be dead.

"But Amma said she was glad he was gone. That he'd been real mean and he deserved what he got. She didn't know that it was me that did it and she never said she thought it had been Dad, but I could tell she was kind of proud of him, so I knew that she did.

"Then the cops got scared that another one of them would get run over next. Amma told me. She said that you" —her slanted blue eyes locked on Roxanne—"took the job here at Fiskar Bay so you wouldn't be messing about with dangerous criminals anymore, and here you were, in charge of the Cop Killer Capital of Canada. That was just too stupid, wasn't it?" She giggled.

"Sergeant Cappelli?" Roxanne asked, struggling to believe what she was hearing.

"Oh, him? Well, he got Amma worried too. 'He's like a machine,' she told me. 'Relentless.' Dissed all the good work she had done. He wanted to pin the murders on some guy Amma knew called McKenzie and that did not sit well with Amma. 'First Ken Roach gets Lex McKenzie—that's right?—blamed for something he didn't do and now Cappelli is going to see if he can hang these murders on him. It's not right,' she said. She knew Cappelli was going to go look at some house that the McKenzies own, out near that old church she likes to visit. I just drove by to see, and there he was, right at the place where people had been leaving flowers for Gilchrist. So, I made sure he'd cause no more trouble."

Killing a serving police officer brought an automatic charge of murder in the first degree. The parents looked stunned as Roxanne made the charges. Then Derek McVicar finally said something.

"There will need to be a psychiatric assessment."

"What?" said Sigrid. "I'm not crazy."

31

"OF COURSE SHE'S crazy," said Izzy next day as she unpinned photographs from the whiteboard. The arrests were the talk of the town and her mom had been hearing her share of the gossip. "She comes by it honestly. Kathy's father was a bit weird. My mom says he should have been locked up. Sounds like he got depressed a lot. And look at Kathy, she's totally OCD. She was in a relationship with Bill Gilchrist all these years, hoping it might actually go somewhere but pretending all the time that nothing was going on? What was she thinking?"

Kathy had turned ashen faced when she had heard that her granddaughter had been charged with killing Ken Roach and Mark Cappelli. "I thought that it was John that did it," she had said.

"You did know," Roxanne had told her, "that Sigrid went out in your truck on Saturday night in the storm and so she must be the person who tried to run me down."

Kathy hadn't replied to that. She crossed her arms and looked the other way.

Now it was Monday morning and what charges would be brought against her and her son was still under discussion. Careless driving causing death, maybe manslaughter in the case of Bill Gilchrist. The question was whether Gilchrist died before or after Kathy's son pushed him into the ditch.

A lawyer who was more up-to-speed than Derek McVicar would get either of them off on a lesser charge. Kathy might get away with a hit-and-run and John with being an accessory to Bill's death. But, in a way, Kathy was responsible for all of these murders.

She had set them all up. She complained about the police she worked with, the ones who died, to her family. She was the driving force behind the killings and she had set an example to Sigrid when she ran down Bill Gilchrist and left him to die.

The whole family was implicated. Melanie Isfeld had gone home and closed her door behind her. She must have had some idea what was going on, but it didn't seem she had suspected her daughter. She had called the hotel asking for leave from her job. Her friends were rallying around her on Facebook and Instagram.

"What's going to happen with the Kuryks?" asked Izzy. "They found Bill's body and failed to report it."

"Charged with concealing evidence. They'll get their knuckles rapped and that'll be all."

Roxanne looked around at the bare room; the paraphernalia of the investigation was almost all stashed away. Jeff Riordan and Rick Peters had driven into Winnipeg the evening before, taking Sigrid Isfeld with them. She was going straight to the Youth Detention Centre and Derek McVicar had been right—there would be a psychiatric assessment scheduled for her.

"The Isfelds are related to half this town, Izzy." Roxanne looked out the window. A street washer was cleaning the road outside. "All of this may not go down well here in Fiskar Bay."

"Just as well you got them," Izzy assured her, taping the final box shut. "You stopped them before they killed anyone else, including yourself. You got this case all cleaned up before tourist season. That's going to win you Brownie points. Al Melnychuk made you cocoa with rum in it. He must think you're not so bad after all. You'll just need to find yourself a new babysitter. And advertise for a new civvie for the office. Bet you'll get plenty of applications." She sat down.

"I talked to Schultzy first thing this morning. He's sending me up to Robson on the plane tonight. They're opening that old case, and I finally get to be primary investigator." She grinned, pleased. "I'm going to go talk to the Featherstones again before I leave here. And I'm moving back to Winnipeg permanently. Matt and I are splitting up."

"You are?"

"Yup. Well, it hasn't been working out between us for a while. He loves it here and I can't wait to leave. He likes kids; I don't want any. Not now, anyhow. He's fine with this, I think. He's been seeing it coming. It's not like we've fallen out or anything. We're just not going to live together anymore. We are done."

"But he's such a good guy. Kind and considerate. He reminds me a bit of Jake, the guy I married."

"Does he now?" said Izzy. "Y'know, Matt and I just drifted together. We get along okay, but that's not enough, is it? He's going to hang out his shingle here one of these days and take over from Derek McVicar. Derek's more than due to retire. And being with him and stuck out here is getting in the way of what I need to do. So, I am off. I'm going to make inspector one of these days." Her big smile lit up her face. "Maybe someday I'll be the boss of you."

MARGO WISHART AND Sasha Rosenberg walked the shoreline south of Cullen Village. Their dogs were off leash. Margo threw a stick into the water so that Bob could swim out to retrieve it. The sand had been compacted by the waves. It was damp and Lenny was having none of it. He sniffed around the bushes that edged the sand where the ground was bone dry.

News was out that arrests had been made. They both knew that the Isfeld family was involved. "The mother worked for the RCMP in Fiskar Bay and I think her granddaughter babysat for Roxanne Calloway," said Margo, swinging a stick, her dog bouncing alongside her, waiting for the next throw.

"Guess that means we can stop worrying that they're going to lock up Julie Gilchrist." Sasha put two fingers to her lips and whistled as Lenny disappeared behind a clump of bush. He trotted back into view.

"She talked to me this morning. She does sound relieved. I think she knows more than she's letting on."

"Well then, we'll have to invite her over soon for lunch." Sasha zipped her jacket up to her neck. "Find out what she can tell us." A light wind was blowing in from the south, stirring up waves on the surface of the lake.

"It's too bad Lex McKenzie got implicated." The dog bounced back to Margo, stick in mouth, splashing water onto her feet. She didn't mind. She was wearing a rain slicker and rubber boots. "He's completely disappeared. Bea Benedict is so annoyed about that. She knows the deputy commissioner of the RCMP. She's going to complain about how the police treated him. Steve Rice has been released. She's told him to pack up his office and leave the Sunnywell Centre, though. You know he's moved back in with Susan?"

Sasha stopped in her tracks. "She's taken him back?" she asked. "What's she thinking? Has she dropped the charges?"

"I expect so. Maybe she thinks it won't happen again."

"Dream on! And what about the money he stole?"

"Bea says he has to go to court for that."

"Huh." Sasha whistled again for her dog and turned to face the wind. "He'll probably say he's sorry and get off with it too. Let's head back. Roberta's coming over later this morning with some lace she's made for those three big sisters I'm building. I want to get some work done on them before she gets here."

They strode, side by side, their dogs tagging along behind them, back to their cars, eager to get out of the wind and back home to some hot tea.

ROXANNE TOOK THE afternoon off and went for a run along the beach. The detachment was quiet once more. The mayor and council had sent an arrangement of spring flowers in a vase, with a thank-you card. She'd put them on her office desk, the one she'd reclaim tomorrow, when she was back in uniform. Inspector Schultz had called.

"Well done," he had said. "I knew you'd be the one to sort that mess out."

Her report was in and her secondment with the Major Crimes Unit was over. She was going to miss overseeing an investigation that had such urgency. But meantime, most of the snowbirds had arrived back with the geese and cottagers were beginning to appear on the weekends, opening their cabins, ready for the summer. It wouldn't be long before the tourists arrived in droves and she would be busier. She needed to spend more time with her son. Some of what Sigrid Isfeld had said about her putting the job first had struck home. She stopped by the school and went to pick him up.

"Good job, Sergeant," said the principal as she passed her in the corridor. A couple of the other parents smiled approval in her direction.

She had just closed the door to her house when her phone buzzed.

"Hi, Matt," she said. "I'm sorry to hear about you and Izzy."

"No worries." He sounded quite cheerful. "I've known for a while that we were over. I told her on Sunday that I was going to be around all summer, helping out in Derek McVicar's practice. And that I was thinking about getting one of those pups that Mo Magnusson's got, to keep Joseph company. I like living here and she can't stand having the family breathing down her neck. I think having to show up at that christening while you were wrapping up this case was the final straw."

"Maybe she'll change her mind after a while."

"I don't think so. Izzy's got career goals."

So had Roxanne, for a while, but that had changed with her move to Fiskar Bay. She might not be going anywhere else for some time, either.

"The lease is up soon on the apartment we were renting in Winnipeg. Izzy's going to renew it so she can move back in by herself. It's all working out fine. What are you doing tonight?" Matt asked.

"I just got home with Finn." She had no plans. There was probably nothing much to eat in the fridge.

"How about I pick up some pizza and drop by? Can I bring the dog? And a bottle of wine?"

"Sure," she heard herself say. "Sounds good. Give me time to do a grocery run. I'll pick up a salad. See you after that?"

He would be there by six, he said.

Roxanne Calloway reached for her jacket, called for her son, and opened the door.

Acknowledgements

THANKS AS ALWAYS to everyone at Signature Editions, my publisher, Karen Haughian, marketing assistant, Ashley Brekelmans, my editor, Douglas Whiteway, and to Terry Gallagher, for the cover design. I feel very lucky to have them take care of my book.

Kirsty Macdonald and Ann Atkey read the manuscript and told me, tactfully but firmly, what worked and what didn't. I am so glad to have their help. I am also grateful to Deborah Romeyn for answering my questions about some anatomical details and Claire Borody for advice about Ukrainian churches in Manitoba. Thanks also to Indigenous Elder and storyteller Ruth Christie for telling me the story about the three sisters of Lake Winnipeg.

Also by Raye Anderson

And We Shall Have Snow

Corporal Roxanne Calloway is new to the RCMP's Major Crimes Unit and keen to make her mark. But when she's called from the big city to tiny Cullen Village to lead the investigation into the death of the talented but devious star of the local music scene she discovers that this close-knit community does not give up its secrets willingly.

ISBN 978-1773240-66-4

And Then Is Heard No More

When Sergeant Roxanne Calloway begins investigating the murder of Prairie Theatre Centre's well-loved Artistic Director she quickly learns that in the world of theatre, fact and fiction merge, lies are delivered as truth, and people with active imaginations conjure up convincing stories. Who is Roxanne supposed to believe?

ISBN 978-1773240-88-6

About the Author

RAYE ANDERSON IS a Scots Canadian who spent many enjoyable years running theatre schools and delivering creative learning programs for arts organizations, in Winnipeg, notably at Prairie Theatre Exchange, and in Ottawa and Calgary. Her work has taken her across Canada, coast to coast, and up north as far as Churchill and Yellowknife. She's also worked as far afield as the West Indies and her native Scotland. She has two daughters and one granddaughter.

Now, she lives in Manitoba's beautiful Interlake and is part of a thriving arts community. *Down Came the Rain* is Anderson's third novel featuring RCMP Sergeant Roxanne Calloway, who made her debut in *And We Shall Have Snow*, and continued her adventures in *And Then Is Heard No More*.